Text Book Of

FUNDAMENTALS OF COMPUTER

For

B.C.A. Science : Semester - I

As Per New Syllabus

Shreeram Gholap
M.E. (Computer)
Lecturer, Dept. of Computer Engineering
Navsahyadri Institute of Technology
A/p Naigoan,Tal. Bhor, Dist. Pune

Sudarshan Lakhdive
M.C.A., M. Phil., NET, Ph.D.
HOD, Dept. of Computer Science
Prof. Ramkrishna More Arts, Commerce & Science
College, Akurdi, Pune

Mrs. Reshma Masurekar
M.C.S.
Assistant Professor, Dept. of Computer Science
Dr. D.Y. Patil Arts, Commerce & Science College
Pimpri, Pune

Mrs. Priyanka Shivarkar
B.E. (Computer)
Lecturer, Dept. of Computer Engineering
Navsahyadri Institute of Technology
A/p Naigoan,Tal. Bhor, Dist. Pune

NIRALI PRAKASHAN
ADVANCEMENT OF KNOWLEDGE

N3861

Fundamentals of Computer **ISBN 978-93-86084-67-5**

First Edition	:	**July 2016**
©	:	**Authors**

Published By :
NIRALI PRAKASHAN
Abhyudaya Pragati, 1312, Shivaji Nagar
Off J.M. Road, PUNE – 411005
Tel - (020) 25512336/37/39, Fax - (020) 25511379
Email : niralipune@pragationline.com

➢ DISTRIBUTION CENTRES

PUNE

Nirali Prakashan : 119, Budhwar Peth, Jogeshwari Mandir Lane, Pune 411002, Maharashtra
Tel : (020) 2445 2044, 66022708, Fax : (020) 2445 1538
Email : bookorder@pragationline.com, niralilocal@pragationline.com

Nirali Prakashan : S. No. 28/27, Dhyari, Near Pari Company, Pune 411041
Tel : (020) 24690204 Fax : (020) 24690316
Email : dhyari@pragationline.com, bookorder@pragationline.com

MUMBAI

Nirali Prakashan : 385, S.V.P. Road, Rasdhara Co-op. Hsg. Society Ltd.,
Girgaum, Mumbai 400004, Maharashtra
Tel : (022) 2385 6339 / 2386 9976, Fax : (022) 2386 9976
Email : niralimumbai@pragationline.com

➢ DISTRIBUTION BRANCHES

JALGAON

Nirali Prakashan : 34, V. V. Golani Market, Navi Peth, Jalgaon 425001,
Maharashtra, Tel : (0257) 222 0395, Mob : 94234 91860

KOLHAPUR

Nirali Prakashan : New Mahadvar Road, Kedar Plaza, 1st Floor Opp. IDBI Bank
Kolhapur 416 012, Maharashtra. Mob : 9850046155

NAGPUR

Pratibha Book Distributors : Above Maratha Mandir, Shop No. 3, First Floor,
Rani Jhanshi Square, Sitabuldi, Nagpur 440012, Maharashtra
Tel : (0712) 254 7129

DELHI

Nirali Prakashan : 4593/21, Basement, Aggarwal Lane 15, Ansari Road, Daryaganj
Near Times of India Building, New Delhi 110002 Mob : 08505972553

BENGALURU

Pragati Book House : House No. 1, Sanjeevappa Lane, Avenue Road Cross,
Opp. Rice Church, Bengaluru – 560002.
Tel : (080) 64513344, 64513355,Mob : 9880582331, 9845021552
Email:bharatsavla@yahoo.com

CHENNAI

Pragati Books : 9/1, Montieth Road, Behind Taas Mahal, Egmore,
Chennai 600008 Tamil Nadu, Tel : (044) 6518 3535,
Mob : 94440 01782 / 98450 21552 / 98805 82331,
Email : bharatsavla@yahoo.com

niralipune@pragationline.com | www.pragationline.com

Also find us on www.facebook.com/niralibooks

Preface ...

We take an opportunity to present this book entitled as **"Fundamentals of Computer"** to the students of **B.C.A. Science, Semester - I** as per the New Syllabus, June 2016-2017.

The book covers theory of Introduction to Computer System, Introduction to Computer Peripherals, Concepts of Software, Editors and Word Processors, Spreadsheets, Presentation Tool, PC Hardware and Troubleshooting (Preventing Problems).

A special words of thank to Shri. Dineshbhai Furia, Mr. Jignesh Furia for showing full faith in us to write this text book. We also thank to Mr. Amar Salunkhe and Mr. Akbar Shaikh of M/s Nirali Prakashan for their excellent co-operation.

We also thank Ms. Chaitali Takale, Mr. Ravindra Walodare, Mr. Sachin Shinde, Mr. Nilesh Deshmukh, Mr. Ashok Bodke, Mr. Moshin Sayyed and Mr. Nitin Thorat.

Although every care has been taken to check mistakes and misprints, any errors, omission and suggestions from teachers and students for the improvement of this text book shall be most welcome.

Authors

Syllabus ...

1. Introduction to Computer System (10 L)

1.1 Introduction, Characteristics of Computers, Block Diagram of Computer.

1.2 Types of Computers and Features - Mini Computers, Micro Computers, Mainframe Computers, Super Computers, Laptops and Tablets.

1.3 Types of Programming Languages - Machine Languages, Assembly Languages, High Level Languages.

1.4 Translators - Assembler, Compiler, Interpreter.

1.5 Data Organization - Drives, Files, Directories.

2. Introduction to Computer Peripherals (08 L)

2.1 Primary and Secondary Storage Devices.

2.2 Primary Storage Devices - RAM, ROM, PROM, EPROM.

2.3 Secondary Storage Devices - CD, HD, Pen Drive.

2.4 I/O Devices - Scanners, Digitizers, Plotters, LCD, Plasma Display.

2.5 Pointing Devices - Mouse, Joystick, Touch Screen.

2.6 Number Systems.

2.7 Introduction to Binary, Octal, Hexadecimal System Conversion, Simple Addition, Subtraction, Multiplication, Division.

3. Concepts of Software (12 L)

3.1 Difference between Imperative Knowledge and Definitional Knowledge. Difference between Fixed Program and Stored Program Computers. Definitions of Syntax, Static Semantics, and Semantics. Explain Straight Line, Branching, And Looping Programs.

3.2 Definition: Software, Types of software: System Software, Application Software. System Software: Operating System. Types of O.S.

3.3 Internal and External Commands, Batch Files.

3.4 Introduction to DOS and its Limitations.

3.5 MS Windows: Desktop, Icons, File and Directory, Structure, Menu Items, Control Panel, File and Directory Search, Notepad, Paintbrush, Utility programs: Anti-virus, DiskCleaning, Defragmentation, Compression/Decompression of Files.

3.6 Application Software: Examples of Commercial Software with Brief Introduction.

4. **Editors and Word Processors** (07 L)

    4.1 Basic Concepts, Examples: MS-Word, gedit, vi.

    4.2 Introduction to Desktop Publishing

5. **Spreadsheets** (08 L)

    5.1 Purpose, Usage

    5.2 Creation of Files in Spreadsheet

6. **Presentation Tool** (05 L)

    6.1 Design Slides (Using Text, Images, Charts, Clipart)

    6.2 Slide Animation

    6.3 Template and Theme Creation

7. **PC Hardware** (05 L)

    7.1 Introduction of Hardware.

    7.2 Type and Working of Hardware parts – Ports, Motherboard, CPU.

    7.3 Basic Input and Output Setting (BIOS), Network Interface Card (NIC),

    7.4 Graphics Card.

8. **Troubleshooting and Preventing Problems** (05 L)

    8.1 Logical Fault Isolation – ADJUST Method, Common Networking Problems, Tools for Gathering Information, Troubleshooting PC Hardware.

Contents ...

CHAPTER 1

Introduction to Computer System

Contents ...

1.1 | INTRODUCTION

- Today's world is an information rich world. In today's world, computers have become an integral part of our lives; computers are being used in every sphere of human activity whether it is at home, at office or at bank.

- Fields such as education, entertainment, medicine, banking, military, weather forecasting and telecommunications have been greatly influenced by the use of computers. This pervading presence of computers has made it necessary for everyone to have a fundamental knowledge of computers.

- A computer is basically a programmable computing machine. Computing is the process of utilizing computer technology to complete a task. Computing machine is a machine for performing particular tasks automatically.

- A computer is an electronic device that performs diverse operations using instructions to process the information in order to achieve the desired result.

1.1.1 Basics of Computer (Meaning and Definition)

- The term computer is derived from the Latin word "compute" means "to calculate".

- A computer is an electronic device, operating under the control of instructions stored in its own memory, that can accept data (input), process the data according to specified rules (process), produce results (output), and store the results (storage) for future use, (See Fig. 1.1).

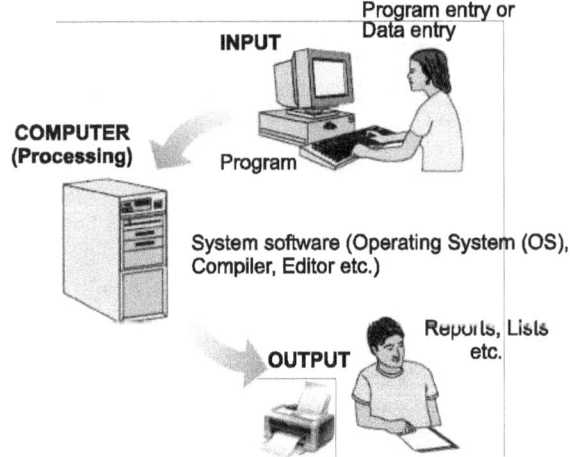

Fig. 1.1: Work Environment of Computer

- A computer is defined as, "an electronic device that performs a given task on the basis of given instructions".

OR

1.2

- A computer can be defined as "a programmable electronic device that can perform mathematical and logical calculations, data processing in accordance with a predefined program of instructions".

OR

- A computer may be defined as "a machine that can solve problems by accepting data, performing certain operations and presenting the results of those operations under the direction of detailed step-by-step instructions i.e., programs".

1.1.2 Computer System

- A system is a group of element or components that work together to carry out some common tasks and to achieve a common goal or objective.

- A computer can be viewed as a system, which consists of a number of interrelated components or elements that work together with the aim/goal of converting data into information.

- A complete computer system consists of four parts components/elements i.e., Hardware, Software, Data and User as shown in Fig. 1.2.

Fig. 1.2: Parts/Elements/Components of Computer System

- Fig. 1.2 shows following components/elements of computer system:

1. **Hardware:**

- The mechanical devices/parts/components that make up the computer are called hardware.

- A computer's hardware consists of interconnected electronic devices that you can use to control the computer's operation, input and output.

2. **Software:**

- It is a set of instructions that makes the computer perform tasks.

- In other words, software tells the computer what to do.

Difference between Hardware and Software:

Sr. No.	Hardware	Software
1.	These are the physical components of a computer system.	These are the logical components of a computer system.
2.	User can see, touch and feel the hardware.	User cannot touch the software.
3.	Hardware works based on the instructions of the software.	Software tell the hardware what do do.
4.	Hardware components are less expensive.	Software are generally costlier and expensive as compare to hardware.

3. **Data:**

- Data is the raw information or raw/basic facts that computer can process. Data by itself does not make much sense to the user. It will give a meaning only when it is processed by the computer.
- A processed data is called as information.
- Data can be text, numbers, audio or video that the computer manipulates.

4. **Users:**

- People who use computers are called users.
- Users are people who write computer programs or interact with the computer.
- They are also known as skinware, liveware, humanware or peopleware.
- Computer programmers, data entry operators, system analyst and computer hardware engineers fall into this category.

1.1.3 Computer Generations

- In computer terminology, the word generation is described as a stage of technological development or innovation.
- A major technological development that fundamentally changed the way computers operate, resulting in increasingly smaller, cheaper, more powerful and more efficient and reliable devices, characterises each generation of computer.
- According to the technology used, there are five generations of computers, which are discussed in the Table 1.1.

Table 1.1: Generations of Computer

Sr. No.	Generations and Year
1.	**First Generation (1942-1955):** Vacuum tube based.
2.	**Second Generation (1955-1964):** Transistor based.
3.	**Third Generation (1964-1975):** Integrated Circuit based.
4.	**Fourth Generation (1975-1989):** VLSI microprocessor based.
5.	**Fifth Generation (1989-onwards):** ULSI microprocessor based.

1. First Generation Computers (1942-1955):

- The first generation computers were using Vacuum Tubes and machine languages were used for giving instructions.
- The computers of this generation were very large in size and their programming was a difficult task.
- The major first generation computers were UNIVAC-1, IBM-701, IBM-650, ENIAC, EDVAC etc.

Advantages:

(i)   First generation computers were fastest calculating devices of their time.

(ii)   Support parallel processing.

Disadvantages:

(i)   Air conditioning is required.

(ii)   Bulky in size (required large rooms) for assembly on installation.

(iii) Vacuum tube required very high power consumption.

(iv)   Time consuming for assembling and installation.

2. Second Generation Computers (1955-1964):

- In second generation computers the vacuum tubes are replaced by Transistors.
- Transistors were highly reliable, requires less power and faster than vacuum tubes. High Level Languages such as FORTRAN, COBOL, BASIC etc., were introduced.
- The practice of writing programs in Machine languages were replaced by High Level Languages. Punched cards were used for input-output operations.
- Major second generation computers were IBM-1400 series, 7000 series, Honeywell 200, CDC 3600, UNIVAC 1108 etc.

Advantages:

(i)   Transistors are faster than vacuum tube.

(ii)   More reliable.

(iii) Cheaper and Smaller in size.

(iv)   Less power consumption.

Disadvantages:

(i)   Time consuming for assembly and installation.

(ii) Air conditioning required.

(iii) Difficult for commercial production.

(iv) Costly for commercial production and Maintenance is high.

3. Third Generation Computers (1964-1975):

- The third generation computers used the new technology, transistor Integrated Circuits (IC) intended by Jack and Noyce in 1958.

- All electronic components like transistors, resistors and capacitors were fabricated on silicon chips. Computers were designed by making use of ICs.

- Major third generation computers were IBM -360 series, ICL -1900 series, CYBER -175, TDC-316, IBM 370/168 etc.

Advantages:

(i)   Required small space (Portable).

(ii) More reliable and Faster.

(iii) Less installation time.

(iv) Low maintenance.

Disadvantages:

(i)   Air conditioning required.

(ii) Cost is more than fourth generation computers.

4. Fourth Generation Computers (1975-1989):

- The ICs used in third generation computers had about 10 to 100 transistors per unit. This technology was called Small-Scale Integration (SSI).

- Later, with the advancement of technology for manufacturing ICs, it is possible to integrate 10,000 transistors in an IC. This technology is called Large-Scale Integration (LSI).

- Very Large Scale Integration (VLSI) can pack a million or more transistors on a single chip. LSI and VLSI technologies led to the introduction of Microprocessors.

- Computers which are designed using Microprocessors become the fourth generation computers. Magnetic disks become the primary means for external storage.

- Intel introduced the first microprocessor 4004 using LSI. The languages C, LISP, Prolog become popular.

- Major fourth generation computers are IBM System 370, HP-3000, CRAY–MPC, WIPRO 860, IBM AS/400/B60, IBM ps/2 MODEL 80, HCL Magnum, etc.

Advantages:

    (i)   Portable in size and Cheaper.

    (ii) More reliable.

    (iii) Easy for installation.

    (iv) Support High Level Language (HLL) and Networking.

Disadvantages:

    (i)   Air conditioning is required.

    (ii) Expensive.

    (iii) Single user oriented.

5. **Fifth Generation Computers (1989 onwards):**

- Fifth generation computers are capable of parallel processing, high speed computing and artificial intelligence.

- They have an architecture which allows more neural problem solving ability. These machines uses the principle of Artificial Intelligence (AI).

- They have the ability to understand natural languages like English, Malayalam etc., it can converse with human beings.

- Computer languages such as LISP, PROLOG, C, C++, etc., are available to program such computers.

- PARAM-10000 (India) and CRAY machines (Japan) are the examples of fifth generation computers.

Advantages:

    (i)   More smaller and handy than computers of fourth generation, allowing users to use the computing facility even while travelling.

    (ii) Very less power required, so no air-conditioning required.

    (iii) Support standard HLLs (High Level Languages).

    (iv) Faster in speed and Easy for installation.

1.2 | COMPUTER CHARACTERISTICS

- The main characteristics of computer, which makes them powerful and useful are:

    1. **Automation:** An automatic machine works by itself without human intervention. Computers has automation (ability to perform the given task automatically) power that means computer can perform the task automatically by using programs.

    2. **Speed:** Computers are of high speed in its operation. The speed is measured in terms of Instructions Per Second (IPS). All modern computers can process information at a speed of a couple of Million Instructions Per Second (MIPS).

3. **Accuracy:** Computers are highly accurate in its operations. They either give correct answer or do not answer at all. Errors can occur in computers but these are mainly due to human rather than technological weakness.

4. **Reliability:** It is the ability of a computer to perform the same job exactly in the same way in any numbers of times.

5. **Versatility:** A computer is capable of performing almost any task provided that the task can be reduced to a series of logical steps.

6. **Integrity:** It is the ability of a computer to carry out a sequence of instructions.

7. **No Feelings:** Computers are devoid of emotions. They have no feeling because they are machines.

8. **Diligence Continuity:** A computer is free from monotony, tiredness, lack of concentration, etc. It can work for hours without creating any error.

9. **Power of Remembering:** Computers can store and recall any amount of information because of its storage capability.

1.3 | BLOCK DIAGRAM OF COMPUTER

- The computer as a machine consists of different components that interact with each other to provide the desired functionality of the computer.

- As a user of the computer, we need:

    1. **Computer Architecture,** refers to the structure and behavior of the computer. It includes the specifications of the components, for example, instruction format, instruction set and techniques for addressing memory, and how they connect to the other components of computer.

    2. Given the components, **Computer Organization** focuses on the organizational structure. The internal arrangement of different parts/components of a computer is called the computer organization. It deals with how the hardware components operate and the way they are connected to form the computer.

    3. Given the system specifications, **Computer Design** focuses on the hardware to be used and the interconnection of parts.

- Different kinds of computer, such as a PC or a mainframe computer may have different organization; however, basic organization of the computer remains the same.

- The major components of a digital computer are CPU (Central Processing Unit), memory, input device and output device. The input and output devices are also known as peripherals.

- Fig. 1.3 shows block diagram of a computer.

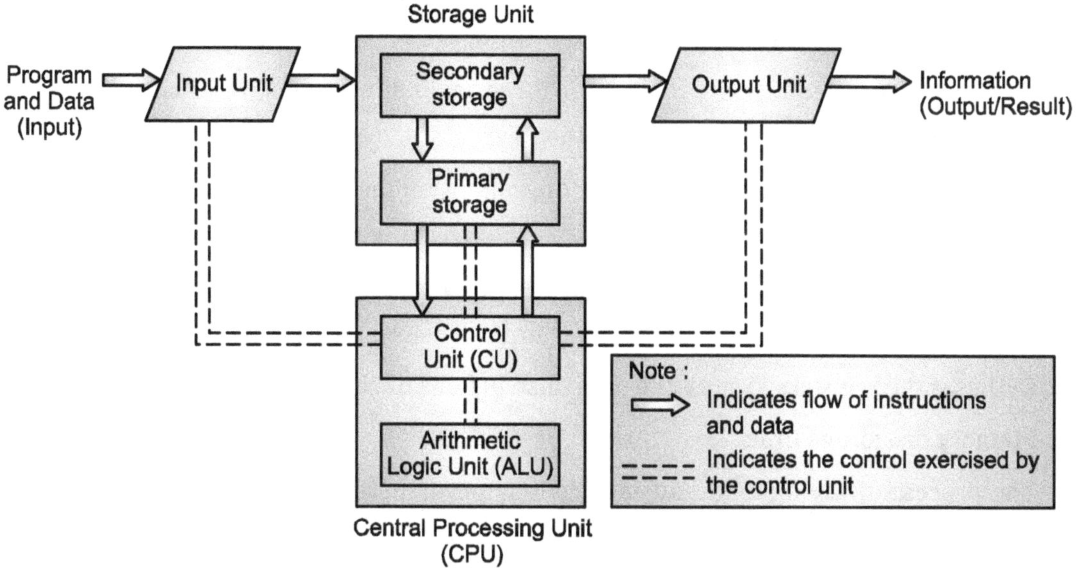

Fig. 1.3: Block diagram of Computer

- Various parts/components of computer in Fig. 1.3 are described below:

1. Input Unit:

- Input is the process of entering data and programs in to the computer system. Input is the raw information entered into a computer from the input device.

- The device that accepts data from the user and communicates the same to the CPU is called as an input device.

- Some common input devices are keyboard, mouse, joystick, light pen, track ball, scanner, graphic tablet, microphone, Magnetic Ink Card Reader (MICR), Optical Character Reader (OCR), Barcode reader, Optical Mark Reader (OMR) etc.

- **Functions of Input Unit:**

    (i)   It accepts or reads data/instructions from outside world.

    (ii)   Input unit converts these data/instructions in computer acceptable form.

    (iii) Input unit supplies the converted data/instructions to the storage unit for storage and further processing.

2. CPU:

- The Central Processing Unit (CPU) is referred to as "brain" of a computer system. CPU converts data (input) into meaningful information (output).

- CPU controls all the internal and external devices, performs arithmetic and logic operations, and operates only on binary data, that is, data composed of 1's and 0's.

- In addition, it also controls the usage of main memory to store data and instructions and controls the sequence of operations.

- The central processing unit consists of three main subsystems, the Arithmetic Logic Unit (ALU), the Control Unit (CU), and the Registers.

- ALU performs the arithmetic and logic operations on the data that is made available to it.

- CU is responsible for organizing the processing of data and instructions. CU controls and co-ordinates the activity of the other units of computer.

- CPU uses the registers to store the data, instructions during processing.

3. **Memory or Storage Unit:**

- The process of saving data and instructions permanently or temporary is known as storage.

- Memory unit can store instruction, data and intermediate results. This unit supplies information to the other units of the computer when needed.

- The memory unit consists of primary memory and secondary memory.

- **Primary Memory (main memory)** of the computer is used to store the data and instructions during execution of the instructions. Random Access Memory (RAM) and Read Only Memory (ROM) are the primary memories.

- **Secondary Memory** is non-volatile and is used for permanent storage of data and programs. A program or data that has to be executed is brought into the RAM from the secondary memory. Magnetic tape, disks are the examples of secondary storage.

4. **Output Unit:**

- The result of computer processing is called as output.

- This result is communicated to user through a device called output devices like Monitors, Plotter, Printer etc.

- **Functions of Output Unit:**

   (i)   Output unit accepts the produced results, which are in the coded form.

   (ii) It converts these coded results to human acceptable form.

   (iii) Output unit supplies the converted results to outside world.

1.4 | TYPES OF COMPUTER AND FEATURES

- Computers can be classified according to purpose, data handling and functionality as shown in Fig. 1.4.

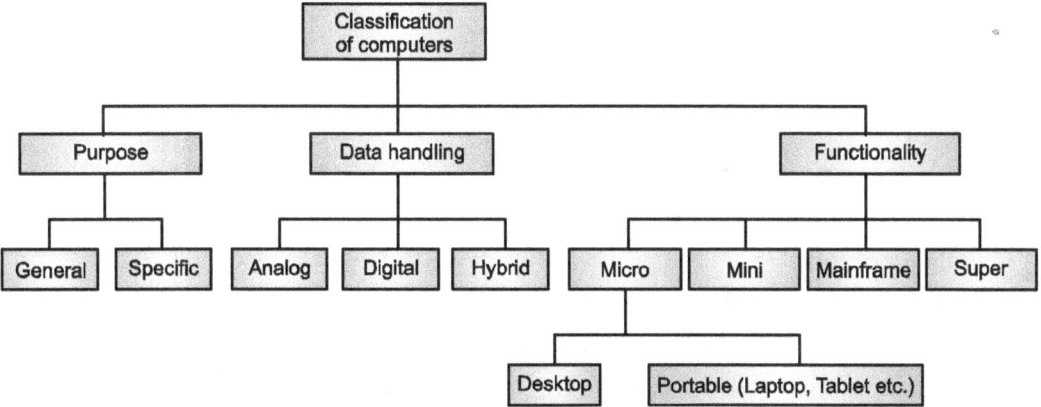

Fig. 1.4: Types of Computer

1.4.1 Types of Computer According to Type of Data Handling Techniques

- Different types of computers process the data in a different manner. According to the basic data handling principle, computers can be classified into three categories i.e., analog, digital and hybrid as discussed below.

1. Analog Computers:

- The earliest computers were analog computers.

- A computing machine that works on the principle of measuring, in which the measurements obtained are translated into desired data is known as analog computer.

- Modern analog computers usually employ electrical parameters, like voltages, resistances or currents, to represent the quantities being manipulated.

- Analog computers do not deal directly with the numbers. They measure continuous physical magnitudes such as temperature, pressure and voltage, which are analogous to the numbers under consideration.

- For example, the petrol pump may have an analog computer that converts the flow of pumped petrol into two measurements – the quantity of petrol and the price for that quantity.

- Slide rule, Antikythera mechanism, astrolabe, differential analyzer, Deltar, Kerrison Predictor are the examples of an analog computers.

- Analog computers are used for scientific and engineering purposes.

Advantages:

    (i)   Continuous representation of all data within the range of the machine.

    (ii)   Fast and inexpensive when implemented with same technology as digital computer.

    (iii) Parallel and real-time operation many signal values can be computed simultaneously.

Disadvantages:

    (i)   Analog computers are not accurate.

    (ii)   Analog computers has lack memory.

2. Digital Computers:

- A computer that operates with information, numerical or otherwise, represented in a digital form (0s an 1s) is known as digital computer.

- Digital computers process data including text, sound, graphics and video into a digital value in 0's and 1's.

- In digital computers, analog quantities must be converted into digital quantity before processing. In this case, the output will also be digital.

- The desktop PC at your home, banks, offices etc., are the examples of digital computers.

Advantages:

    (i)   Digital computers are accurate.

    (ii)   It can store large amount of facts, instructions, and information.

    (iii) Digital computers are easy to design.

Disadvantage:

    (i)   Digital computers are slow as compared to analog computers.

    (ii)   It has higher cost and complexity.

3. Hybrid Computers:

- Those computers which employ both the features of analog and digital computers are known as Hybrid computer.

- The use of hybrid computer day to day as there are number of areas in the real world where need both analog and digital computers. Consider the example of an hospital, in a hospital there may be number of devices like E.C.G. machine etc. which are used to measure the person's heart beat, temperature and other information.

- EAI 180, HPLC and EAI 185 are the examples of hybrid computers.

Advantages:

    (i) Less expensive than the digital computer.

    (ii) Hybrid computers have tremendous computing speed.

Disadvantages:

(i) Hybrid computers required detailed knowledge of operation for both the analog and digital computers.

(ii) Hybrid computer simulations were composed of two parts i.e., the analog and digital computer portions. This made debugging complicated, since both parts had to be debugged and then integrated.

(iii) Simulations using hybrid computers were extremely time consuming.

Difference between Analog, Digital and Hybrid Computers:

Sr. No.	Analog Computer	Digital Computer	Hybrid Computer
1.	Analog computers are used to process analog data.	Digital computers are used to process digital (letters, numerals, special symbols) data.	A hybrid computer can process both digital and analog data.
2.	Speed is a faster than digital computer.	Speed is slower than hybrid computer and to analog computer.	It has high speed than digital and analog computers.
3.	Analog computer do not requires any storage capability because they measure quantities in a single operation.	Digital computers requires storage capability.	Hybrid computer requires storage capability.
4.	Data in analog computer is of continuous in nature.	Data in digital computer is discrete in nature.	Hybrid computer process both continuous and discrete data.
5.	Analog computer can process only numeric data.	Digital computer process number as well as non-numeric data.	It process both numeric and non-numeric data.
6.	Examples: Slide rule, Delta.	Examples: Desktop computers.	Examples: EAI-185, HPLC.

1.4.2 Types of Computers According to Functionality

- Based on physical size, performance and application areas, we can divide computers generally into four major categories i.e., micro, mini, mainframe and super computers.

1.4.2.1 Super Computers

- The super computer were first presented in the year 1960 by Seymour Cray at CDC (Control Data Corporation).
- A super computer is the fastest type of computer that can perform complex operations at a very high speed. These computers can process billions of instructions per second.
- Super computers are more expensive than the other categories of computers and are specially designed for the applications in which large number of complex calculations have to be carried out to get the desired output.
- Some of the manufacturers of super computers are IBM, Silicon Graphics, Fujitsu, Intel, etc. Examples of super computers are, CRAY 3, Cyber 205, NEC SX-3 and PARAM from India.

Features of Super Computer:

1. A super computer utilizes all its processing speed and power in executing a few programs as fast as possible.
2. The performance of super computer is measured in terms of Flop/s (Floating Point Operations per Second).
3. Super computer executes complicated computations and utilizes large memory.
4. Super computers are purpose built for tasks like simulation, modelling, research etc.

Advantages of Super Computers:

1. Run more problems in shorter time i.e. they are very fast.
2. They have very high storage capacity.

Disadvantages of Super Computers:

1. They require very high power.
2. Takes up a lot of space i.e. they are larger in size.
3. They are more costly and Maintenance cost is very high.
4. Difficult to assembly.

Fig. 1.5: Super Computer

Applications of Super Computers:

1. Weather forecasting, 2, Animated graphics, 3. Fluid mechanics,
4. Nuclear energy research, 5. Petroleum exploration.

1.4.2.2 Mainframe Computers

- The mainframes are 32-bit or 64-bit computers and have large storage capacity and can support a large number of terminals (ranges from 64 to 100).
- A mainframe is an ultra-high performance computer made for high-volume, processor-intensive computing.

- Mainframe computer colloquially referred as "big-iron".

- Mainframe computer consists of a high-end computer processor, with related peripheral devices, capable of supporting large volumes of data processing, high performance on-line transaction processing systems, and extensive data storage and retrieval.

- Normally, it is able to process and store more data than a mini computer and far more than a micro computer. Moreover, it is designed to perform faster than a mini computer and much faster than a micro computer.

- Examples of mainframe computers are, DEC-1090, IBM 308-580 series, IBM 4300, ICIM 2904, etc.

Features of Mainframe Computer:

1. Mainframe uses its processing power to execute multiple programs concurrently.

2. For mainframe, performance is measured in terms of MIPS (Millions of Instructions Per Second).

3. Mainframes undertake simple computational task that involves huge amount of external data.

Advantages:

1. Huge memory.
2. High speed compared to volume of data.
3. No virus attack so far reported in last 50-60 years.
4. Superb virtualization.
5. Huge data processing.

Fig. 1.6: Mainframe Computer

Disadvantages:

1. Cost of hardware is high.
2. Special operating systems/software require so higher cost.
3. Intense human and space attention required.
4. More resource consumption.

Applications:

1. Normally, they are used in banking, airlines and railways etc. for their applications.

2. Both e-business and e-commerce use mainframe computers to perform business functions and exchange money over the Internet.

3. The military one of the first users of mainframe computers continues employing this technology in combat and for keeping the country's borders secure.

4. Satellites that were once a science fiction fantasy continue to operate mainframe computers in their intelligence and spying efforts.

5. Public and private libraries, as well as colleges and universities, use mainframe computers for storage of critical data.

1.4.2.3 Mini Computer

- A mini computer is a small digital computer. Normally, mini computer is able to process and store less data than a mainframe but more than a micro computer, while doing so less rapidly than a mainframe but more rapidly than a micro computer.

- Mini computer sometimes called a mid-range computer. Mini computer is designed to meet the computing needs for several people simultaneously in a small to medium size business environment.

- It is capable of supporting from 4 to about 200 simultaneous users.

- Some of the widely used mini computers are, PDP 11, IBM (8000 series), and VAX 7500.

Characteristics/Features of Mini Computers:

1. Small in size and require small space.
2. More reliable and less power required.
3. Faster in speed.
4. Larger primary and secondary storage capacity.
5. Use for scientific and commercial use.
6. Standardization of high level language.

Fig. 1.7: Mini Computer

Advantages:

1. They are faster and powerful than other computers.
2. Smaller in size and More reliable.
3. Less power required.
4. Larger storage capacity and Support standardized high level languages.

Disadvantages:

1. Air-conditioning required.
2. Cost is more than micro computer.

Applications:

1. Mini computers used for data management can be employed to acquire data, as in process control, generate data, or simply as a storage system for information.
2. Mini computers can be used as a communications tool in a larger system.

1.4.2.4 Micro Computers

- Micro computers are small, low-cost and single-user digital computer.

- A micro computer usually consists of a microprocessor, a storage unit, an input device, and an output device, all of which may be on one chip inserted into one or several PC boards. The addition of a power supply and connecting cables, appropriate peripherals (keyboard, monitor, printer, disk drives, etc.), an Operating System (OS) and other software programs can provide a complete micro computer system.

- The micro computer is generally the smallest of the computer family. Originally, they were designed for individual users only, but now-a-days they have become powerful tools for many businesses that, when networked together, can serve more than one user.

- IBM-PC Pentium 100, IBM-PC Pentium 200, and Apple Macintosh are some of the examples of micro computers.

- Micro computers include desktop, (See Fig. 1.8) laptop (See Fig. 1.9) and hand-held computers (See Fig. 1.10).

Characteristics/Features of micro computers:

1. Support Graphical User Interface (GUI).
2. Speed is faster and larger storage capacity.
3. More powerful.
4. Smaller in size and cheaper.
5. Uses standard high level programming.

Advantages of Micro Computers:

1. Smaller in size and Cheaper in cost.
2. More powerful and Easy for installation.
3. Air-conditioning not required.
4. Faster in speed.
5. Larger primary and secondary storage.
6. Sharing resources in networking.
7. More reliable and Less hardware failure.

Disadvantages of Micro Computers:

1. Non-portable.
2. Single user oriented.
3. More maintenance.

Applications of Micro Computers:

1. Families use micro computers for education; software can hold thousands of book volumes worth of information. Also, the first portable video games were built for the micro computers. The home micro computers paved the way for the invention of laptops.

2. Businesses took a huge leap forward in book-keeping, inventory, medical records and communication when micro computers were made readily available.

1.4.2.5 Types of Micro Computers like Laptop and Tablets

1. Desktop Computers:

- Desktop Computer or Personal Computer (PC) is the most common type of micro computer.

- Desktop computer is a stand-alone machine that can be placed on the desk. Externally, it consists of three units i.e., keyboard, monitor and a system unit containing the CPU, memory, hard disk drive, etc., (See Fig. 1.8).

- It is not very expensive and is suited to the needs of a single user at home, schools, small business units and organisations.

- Microsoft, Apple, HP, Lenovo and Dell are some of the PC manufacturers.

Advantages of Desktop PC:

(i) Lots of memory space.

(ii) Easy to upgrade and Fast processors.

(iii) Large screen (depending on the monitor).

(iv) Cheaper than laptops and tablets.

Fig. 1.8: Desktop Computer

Disadvantages of Desktop PC:

(i) Need keyboard, mouse and monitor etc.

(ii) Big and heavy and require space.

(iii) Probably without wireless connection.

(iv) Not portable.

2. Laptop Computers:

- Laptop computers are portable and light weight personal computers.

- Laptop computer can be taken from one place to another at any time very easily. It is also known as notebook computer, notepad or mobile computer.

- The laptop computer is a small-size computer that incurporates all the features of a typical desktop computer. Laptop computers are provided with a rechargeable battery that removes the need of continuous external power supply. However, these computer systems are more expensive than desktop computers.

Fig. 1.9: Laptop Computer

- The different manufacturers of laptop computers are, Acer, Apple, Panasonic, Sony and HP.

Advantages of Laptop PC:

(i)   Easy to carry because of smaller in size.

(ii) Light weight.

(iii) Portable.

Disadvantages of Laptop PC

(i)   Very expensive.

(ii) Less ergonomic than a desktop.

(iii) Easy to steal or loose or theft.

3. Hand-held Computers:

- Hand-held PCs are small computing devices which we can hold them in the hands for this reason they are called as hand-held devices or hand-held PCs.

- Hand-held computers also called Personal Digital Assistant (PDA), is a computer that can conveniently be stored in a pocket (of sufficient size) and used while the user is holding it.

- A PDA user generally uses a pen or electronic stylus, instead of a keyboard for input.

- As shown in Fig. 1.10, the monitor is very small and is the only apparent form of output. Since, these computers can be easily fitted on the palmtop.

- Hand-held computer are also known as palmtop computers.

- Hand-held computers usually have no disk drives, rather they use small cards to store programs and data. However, they can be connected to printer or a disk drive to generate output or store data.

- Hand-held computers have limited memory and are less powerful as compared to desktop computers.

- Some examples of PDAs are Apple Newton, Casio Cassiopeia, and Franklin eBookMan.

- Over the last few years, PDAs have merged into mobile phones to create smart phones.

- Smartphone a mobile phone that performs many of the functions of a computer.

- Smartphones are a handheld device that integrates mobile phone capabilities with the more common features of a handheld computer or PDA.

Fig. 1.10: Hand-held Computer

Advantages of PDA:

(i)   PDAs have increased in power and decreased in size.

(ii) PDA allows you to automatically store everything in one place and then synchronize it with the data already on your PC.

(iii) PDAs have GPS, Wi-Fi, E-mail and Bluetooth connectivity, along with a host of other applications. They also allow you to connect with other PDAs.

Disadvantages of PDA:

(i) PDAs are not designed for rough use. They are delicate devices that are vulnerable to bumps, scratches and even fractures.

(ii) PDAs are expensive. The typical costs associated with them include their cost of purchase and upgrades and cost of maintenance (servicing and batteries).

(iii) PDAs are limited in scope. They are neither laptop replacements nor can they be effectively used to replace cellular phones. PDAs are not equipped to deal entirely with micro-processing capabilities. Their display screens are small and most users find it difficult to navigate data on them.

(iv) PDAs are limited in terms of memory and many require additional memory upgrades.

4. Tablet Computers:

- A tablet is a wireless, portable personal computer with a touch screen interface.

- In this screen interface we can write or type the data and instructions. It uses a touch screen and digitizing tablet technology to accept data and information for processing.

- The tablet form factor is typically smaller than a notebook computer but larger than a smart phone.

- Tablet computer has features of the notebook computer but it can accept input from a stylus or a pen instead of the keyboard or mouse.

Fig. 1.11: Tablet Computer

Advantages of Tablet PC:

(i)   Small and light weight.

(ii)   Recognizes handwriting.

(iii) Great for note taking and multi-touch screen.

(iv)   Long battery lifetime.

Disadvantages of tablet PC:

(i)   Easy to damage.

(ii)   Small screen.

(iii) High cost.

- Difference between All Types of Computers:

Sr. No.	Types of Computer / Key features	Mini computers	Micro computers (Personal Computers)	Mainframe computers	Super computer
1.	Size	Small	Small	Large	Large
2.	Processing power	Low	Low	Higher	Highest
3.	Main memory capacity	Low	Low	Higher	Highest
4.	Single/Multiple processors	Single	Single	Multiple	Multiple
	Single/Multiple user oriented	Single	Single	Multiple	Multiple
5.	Hard Disk Storage Capacity	Low	Low	Highest	Higher
6.	Popular operating systems	MS-DOS, MS-Windows	MS-DOS, MS-Windows, Window-NT, Linux, Unix	Unix	Unix
7.	Display facility	Small display	Medium size display	Generally not available	Generally not available
8.	Examples:	(i) PDP-II (ii) PDP-45	(i) PC-XT (ii) PC-AT	(i) IBM 4381 (ii) NEC 610 (iii) DEC 10	(i) CRAY-XP (ii) ETA-10 (iii) PARAM

1.4.3 Types of Computers According to Purpose

- There are two types of computers according to their purpose i.e., general-purpose computers and special-purpose computers.

1. **General-purpose Computers:**
- A general-purpose computer, as the name suggests, is designed to perform a range of tasks.
- The computer that you use in your schools and homes are general-purpose computers.
- General-purpose computers have the ability to store numerous programs. These machines can be used for various applications, ranging from scientific as well as business purpose applications.

2. **Special-purpose Computers:**
- Special-purpose computers are designed to handle a specific problem or to perform a single specific task.
- A set of instructions for the specific task is built into the machine. Hence, they cannot be used for other applications unless their circuits are redesigned, that is, they lacked versatility.

- Most analog computers are special purpose computers.
- Special-purpose computers are used for airline reservations, satellite tracking, and air traffic control.

Difference between General-purpose and Special-purpose Computers:

Sr. No.	General-purpose Computer	Special-purpose Computer
1.	General-purpose computers are used for general purposes.	Special-purpose computers are used for specific purposes.
2.	General-purpose computer's has versatility because they able to perform a wide variety of operations.	Special-purpose computer's has the lack of versatility. It cannot be used to perform other operations.
3.	Usually inexpensive.	Usually expensive.
4.	It is more popular as they are cheap and can perform a variety of work.	Cost is high.

1.5 TYPES OF PROGRAMMING LANGUAGES

- Everyone in this world communicates with each other through some means or other. The sensible mean of communication is called as a language.
- A language is a medium for communication.
- Humans need languages like Marathi, English, Hindi, Punjabi, Tamil, and Bengali etc., to communicate with each other. But computers are machines. Unfortunately, they cannot understand natural languages. Therefore, they need some special languages to gives them instructions. This language is called a programming language.
- A computer language is also known as programming language. A programming language is a set of commands, instructions, and other syntax use to create a software program.
- A program is a set of instructions for performing a particular task. A program is also called as software. The art of writing a program is called as programming.
- Computer languages may be basically classified in three major categories as shown in Fig. 1.12.

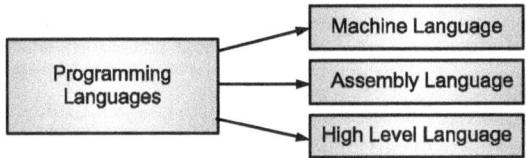

Fig. 1.12: Types of Programming Languages

1.5.1 Machine Language

- The set of instruction codes, whether in binary or decimal, which can be directly understood by the CPU of a computer without the help of translating program, is called a Machine Language. Thus, machine language programs need to be coded as strings of binary digits i.e., 0's and 1's.

- Machine code is the fundamental language of a computer. The circuitry of a computer is wired in such a way that it immediately recognizes the machine language and converts it into electrical signals to run the computer.

- An instruction prepared in any machine language has a two part format. The first part is the **command or operation**, and it tells the computer what function to perform. The second part of the **instruction is the operand**, and it tells the computer where to find or store the data or other instructions that are to be manipulated.

- Typical operations involve reading, adding, subtracting, writing and so on. For example typical program instruction to print out a number on the printer might be,

  001100101010

- Machine language is usually used for complex applications such as space control system, nuclear reactors, and chemical processing.

Advantages of Machine Language:

1. **Translation Free:** Machine language written in 0's and 1's so, CPU directly understands machine instructions and no translation of the program is required.

2. **High Speed:** Since, no translation is needed, the applications developed using machine language is extremely fast.

Disadvantages of Machine Language:

1. **Machine-Dependent:** Machine language differs from computer to computer. Hence, the program written for one machine cannot be executed on other machines.

2. **Difficult to Write or Program:** Writing a program in machine language is very tedious because it is difficult to learn and understand the language, which is in strings of 0's and 1's.

3. **Difficult to Modify:** Checking machine instructions to locate errors is very difficult and time consuming.

4. **Error Prone:** Programmers have to remember the opcodes and must keep track of the storage locations of the data and instructions; hence, it becomes very difficult to concentrate fully on the logic of the problem.

1.5.2 Assembly Language

- As computer became more popular, it became quite apparent that machine language programming was simply too slow, tedious for most programmers.

- The language which substitutes letters and symbols for the numbers in the machine language program is called an Assembly Language or Symbolic Language.

- A program written in symbolic language that uses symbols instead of numbers is called assembly code or symbolic code i.e. MNEMONICS.

- The computer instructions are written in easily understandable short words which are called MNEMONICS. For example, MOV stands for moving the data, SUB stands for subtraction, ADD stands for addition, etc. All instructions are written in capital letters.

- A program in assembly language needs software known as an assembler which converts the program consisting of mnemonics and data into machine language.

- Fig. 1.13 shows mnemonic code converted into machine code.

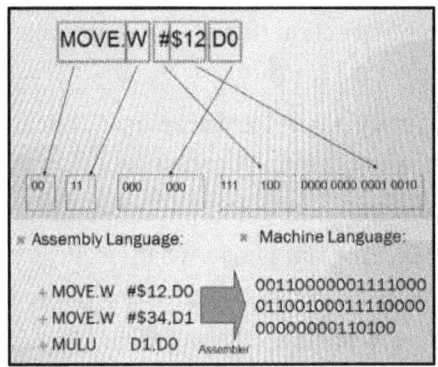

Fig. 1.13

Advantages of Assembly Language:

1. **Faster:** Assembly level language programs can run much faster and use less memory and other resources than a similar program written in a high level language.

2. **Easier to Understand and Use:** Assembly language is easier to understand and use because mnemonic is used instead of numeric op-codes and suitable names are used for data.

3. **Easy to Locate and Correct Errors:** While writing programs in assembly language, fewer errors are made and those errors are easier to find and correct because of the use of mnemonics and symbolic field names. Programmers can easily track and locate errors.

4. **Easier to Modify:** Assembly language programs are easier for people or user to modify than machine language programs.

Disadvantages of Assembly Language:

1. **Slow Development Time:** Assembly level language generated applications are slower and time consuming to develop.

2. **Machine Dependent:** Assembly language programs are machine dependent i.e., assembly language is differ from computer to computer.

3. **Knowledge of Hardware Required:** Since, assembly languages are machine dependent, so the programmer must be aware of a particular machine's characteristics and requirements as the program is written.

4. **Machine Level Coding:** A machine cannot execute an assembly language program directly. It needs to be first translated into machine language code. This is done by an assembler.

1.5.3 High Level Language

- During 1960s computers started to gain popularity and it became necessary to develop languages that were more like natural languages such as English so that a common user could use the computer efficiently.

- High level languages are similar to English language. Programs written using these languages can be machine independent.

- A single high-level statement can substitute several instructions in machine or assembly language.

- In high-level language, programs are written in a sequence of statements to solve a problem. For example: sum = x + y.

- Languages such as COBOL, FORTRAN, BASIC, and C are considered high-level languages.

Advantages:

1. **Machine Independent:** High-Level Language (HLL) are machine independent in the sense that a program created using HLL can be used on different platforms with very little or no change at all.

2. **Fewer Errors:** In case of high level languages, since the programmer need not write all the small steps carried out by the computer, for this reason the computer is much less likely to make an error.

3. **Easier to Maintain:** Program written in high level languages are easier to maintain than assembly or machine language programs.

4. **Easy to Learn and Use:** These languages are very similar to the languages normally used us in our day to day life. Hence, they are easy to learn and use.

5. **Lower Program Preparation Development Cost:** Writing programs in high level languages requires less time and effort, which ultimately leads to lower program preparation cost.

Disadvantages:

(i) **Lack of Flexibility:** Because the automatic features of high level languages always occur and are not under the control of the programmer, they are less flexible than assembly languages.

(ii) **Lower Efficiency:** The programs written in high level languages take more time to run and require more main storage.

(iii) **Poor Control on Hardware:** Sometimes, the applications written in high level languages cannot completely harness the total power available at hardware level.

Comparison of Machine, Assembly and High Level Languages:

Sr. No.	Machine Language	Assembly Language	High Level Language
1.	It is in the form of 0's and 1's.	It is in the form of symbolic phrases called as mnemonic like ADD, MOV etc.	It is in the form of English words.
2.	Machine dependent language.	Machine dependent language.	Machine independent language.
3.	It does not need any language translators like assembler or compiler.	A translator 'assembler' is required to convert assembly language into machine code.	A translator like 'compiler or interpreter' is required to translate high level language into machine level languages.
4.	It is difficult to programming.	It is difficult to programming.	Easy to programming.
5.	Speed is high.	Speed is high.	Slow speed.
6.	Hard and difficult to understand.	Hard and difficult to understand.	Easy and simple to understand.
7.	Not user friendly.	Not user friendly.	User friendly.

1.6 | TRANSLATORS

- We know that a program is a set of instructions for performing a particular task.

- Translator is a general term used far converting one form of computer language into another form, (See Fig. 1.14).

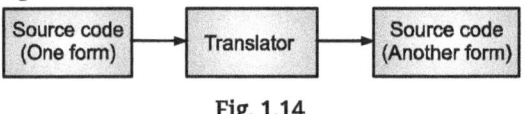

Source code (One form) → Translator → Source code (Another form)

Fig. 1.14

- Translators are software packages, which accept the source language code as input and produce either the object language, target language or machine language code as output.

- The written program is called the source program. The source program is to be converted to the machine language, which is called an object program.

- A list of translators is given in Fig. 1.15.

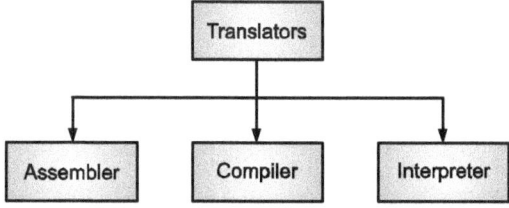

Fig. 1.15: Types of Translators

1.6.1 Assembler

- It is a software which translates an assembly language into a machine code.

- An assembler translates the symbolic codes of programs of an assembly language into machine language instructions as shown in Fig. 1.16.

- The input of the assembler is called a source program that contains only assembly level instructions. The output that are generated by the assemblers are called an object code or a machine level code of a particular computer hardware.

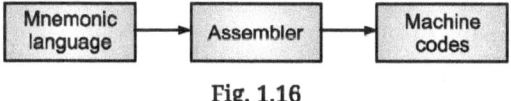

Fig. 1.16

- Examples of assemblers are TASM (Turbo ASseMbler), Microsoft MASM (Macro ASeMbler).

1.6.2 Compiler

- A program that translates a high level language program into machine language program is called a complier.

- Programming languages like TURBO C, TURBO PROLOG, C++, Pascal, COBOL are the some examples of compilers.

- Compiler can be defined as "a system program, which converts a HLL (High Level Language) program into its MLL (Machine Level Language) equivalent".

- A program written in a HLL is called a source program and the machine code obtained after conversion is called object program.

- The process of converting a high level language program into machine level language using a compiler is called as compilation.

- Fig. 1.17 shows compiler process.

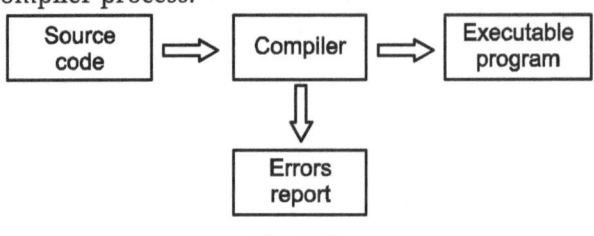

Fig. 1.17

1.6.3 Interpreter

- An interpreter is a software which converts a program that is written in a high level language into a machine level code line by line.

- An interpreter translate a statement in a program and executes the statements immediately, before translating the next source language statement.

- The input file or text of the interpreters is called a source program that contains a program written in a high level language. The output of the interpreter is known as an object program, (See Fig. 1.18).

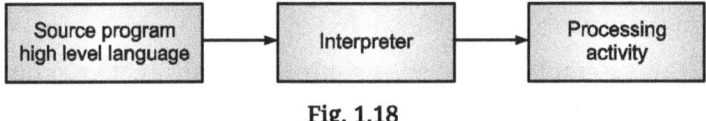

Fig. 1.18

Characteristics of Interpreter:

1. Interpreter detects only one error at a time.
2. It translates line by line into a machine language.
3. Special instruction is required to store it in the memory.
4. It relatively requires less memory space.

- Programming languages like PHP, BASIC, LOGO, LISP are uses of interpreter.

Comparison between Compiler and Interpreter:

Sr. No.	Interpreter	Compiler
1.	Interpreter program works line-by-line. It takes one statement at a time as input.	Compiler works on the complete program at once. It takes the entire program as input.
2.	Interpreter does not generate intermediate object code or machine code.	Compiler generates intermediate code, called the object code or machine code.

contd. ...

3.	Requires less main memory.	Requires more main memory.
4.	Each time program is executed, every time is checked for syntax and then converted into equivalent machine code.	Converts entire program to machine code, when all syntax errors are removed and, executes object code directly.
5.	Source program and interpreter both are required for execution.	Neither source nor compiler are required for execution.
6.	Easily debugging and testing.	Slow for debugging and testing.
7.	Execution time is more.	Execution time is less.
8.	Examples of programming languages that use compilers: C, C++, COBOL.	Examples of programming languages that use interpreters: BASIC, Visual Basic (VB), Python, Ruby, PHP, Perl, MATLAB, Lisp.

1.7 | DATA ORGANIZATION

- Data organisation refers to the systematic organisation of data, often in a hierarchical form. It is a way of grouping data or information.

- Data organisation involves files, directories, drives etc. Some common terms in data organisation is given below:

  1. **Bit (Binary Digit):** A bit is the smallest unit in digital representation of information. A bit has only two values, ON and OFF where ON is represented by 1 and OFF by 0.

  2. **Nibble:** A group of 4 bits is called nibble.

  3. **Byte:** A group of 8 bits is called byte. A byte is the smallest unit which can represent a data item or a character.

  4. **Word:** A computer word, like a byte, is a group of fixed number of bits processed as a unit which varies from computer to computer but is fixed for each computer. The length of a computer word is called word-size or word length and it may be as small as 8 bits or may be as long as 96 bits. A computer stores the information in the form of computer words.

     Few higher storage units are following

     (i)   Kilobyte (KB)   1 KB = 1024 Bytes

     (ii)   Megabyte (MB) 1 MB = 1024 KB

     (iii) GigaByte (GB)   1 GB = 1024 MB

     (iv) TeraByte (TB   1 TB = 1024 GB

     (v)   PetaByte (PB)   1 PB = 1024 TB

5. **Datafield:** It holds a single fact or attribute of an entity.
6. **Record:** It is a collection of related fields.
7. **File:** It is a collection of related records.
8. **Directory:** It is a group of files, also called as folder.
9. **Database:** It is a collection of related data.
10. **DBMS:** Files are integrated into database, this is done using DBMS (DataBase Management System).

1.7.1 Files

- In Information Systems (ISs) we deal with data. This data has to be arranged in a proper way to accept process and communicate operations and results. For arranging the data, we need files.
- A file is an organized collection of data/information stored on a storage device such as floppy, hard disk or magnetic tape.
- A file can be defined as "a named collection of related data". A file is identified by its file name.
- A file system is the way your computer stores and organizes its files.
- All files can be broadly classified as either text files or binary files. In a text file, the bytes of data are organized as characters from the ASCII or Unicode character sets. A binary file requires a specific interpretation of the bits based on the data in the file.
- The files that containing data is called as data files such as transaction file, report file etc., while the files containing software instructions called as program files.

1.7.2 Directory

- A typical computer system today may store thousands or even tens of thousands of files on its secondary storage. Apart from the files created by users, a large number of files are placed in secondary storage by the Operating System (OS) and by the application software.
- For effective and efficient organisation of information; it is necessary to group related files together into a structure of directories and sub-directories.
- A directory is special type of file that contains other files. It is also called as folder.
- In short, a group of files can be stored in a directory.
- A directory may also contain directories within it. Such directory within a directory is called sub-directory.
- A directory is nothing but a special type of file which records information about other files and sub-directories.

- Fig. 1.19 shows a typical directory structure, note that, since directories can contain sub-directories, the resulting structure becomes a hierarchy of directories.

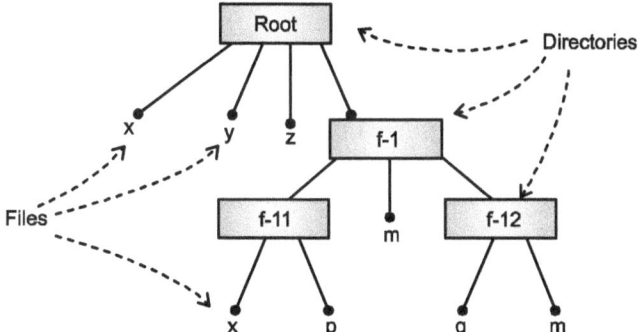

Fig. 1.19: Hierarchical Structure of Files and Directories

1.7.3 Drives

- A computer drive is a piece of hardware that is used to read and store information on the computer and that is usually not as easily removed as a disk.
- There are many different kinds of drives available for computers. One example is the hard drive, which serves as the main storage area in a computer. Hard drives are not removable.
- There are also disk drives for CDs, DVDs, Blu-rays, CD-RWs and other types of removable media that are inserted into the drive where information is read. Portable drives are another type of drive that usually plugs into a computer by way of a USB connection.
- Hard disk drives (also called hard drives or disk drives) is the mechanism that reads and writes data on a hard disk (a magnetic disk on which you can store computer data).
- Hard Drive (HD) is a magnetic media device. It is the traditional non-volatile storage used by computers and is reasonably fast, able to store vast amounts of data and very competitive price-wise per Gb of storage.
- Fig. 1.20 shows parts of hard drive.
- A drive is a group of directories or files themselves and it is represented by a letter like A, B, C, D....etc. It can be a floppy drive (Usually designed as A and B) or a HDD designated as C, D.... etc.
- The Fig. 1.20 is an example of different drives listed in Microsoft Windows 7.

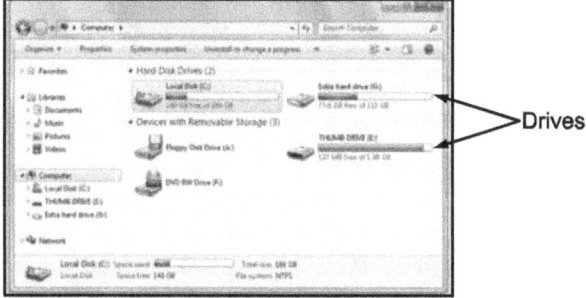

Fig. 1.20

- In the Fig. 1.20 drive A: is the floppy drive, C: is the hard disk drive, G: and E: partitions of the hard drive, and F: is the DVD-RW drive.

PRACTICE QUESTIONS

1. What is computer?
2. Explain generations of computer in detail.
3. Define the following terms:
    (i)   Computer,
    (ii) Software,
    (iii) Hardware, and
    (iv) User.
4. What is analog computer? Explain its applications.
5. What is file and directory?
6. Compare analog and digital computer.
7. What are the types of computers? Explain two of them in detail.
8. Describe general and special purpose computer in detail.
9. Write short note on : Drives.
10. What is super computer? State its advantages and disadvantages.
11. What is mini computer? State its advantages and disadvantages.
12. What is mainframe computer? State its advantages and disadvantages.
13. What is micro computer? State its advantages and disadvantages.
14. Distinguish between:
    (i) Mini and micro computers.
    (ii) Super and mainframe computers.
15. What are the types of micro computer?
16. Explain hybrid computer in detail.
17. What is machine language? State its advantages and disadvantages.
18. Write short note on: Assembly language.
19. With the help of diagram describe compiler.
20. What is interpreter? Explain its working diagrammatically.
21. Explain the term assembler in detail.
22. Describe block diagram of computer in detail
23. Explain computer system in detail.
24. Define the following terms:
    (i) Program,
    (ii) Programming.
25. Describe compiler in detail.

■■■

Introduction to Computer Peripherals

Contents ...

2.1 | INTRODUCTION

- A computer interacts with the external/outside environment via the input-output (I/O) devices attached to it.
- Input device is used for providing data and instructions to the computer. After processing the input data, computer provides output to the user via the output device.
- The I/O devices that are attached, externally, to the computer machine are also called peripheral devices.
- Different kinds of input and output devices are used for different kinds of input and output requirements.
- Today's peripherals devices will have wired or wireless connectivity with the CPU.

2.2 | PRIMARY AND SECONDARY STORAGE DEVICES

- A memory is just like a human brain. It is used to store data and instruction in computer.
- The primary goal of computer memory is to store data.
- There are two types of memories:
  1. **Volatile Memory** is a type of memory (storage) whose contents are erased when the system's power is turned off or interrupted.
  2. **Non-volatile Memory** is any memory or storage that will be saved regardless if the power to the computer is on or off.
- Computer memory or storage is divide into primary storage and secondary storage.

1. **Primary Storage:**
- Primary storage (or main memory or internal memory), often referred to simply as memory, is the only one, directly accessible to the CPU.
- The CPU continuously reads instructions stored there and executes them as required.
- Any data actively operated on, is also stored there in uniform manner.
- Primary memory holds only those data and instructions on which computer is currently working. It has limited capacity and data get lost when power is switched off so, it is volatile in nature.
- It is generally made up of semiconductor device. These memories are not as fast as registers. The data and instruction required to be processed earlier reside in main memory.
- Primary memory is divided into two sub-categories RAM and ROM.

2. **Secondary Storage:**
- Secondary storage (also known as external memory or auxiliary storage), differs from primary storage in that it is not directly accessible by the CPU.

- The computer usually uses its input/output channels to access secondary storage and transfers the desired data using intermediate area in primary storage.

- Secondary storage does not lose the data when the device is powered off – it is non-volatile.

- Contents of secondary memories are first transferred to main memory, and then CPU can access it. For example: Disk, CD-ROM, DVD etc.

Comparison between Primary and Secondary Storages (Memories):

Sr. No.	Primary Storage	Secondary Storage
1.	It is a part of CPU.	It is not a part of CPU.
2.	Most primary storage is temporary i.e. volatile in nature.	All secondary storage is permanent i.e. non-volatile in nature.
3.	It is the internal or main memory.	It is the external memory.
4.	The access time is less a few nanoseconds.	The access time is more a few milliseconds.
5.	It is a medium capacity memory.	It is a high capacity memory.
6.	It is further classified as RAM and ROM.	There are different types of secondary storage devices such as Hard Disk, Floppy Disk, CD-ROM etc.
7.	Primary storage is usually faster therefore more expensive.	Secondary storage connects to the CPU via cables or USB and therefore is slower.
8.	Examples: RAM, ROM etc.	Examples: Hard disk, CDs, DVDs etc.

2.2.1 Primary Storage Devices

- Fig. 2.1 shows primary storage devices.

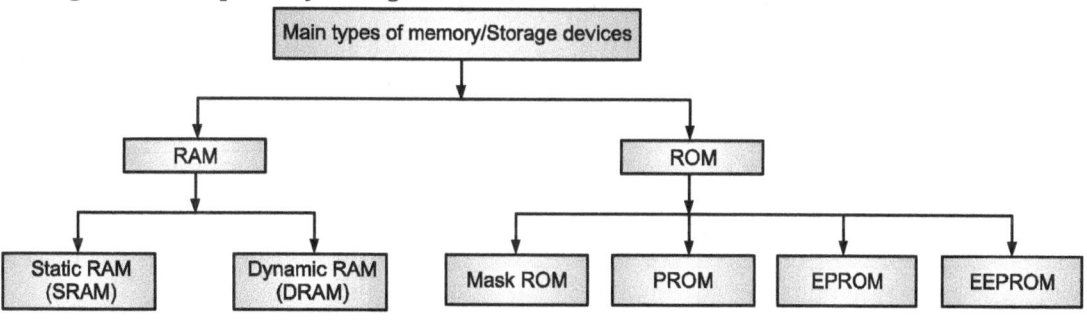

Fig. 2.1: Primary Storage Devices

2.2.1.1 RAM

- RAM stands for Random Access Memory.
- A RAM constitutes the internal memory of the CPU for storing data, program and program result.
- RAM is read/write memory.
- RAM is used to store data and instructions during the operation of computer.
- RAM is volatile in nature, i.e. data stored in it is lost when we switch off the computer or if there is a power failure.
- This memory is accessible from any memory location anytime; one can switch to one place to another place in memory randomly.
- RAM is of two types i.e. Static RAM (SRAM) and Dynamic RAM (DRAM).

1. SRAM:

- SRAM (Static Random Access Memory) is a type of semiconductor memory where the word static indicates that, it does not need to be periodically refreshed, as SRAM uses bi-stable latching circuitry to store each bit.
- SRAM is volatile in the conventional sense that data is eventually lost when the memory is not powered.
- Static RAM is used as cache memory needs to be very fast and small.

2. DRAM:

- DRAM (Dynamic Random Access Memory) is a type of random access memory that stores each bit of data in a separate capacitor within an integrated circuit.
- Since, real capacitors leak charge, the information eventually fades unless the capacitor charge is refreshed periodically. Because of this refresh requirement, it is a dynamic memory as opposed to SRAM and other static memory.

Comparison between Static RAM and Dynamic RAM:

Sr. No.	Static RAM (SRAM)	Dynamic RAM (DRAM)
1.	Each static RAM cell is a flip-flop.	A dynamic RAM cell consists of a MOSFET and a capacitor.
2.	Less number of memory cells/unit area.	More number of memory cells/unit area.
3.	More number of components per cell.	Only two components per cell.
4.	Does not require refreshing.	Require refreshing.
5.	Faster memories.	Slower memories.
6.	Power consumption is less.	More power consumption.

Advantages of RAM:

1. RAM uses much less power than disk drives. Reduce your CO_2 emissions and extend your battery life.
2. RAM is the fastest storage medium outside of the CPU.

Disadvantages of RAM:

1. A power outage will cause irrecoverable data loss.
2. RAM cost per bit is high.
3. RAM has limited memory space.

2.2.1.2 ROM

- ROM stands for Read Only Memory.
- ROM is the memory from which we can only read but cannot write on it.
- ROM is a non-volatile primary memory. It does not lose its content when the power is switched off.
- Read only memory, also known as firmware, is an integrated circuit programmed with specific data when it is manufactured. ROM chips are used not only in computers, but in most other electronic items as well like washing machine and microwave oven.
- A ROM, stores such instruction as are required to start computer when electricity is first turned on, this operation is referred to as bootstrap.

Types of ROM:

1. MROM:

- MROM stands for Masked ROM.
- The very first ROMs were hard-wired devices that contained a pre-programmed set of data or instructions. These kinds of ROMs are known as masked ROMs.
- MROM is inexpensive ROM.

2. PROM:

- PROM stands for Programmable Read Only Memory.
- PROM is read-only memory that can be modified only once by a user. The user buys a blank PROM and enters the desired contents using a PROM programmer.
- Inside the PROM chip there are small fuses which are burnt open during programming.
- PROM can be programmed only once and is not erasable.

3. EPROM:

- EPROM stands for Erasable and Programmable Read Only Memory.
- An EPROM is a type of memory chip that retains its data when its power supply is switched off.
- The EPROM can be erased by exposing it to ultra-violet light for a duration of up to 40 minutes. Usually, a EPROM eraser achieves this function.

4. EEPROM:

- EEPROM stands for Electrically Erasable and Programmable Read Only Memory. EEPROM also written as E^2PROM.

- EEPROM is a type of non-volatile memory used in computers and other electronic devices to store small amounts of data that must be saved when power is removed,

- The EEPROM is programmed and erased electrically. It can be erased and reprogrammed about ten thousand times. Both erasing and programming take about 4 to 10 ms (milli second).

- In EEPROM, any location can be selectively erased and programmed. EEPROMs can be erased one byte at a time, rather than erasing the entire chip. Hence, the process of re-programming is flexible but slow.

Comparison between PROM, EPROM and EEPROM:

Sr. No.	PROM	EPROM	EEPROM
1.	PROM stands for Programmable Read Only Memory.	EPROM stands for Erasable Programmable Read Only Memory.	EEPROM stands for Electrically Erasable Programmable Read Only Memory.
2.	PROM is a memory chip on which data can be written only once.	EPROM is a special type of PROM that can be erased by exposing it to ultra-violet light.	EEPROM is a special type of PROM that can be erased by exposing it to an electrical charge.
3.	Once, a program has been written onto a PROM, it remains there forever.	Once, it is erased, it can be reprogrammed.	EEPROM retains its contents even when the power is turned OFF.
4.	Data alteration or updation is not possible in PROM.	Data alteration or updation is possible in EPROM.	Data alteration or updation is possible in EEPROM.

Advantages of ROM:

1. Non-volatile in nature.
2. Cheaper than RAMs.
3. Easy to test.
4. More reliable than RAMs.
5. These are static and do not require refreshing.

Disadvantages of ROM:

1. More power consumption.
2. For functions with more inputs a ROM based circuit is impractical because of the limit on ROM sizes that are available.
3. Increase in size with increase in number of input variables.

Comparison between RAM and ROM:

Sr. No.	RAM	ROM
1.	RAM stands for Random Access Memory.	ROM stands for Read Only Memory.
2.	It is a read/write memory.	It is a read only memory.
3.	It is volatile storage device.	It is a non-volatile storage device.
4.	Faster in speed.	Slower in speed.
5.	Data is erased as soon as power supply is turned off.	Data remains stored even after power supply has been turned off.
6.	It is used as the main memory of a computer system.	It is used to store Basic Input Output System (BIOS).

2.2.2 Secondary Storage Devices

- Secondary storage devices facilitate storing of data and instructions permanently.
- Fig. 2.2 shows types of secondary storage devices.

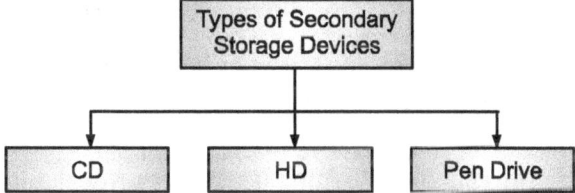

Fig. 2.2: Types of Secondary Storage Devices

2.2.2.1 CD

- CD stands for Compact Disk.
- CD is an optical storage medium that can store upto 700 MB of data.
- A CD is an optical storage medium with digital data recorded on its surface.
- Several other formats were further derived from these, including write-once audio and data storage (CD-R), rewritable media (CD-RW), Video Compact Disc (VCD), Super Video Compact Disc (SVCD), Photo CD, PictureCD, CD-i, and Enhanced Music CD.
- CD-ROM stands for "Compact Disc Read-Only Memory". Computers can read CD-ROMs, but cannot write to CD-ROMs which are not writable or erasable.

- A CD-ROM drive is a type of device used by your computer to read CDs. These CDs are used for a variety of purposes such as installing software and playing music.

- Fig. 2.3 shows a typical CD-ROM.

Fig. 2.3: CD-ROM

- A CD-ROM drive operates by using a laser to reflect light off the bottom of the disc.
- The reflected light is then read by a photo detector. The overall operation of a CD-ROM drive is as shown in Fig. 2.4.

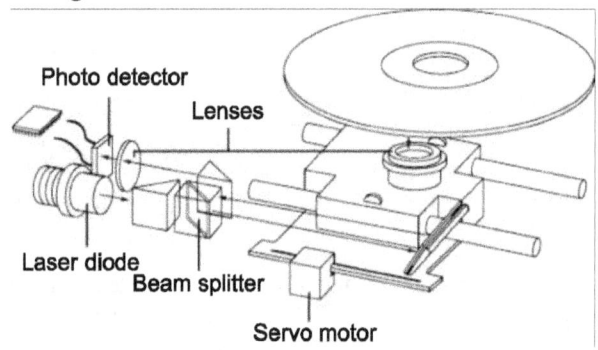

Fig. 2.4: Typical Components inside a CD-ROM Drive

1. The laser diode emits a low-energy infrared beam toward a reflecting mirror.
2. The servo motor, on command from the microprocessor, positions the beam onto the correct track on the CD-ROM by moving the reflecting mirror.
3. When the beam hits the disc, its refracted light is gathered and focused through the first lens beneath the platter, bounced off the mirror, and sent toward the beam splitter.
4. The beam splitter directs the returning laser light toward another focusing lens.
5. The last lens directs the light beam to a photo detector that converts the light into electric impulses.
6. These incoming impulses are decoded by the microprocessor and sent along to the host computer as data.

DVD:

- DVD is an abbreviation of Digital Versatile Disc, and is an optical disc storage media format that can be used for data storage.
- The DVD supports disks with capacities of 4.7 GB to 17 GB and access rates of 600 Kbps to 1.3 mbps.
- A standard DVD disc store up to 4.7 GB of data. There are two types of DVD's: DVD-ROM and DVD-RW.

Advantages of Optical Disk:

1. It is not affected by magnetic field.
2. The life span for data storage in optical disk is considered to be more, about 10-20 years as compared to magnetic disks.
3. It possesses large capacity to store data/information in the form of multimedia, graphics, and video files.
4. Due to its small size and lightweight, it is easily portable and stored.
5. It holds more data recording density as compared to other storage media; therefore, it has low cost per bit of storage.
6. It is tougher than magnetic tapes or floppy disks. It is physically harder to break or melt.

Disadvantages of Optical Disk:

1. It possesses slow data access speed as compared to magnetic disks.
2. It is not easy to write as a floppy disk. One needs to use both software and hardware for writing optical disks.
3. The drive mechanism of optical disk is more complicated than the magnetic and floppy disks.

2.2.2.2 HD

-   The hard disk, also called the hard drive or fixed disk, is the primary storage unit of the computer.
-   It is a non-volatile, random access digital magnetic data storage device.
-   A Hard Disk (HD) consists of one or more platters divided into concentric tracks and sectors. It is mounted on a central spindle, like a stack. It can be read by a read/write head that pivots across the rotating disks.
-   The data is stored on the platters covered with magnetic coating as shown in Fig. 2.5.

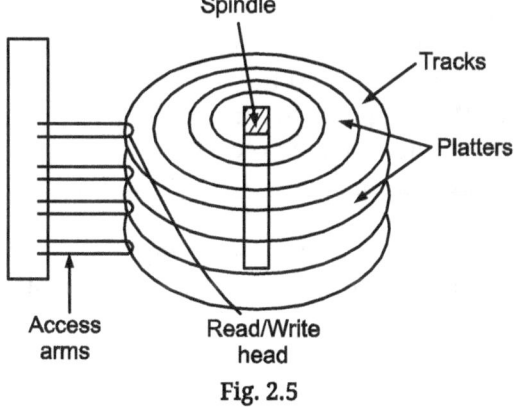

Fig. 2.5

- Fig. 2.6 shows internal construction of hard disk.

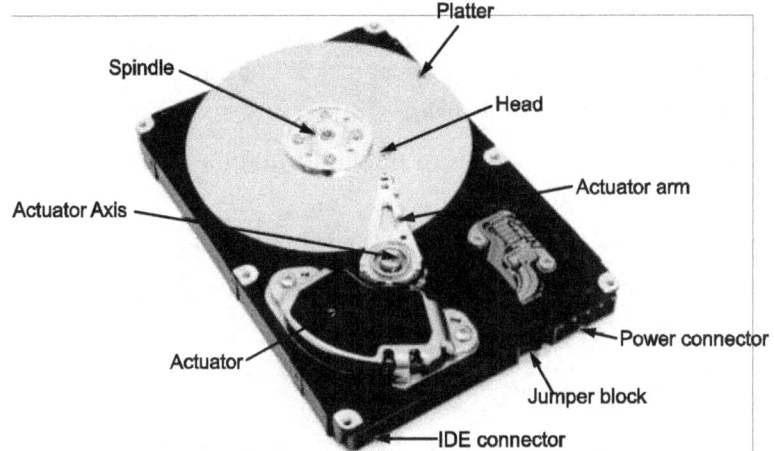

Fig. 2.6: Internal Construction of Hard Disk

- When you store information on your hard drive the computer allocates tracks and sectors to store that information in. Tracks are concentric circles and the sectors are portions of those tracks as shown in Fig. 2.7.

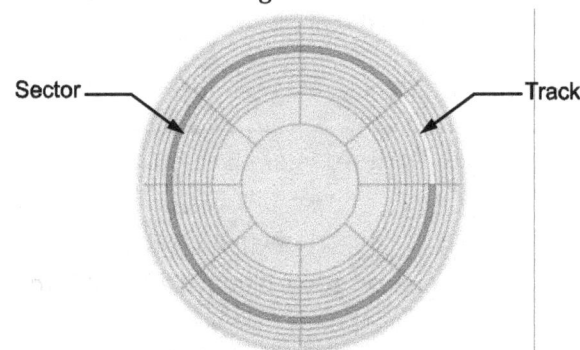

Fig. 2.7: Sectors and Tracks in Hard Disks

Advantages:

1. Large storage capacity.
2. Stores and retrieves data much faster than a floppy disk or CD-ROM.
3. Data is not lost when you switch off the computer.
4. Usually fixed inside the computer so cannot get mislaid.
5. Cheap on a cost per megabyte compared to other storage media.
6. Hard disks can be replaced and upgraded as necessary.

Disadvantages:

1. Hard disks eventually fail which stops the computer from working.
2. Regular 'head' crashes can damage the surface of the disk, leading to loss of data in that sector.
3. The disk is fixed inside the computer and cannot easily be transferred to another computer.

Comparison between Hard Disk (HD) and CD-ROM:

Sr. No.	Hard Disk	CD-ROM
1.	Hard disks are also known as fixed disks.	CD-ROMs are also known as optical disks.
2.	Hard disks are not portable.	CD-ROMs are portable.
3.	It is costly.	It is cheap.
4.	The computer takes less time to read from hard disk. It is in the range of 10 to 30 milliseconds.	The computer takes more time to read from CD-ROM. It is in the range of 100 to 300 milliseconds.
5.	Data can be read or written as and when required. These can be reused.	It is a permanent storage medium. Data once recorded, cannot be erased and hence, the CD-ROMs cannot be reused.
6.	Hard disk require a less complicated drive mechanism.	CD-ROMs required a more complicated drive mechanism.
7.	Hard disks have a very large storage capacity.	It has a storage capacity of about 650 Mega-bytes.

2.2.2.3 Pen Drive

- A pen drive is a removable storage device that is frequently used nowadays to transfer audio, video, and data files from one computer to another.

- Pen drive also called as flash drive.

- A pen drive consists of a small printed circuit board, which is fitted inside a plastic, metal, or rubber casing to protect it.

- The USB connector which is present at one end of pen drive is protected by either a removable cap or pulling it back in the casing.

- Fig. 2.8 shows a pen or flash drive.

- Pen drive is a high storage (ranging from 1 GB to 32 GB) capacity device and is physically small enough to fit into a pocket.

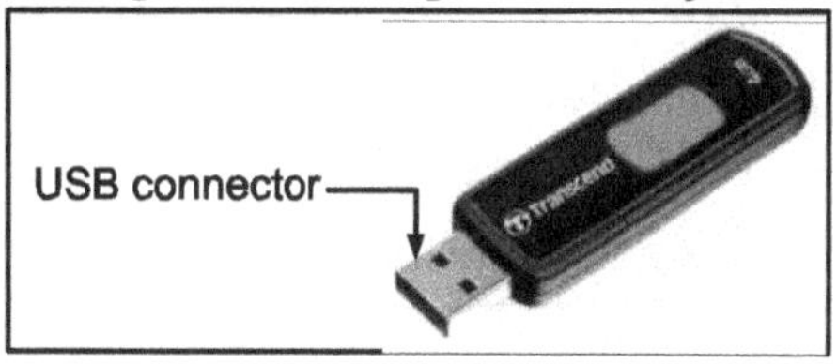

USB connector

Fig. 2.8: Pen Drive

Advantages:

1. Smaller in size.

2. Faster read and write compared to traditional hard disk drives.

3. Uses less power than traditional hard disk drives.

4. Less prone to damage.

5. Cheaper than traditional drives in small storage capacities.

Disadvantages:

1. Most flash drives do not have have a write-protection mechanism.

2. Smaller size devices, such as flash drives make them easier to lose.

2.3 | I/O DEVICES

- Input/Output devices abbreviated as I/O devices and they provides way of computer and user interaction.

- Fig. 2.9 shows the role of I/O devices in a computer system.

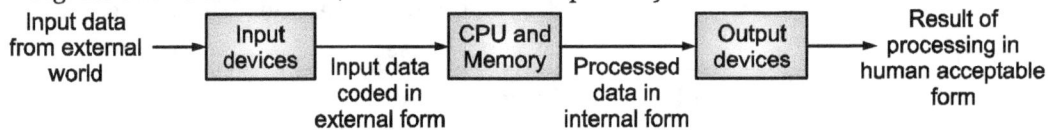

Fig. 2.9: Role of I/O Devices in Computer

- An input device is an electro-mechanical device that accepts data from outside world and translates them into a form of computer can interpret. Some examples of input devices are keyboard, mouse, trackball, joystick, scanner, etc.

- After processing the input data, the computer provides the results with the help of output devices. An output device converts machine-readable information into human-readable form. Some examples of output devices are printers, plotters, monitors, projectors, etc.

2.3.1 Scanners

- Scanner is an input device which works more like a photocopy (Xerox) machine.

- Scanners are peripheral devices used to digitize (convert to electronic format) artwork, photographs, text, or other items from hard copy.

- Scanner is used for direct data entry form the source document into the computer system.

- It converts the document image into digital form so that it can be fed into the computer. Capturing information like this reduces the possibility of errors typically experienced during large data entry.

Fig. 2.10: Scanner

- There are several types of scanners, all of which serve a variety of functions:
   1. **Flat-bed Scanner:** This scanner allows the user to place a full piece of paper, book, magazine, photo or any other object onto the bed of the scanner and have the capability to scan that object.
   2. **Sheet-fed Scanner:** This scanner allows user to scan pieces of paper. The sheet-fed scanner is a less expensive solution when compared to the flatbed scanner.
   3. **Hand-held Scanner:** The hand-held scanner allows the user to drag over select sections of pages, books, magazines, and other objects scanning only sections.

Advantages:
1. Fast and convenient way of copy an image.
2. Flat bed scanners are very accurate and can produce reasonably high quality images.
3. Hand-held scanners are portable and small in size.

Disadvantages:
1. Scanners are relatively slow.
2. Scanned images take up a lot of memory space.
3. Quality of scan not the same as original.

2.3.2 Digitizers

- Digitizer is an input device which converts analog information into a digital form.
- Digitizer is also known as Tablet or Graphics Tablet because it converts graphics and pictorial data into binary inputs.
- A graphic tablet as digitizer is used for doing fine works of drawing and image manipulation applications.
- A tablet or digitizer consists essentially of three interconnected parts:
   1. **A thin flat plate** (known as the platen or, confusingly, the tablet) which forms the work surface or active area.
   2. **A pointing device** which can be moved about the platen,
   3. **A controller** which converts the electrical signals arising from the interaction of the pointer and the platen into location information relative to some origin.

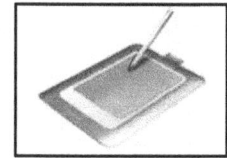

- Digitizing is the process of indentifying, locating or selecting a menu item, entity or point through an input device.

Fig. 2.11: Digitizer

Advantages:
1. Lighter weight, lower power models can function similarly to dedicated E-book readers like the Amazon, Kindle etc.

2. Touch environment makes navigation easier than conventional use of keyboard and mouse or touch pad.

3. Digital painting and image editing are more precise and intuitive than painting or sketching with a mouse.

4. The ability for easier or faster entry of diagrams, mathematical notations, and symbols.

Disadvantages:

1. Higher price.

2. It requires more knowledge of the programs is needed – because information on e.g. icons isn't obtained by pointing at them.

3. They have weaker video capabilities.

4. Their screens also serve as input devices, they run a higher risk of screen damage from impacts and misuse.

2.3.3 Plotters

- A plotter is a device that draws images on paper after receiving a command from a computer.
- A plotter is a special output device used to produce hardcopies of graphs and designs on the paper.
- A plotter is typically used to print large-format graphs or maps such as construction maps, engineering drawings and big posters.
- Computer Aided Engineering (CAE) applications like CAD (Computer Aided Design) and CAM (Computer Aided Manufacturing) are typical usage areas for plotters.
- Plotters are divided into two types drum plotter and flatbed plotter.

1. Drum Plotter:

- A drum plotter is also known as roller plotter.
- Drum plotter consists of a drum or roller on which a paper is placed and the drum rotates back and forth to produce the graph on the paper.
- Drum plotter also consists of mechanical device known as Robotic Drawing Arm that holds a set of colored ink pens or pencils.
- The robotic drawing arm moves side to side as the paper are rolled back and forth through the roller. In this way, a perfect graph or map is created on the paper. This work is done under the control of computer.

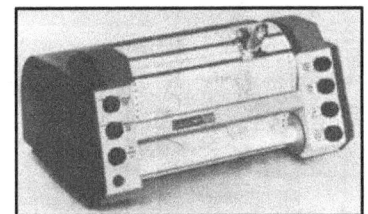

- Drum plotters are used to produce continuous output, such as plotting earthquake activity.

Fig. 2.12: Drum Plotter

2. Flatbed Plotter:

- A flatbed plotter is also known as table plotter.
- Flatbed plotter plots on paper that is spread and fixed over a rectangular flatbed table.
- The flatbed plotter uses two robotic drawing arms, each of which holds a set of colored ink pens or pencils. The drawing arms move over the stationary paper and draw the graph on the paper. Typically, the plot size is equal to the area of a bed.
- The plot size may be 20 by 50 feet. It is used in the design of cars, ships, aircrafts, buildings, highways etc. Flatbed plotter is very slow in drawing or printing graphs. The large and complicated drawing can take several hours to print.

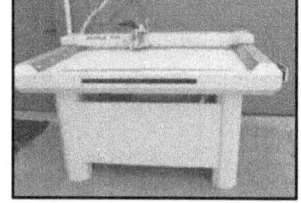

Fig. 2.13: Flatbed Plotter

- The main reason of the slow printing is due to the movement mechanical devices.
- Today, mechanical plotters have been replaced by thermal, electrostatic and inkjet plotters. These systems are faster and cheaper. They also produce large size drawings.

Advantages:

1. Plotters are faster than other types of printing machines, including the desktop printer.
2. The precision of the plotter is the main advantage for engineering drawings.
3. The versatility of plotters is another major advantage. A plotter can be hooked up to any computer. There are a number of plotter configuration options as well, depending on the model and series we buy.
4. Color accuracy and picture quality are also improved with the overall precision of the plotter. This is an advantage for a business looking for an inexpensive and efficient way to print promotional materials, banners and more.

2.3.4 LCD

- LCD stands for Liquid Crystal Display. LCD monitors are much thinner, use less energy, and provide a greater graphics quality.
- It uses liquid crystals technology to display the images. The liquid crystals are actually the molecules of the liquid filled in the LCD.
- These LCD molecules easily flow in different directions and have the capability to bend a beam of light. Each pixel on the LCD screen contains a number of liquid molecules layered between two transparent electrodes and crossed polarising filters.
- The liquid molecules uphold their directions and remain in the same position with respect to each other.

- As the light falls on the molecules, they bend the light and direct them towards a polarising filter.
- The polarising filter absorbs the light making the polariser appear dark for the display of images.

- Fig. 2.14 shows an LCD monitor.

Fig. 2.14: LCD

- LCD monitors have completely obsoleted CRT monitors due to their higher quality, smaller footprint on the desk, and decreasing price.
- The flat-panel display refers to a class of video devices that have reduced volume, weight and power requirement compared to the CRT.
- The flat-panel display are divided into two categories:

    1. **Emissive Displays:** The emissive displays are devices that convert electrical energy into light. Example are plasma panel and LED (Light-Emitting Diodes).

    2. **Non-Emissive Displays:** The Non-emissive displays use optical effects to convert sunlight or light from some other source into graphics patterns. Example is LCD (Liquid-Crystal Device).

Advantages:

1. Small in size.
2. Less power consumption and Radiation emission.
3. Compact and Lightweight
4. Cost is low.
5. Multiple video resolutions.

Disadvantages:

1. It has narrow viewing angle.
2. Do not refresh the pixels very quickly.
3. LCD display is that their images can be difficult to see in bright light.

2.3.5 Plasma Display

- Plasma display panel is a type of flat panel display common to large TV displays 30 inches (76 cm) or larger.
- PDPs (Plasma Display Panels) are also called as gas-discharge displays. They are essentially a matrix of very small fluorescent tubes with RGB phosphors.
- Fig. 2.15 shows construction of plasma panel display.

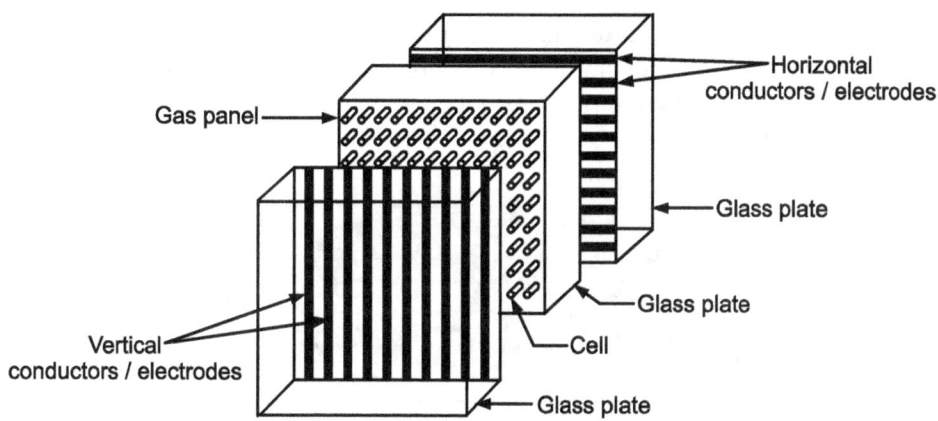

Fig. 2.15: Construction of Plasma Panel

- It consist of two sheets of glass with thin and closed spaced gold electrodes attached to inner faces and covered with dielectric material. These are attached as series of vertical conductors on one glass plate and horizontal on other glass plate.
- The space between two glass plate, is filled with neon based gas and is sealed. By applying voltage between electrodes the gas within panel is divided into tiny cells and each cell is independent of its neighbours.
- Firing voltage applied to pair of horizontal and vertical conductors cause the gas at intersection cell to break down into glowing plasma. This glow can be sustained by maintaining high frequency alternating voltages across cell.

Advantages:
1. Light weight, less bulky than CRTs.
2. Produces flicker free image.
3. Refreshing is not required.
4. They have excellent color reproduction property.
5. They have large viewing angle.
6. They are promising for large format displays.

Disadvantages:
1. Cost is high.
2. They have poor resolutions (about 60 dpi).
3. They have complex addressing and writing requirement.
4. It is an expensive device.

2.3.6 Keyboard

- A keyboard is the most common data entry input device.
- Using a keyboard, the user can type text and commands. Keyboard is designed to resemble a regular typewriter with a few additional keys.
- Data is entered into computer by simply pressing keys.
- The layout of the keyboard has changed very little ever since it was introduced. The number of keys on a typical keyboard varies from 84 keys to 104 keys.

- Keyboard is the easiest input device, as it does not require any special skill. Usually, it is supplied with a computer and so no additional cost is incurred. The maintenance and operational cost of keyboard is also less.
- Fig. 2.16 a typical keyboard.

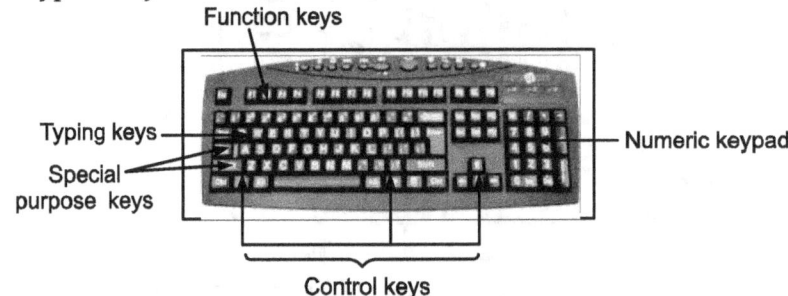

Fig. 2.16: Typical Keyboard

- The keys on the keyboard are as follows:
  1. **Typing Keys:** These keys include the letter keys (A-Z) and digit keys (0-9) which generally give same layout as that of typewriters.
  2. **Numeric Keypad:** It is used to enter numeric data or cursor movement. Generally, it consists of a set of 17 keys that are laid out in the same configuration used by most adding machines and calculators.
  3. **Function Keys:** The 12 function keys are present on the keyboard which are arranged in a row at the top of the keyboard. Each function key has unique meaning and is used for some specific purpose.
  4. **Control keys:** These keys provide cursor and screen control. It includes four directional arrow keys. Control keys also include Home, End, Insert, Delete, Page Up, Page Down, Control(Ctrl), Alternate(Alt), Escape(Esc).
  5. **Special Purpose Keys:** Keyboard also contains some special purpose keys such as Enter, Shift, Caps Lock, Num Lock, Space bar, Tab, and Print Screen.

2.3.7 Printers

- A printer is a device that accepts text and graphic output from a computer and transfers the information to paper, usually to standard size sheets of paper.
- Printers are used to produce paper (commonly known as hard copy) output.
- Based on the technology used they can be classified as impact and non-impact printers.

1. **Impact Printers:**
- The printer that prints the characters by striking the ribbon and onto the paper, are called impact printers.
- For example, dot-matrix printers, daisy wheels, line printers and drum printers etc.

2. Non-Impact Printers:

- Those printers that print a complete page at a time are called as non-impact or page printers. The print head does not make any contact with the paper. No ink ribbon is required.
- For example, ink jet and laser printers.
- Impact printers are of two types i.e., character printers and line printers.

1. Character Printers:

- Character printer are the printers which print one character at a time. These are further divided into two types i.e. Dot Matrix Printer (DMP) and Daisy Wheel Printer.

(i) Dot Matrix Printer:

- In the market one of the most popular printers is Dot Matrix Printer. These printers are popular because of their ease of printing and economical price.
- Dot matrix is a character printer, which prints one character at a time.
- Each character printed is in form of pattern of dots and head consists of a Matrix of Pins of size (5*7, 7*9, 9*7 or 9*9) which come out to form a character that is why it is called Dot Matrix Printer.

Advantages of Dot-matrix Printers:

1. Lower printing costs compared with inkjet or laser printers.
2. These can withstand unclean or dusty environment whereas inkject or laser jet printers require clean environment.

Disadvantages of Dot-matrix Printers:

1. Slow speed.
2. Poor quality.
3. Noisy.

(ii) Daisy-wheel Printers:

- In this printer the head is lying on a wheel and pins corresponding to characters are like petals of Daisy (flower name) that is why it is called as Daisy-wheel printer.
- These printers are generally used for word-processing in offices which require a few letters to be sent here and there with very nice quality.
- A daisy-wheel printer works on the same principle as ball-head typewriter. The daisy wheel printer consists of a disk made of plastic or metal on which characters stand out along the outer edge.
- The printer rotates the disk to print a character until the desired letter is facing the paper, after which a hammer called solenoid strikes forcing the character to hit an ink ribbon making a mark of the character on the paper.

Advantages:

1. More reliable than DMP.
2. Better quality.
3. The fonts of character can be easily changed.

Disadvantages:

1. Noisy when they printing.
2. These kinds of printers cannot print graphics.
3. Printing speed is slow.
4. More expensive than DMP.

2. Line Printers:

- Line printers are the printers which print one line at a time. These are of further two types i.e., Drum Printer and Chain Printer.

(i) Chain Printer:

- An early line printer that used type slugs linked together in a chain as its printing mechanism. In this printer, chain of character sets are used so it is called Chain Printer.

- A standard character set may have 48, 64, or 96 characters. The chain spins horizontally around a set of hammers.

- When the desired character is in front of the selected print column, the corresponding hammer hits the paper into the ribbon and onto the character in the chain.

Advantages:

1. Character fonts can easily be changed.
2. Different languages can be used with the same printer.

Disadvantages:

1. Noisy.

(ii) Drum Printers:

- This printer is like a drum in shape so it is called drum printer. Drum printer consists of a cylindrical drum.

- The surface of drum is divided into number of tracks. Total tracks are equal to size of paper i.e. for a paper width of 132 characters, drum will have 132 tracks.

- A character set is embossed on track. The different character sets available in the market are 48 character set, 64 and 96 characters set. One rotation of drum prints one line.

- Drum printers are fast in speed and can print 300 to 2000 lines per minute. One complete set of characters is embossed on all the print positions on a line. The character to be printed is adjusted by rotating drum.

Advantages:

1. Very high speed.

Disadvantages:

1. Very expensive.
2. Characters fonts cannot be changed.

- Non-impact printers are of two types i.e., Laser Printers and Inkjet Printers.

(i) Laser Printer:

- Laser printers are the fastest and most popular printers on the market today. They produce extremely high quality images – some near photo quality.

- The main principle in the working of laser printer is static electricity i.e., they use electro photography, or an electrophotostatic process, to form images on paper. The basis of the principles involved here is the science of atoms – oppositely-charged atoms are attracted to each other, so opposite static electricity fields cling together.

- The basic parts that a laser printer consists of are toner cartridges, photosensitive drum, erase lamp, primary corona, transfer corona, fuser assembly. Each of these parts have a very important role to play in the printing process.

Advantages:

1. Very high speed.
2. Very high quality output.
3. Give good graphics quality.
4. Support many fonts and different character size.

Disadvantages:

1. Expensive.
2. Cannot be used to produce multiple copies of a document in a single printing.

(ii) Inkjet Printers:

- Inkjet printers are non-impact character printers based on a relatively new technology.

- Inkjet printers produce high quality output with presentable features. Inkjet printers are those that place extremely small droplets of ink onto paper to create an image. They use a reservoir of aqueous ink, a pump and an ink nozzle to accomplish this.

- These dots are extremely small and can have different colors combined together to create photo-quality images. They essentially work by shooting ink onto paper.

- Both inkjet and laser printers are non-impact printers in the sense that they do not have mechanisms that physically touch paper in order to create images.

- However, unlike laser printers, inkjet printers use aqueous ink that spontaneously colors the paper (unlike toner from laser printers that has to be fused into the paper with a fuser).

Advantages:
1. High quality printing.
2. More reliable.

Disadvantages:
1. Expensive as cost per page is high.
2. Slow as compared to laser printer.

2.4 | POINTING DEVICES

*   Pointing devices in computer are used for providing the input to computer by moving the device to point to a location on computer monitor.
*   The cursor on the computer monitor moves with the moving pointing device. Operations such as move, click and drag can be performed using the pointing devices.
*   Mouse, trackball, joystick etc., are some of the common pointing devices.

2.4.1 Mouse

*   Mouse is an input device.
*   It is a small hand-held pointing device with a rubber ball embedded at its lower side and buttons on the top.
*   Usually, a mouse contains two or three buttons, which can be used to input commands or information.
*   Mouse may be classified as:
    1. **Mechanical Mouse:** It uses a rubber ball at the bottom surface, which rotates as the mouse is moved along a flat surface, to move the cursor. It is the most common and least expensive pointing device. Fig. 2.17 (a) shows a mechanical mouse.
    2. **Optical Mouse:** It uses a light beam instead of a rotating ball (scroll) to detect movement across a specially patterned mouse pad. As the user rolls the mouse on a flat surface, the cursor on the screen also moves in the direction of the mouse's movement. Fig. 2.17 (b) shows a optical mouse.

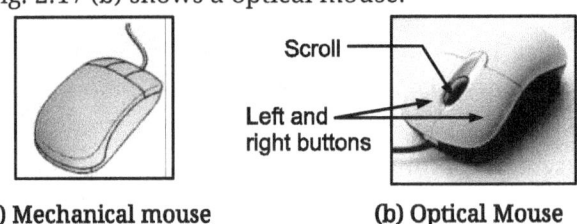

| (a) Mechanical mouse | (b) Optical Mouse |

Fig. 2.17

Advantages:
1. Easy to use.
2. In expensive.
3. Moves the cursor faster than the arrow keys of keyboard.

2.4.2 Joystick

- Joystick is also a pointing device which is used to move cursor position on a monitor screen.
- Joystick is a stick having a spherical ball at its both lower and upper ends. The lower spherical ball moves in a socket. The Joystick can be moved in all four directions.
- The function of joystick is similar to that of a mouse.

Fig. 2.18: Joystick

- A joystick is generally used to control the velocity of the screen cursor movement rather than its absolute position. It is used for computer games. The other applications in which it is used are flight simulators, training simulators, CAD/CAM systems, and for controlling industrial robots.

Advantages:

1. A joystick is that it is very easy to learn to use and they have a very simple design so they can be inexpensive.
2. The advantage of joystick is that it gives the player a real-time or virtual experience of the game.

Disadvantage:

1. A joystick has more difficult to control than using a mouse.
2. Joysticks are only limited to forward, backward, left and right.

2.4.3 Touch Screen

- A touch screen is a display screen that is an input device.
- A touch screen allows the direct selection of a menu item or the desired icon with the touch of finger. Essentially, it registers the input when a finger or other object is touched to the screen.
- Typically, it is used in information-providing systems like the hospitals, airlines and railway reservation counters, amusement parks, etc.
- A basic touch screen has three main components i.e., a touch sensor, a controller, and a software driver as shown in Fig. 2.19.
    1. **The Touch Sensor or Panel:** It is a clear glass panel with a touch-responsive surface. It is placed over a display screen so that the responsive area of the panel covers the viewable area of the video screen. There are several different touch sensor technologies in the market today, each using a different method to detect touch input. These methods are optical, acoustical, and electrical methods.

2. **The Controller:** It connects the touch sensor and the computer. It takes information from the touch sensor and translates it into information that a computer can understand.

3. **The Driver:** It is a software update for the computer system that allows the touch screen and the computer to work together. It tells the Operating System (OS) how to interpret the touch event information that is sent from the controller.

Advantages:

1. They are very intuitive (easy and simple to use and understand).

2. They saves space as there is no mouse, keyboard etc.

3. They are the fastest pointing devices.

4. Easier hand eye co-ordination.

Disadvantages:

1. Could be at arm reach from the device and might not beable to see anything on it.

2. Cost more than alternative devices.

3. Screens need to be installed at a lower position and tilted to reduce arm fatigue (pain).

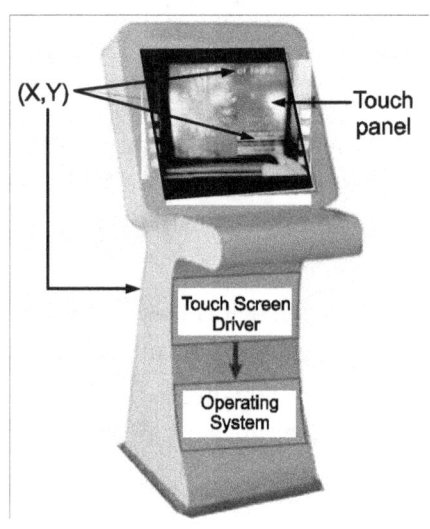

Fig. 2.19: Components of a Touch Screen

2.5 | NUMBER SYSTEM

- Number systems are very important to understand because the design and organisation of a computer depends on the number systems.

- We are all familiar with number system which is an ordered set of ten (0, 1, 3, 4, 5, 6, 7, 8, 9) the symbols or digits.

- In computers we use data in numeric (0, 1, ... 9), alphabets (a, b, c, ... z or A, B, ... Z) or special characters (· ; ,) etc.

- The system in which an ordered set of digits are used to specify any number is called number system.

- There are two types of number system as explained below:

1. **Non-positional Number Systems:**

- In ancient times, people used to count with their fingers. When fingers became insufficient for counting, stones and pebbles were used to indicate values. This method of counting is called the non-positional number system.

- In non-positional number system, we have symbols like I for 1, II for 2, III for 3, IIII for 4 etc. Each symbol represents the same value regardless of its position in a number and to find the value of a number, one has to count the number of symbols present in the number.

- The most common non-positional number system is the Roman Number System.

2. **Positional Number Systems:**

- A positional number system is any system that requires a finite number of symbols/digits of the system to represent arbitrarily large numbers.

- When using these systems the execution of numerical calculations becomes simplified, because a finite set of digits is used. The value of each digit in a number is defined not only by the symbol, but also by the symbol's position.

- The most popular positional number system being used today is the Decimal Number System.

- The word base (or radix) means the quality of admissible marks used in a given number system. The admissible marks are the characters, such as Arabic numerals, Latin letters, or other recognizable marks, which are used to present the numerical magnitude of a "quantity".

- Following table shows types of number system:

Sr. No.	Number System	Radix Value	Set of Digits	Example
1.	Decimal	R = 10	(0, 1, 2, 3, 4, 5, 6, 7, 8, 9)	$(25)_{10}$
2.	Binary	R = 2	(0, 1)	$(11001)_2$
3.	Octal	R = 8	(0, 1,2 , 3, 4, 5, 6, 7)	$(31)_8$
4.	Hexadecimal	R = 16	(0, 1, 2, 3, 4, 5, 6, 7, 8, 9, A, B, C, D, E, F)	$(19)_{16}$

2.5.1 Decimal Number System

- Deci means 10. There are only 10 basic digits in decimal number system from 0 to 9.

- The number system which uses ten digits or symbols, (0, 1, 2, 3, 4, 5, 6, 7, 8 and 9) is called a decimal number system.

- The weight associated with each symbol can be expressed as shown in following table.

MSD   LSD

10^4	10^3	10^2	10^1	10^0	.	10^{-1}	10^{-2}	10^{-3}	10^{-4}
10000	1000	100	10	1	.	1/10	1/100	1/1000	1/10000

↑   ↑
Weight   Decimal
                                            point

- In this case the Most Significant Digit (MSD) and Least Significant Digit (LSD) are the left most and the right most digit respectively.

- For example, the decimal number 1275 (written 1275_{10}) can be expanded as follows :

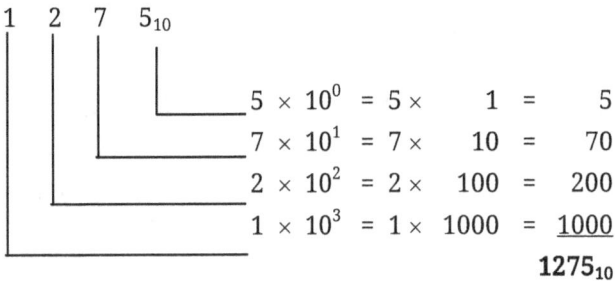

$$1\quad 2\quad 7\quad 5_{10}$$

$$5 \times 10^0 = 5 \times \quad 1 \quad = \quad 5$$
$$7 \times 10^1 = 7 \times \quad 10 \quad = \quad 70$$
$$2 \times 10^2 = 2 \times \quad 100 \quad = \quad 200$$
$$1 \times 10^3 = 1 \times \quad 1000 \quad = \quad \underline{1000}$$
$$\mathbf{1275_{10}}$$

- For example, $(4234)_{10}$ in decimal number system can be written as,

$$= (4 \times 10^3) + (2 \times 10^2) + (3 \times 10^1) + (4 \times 10^0)$$

$$= (4 \times 1000) + (2 \times 100) + (3 \times 10) + (4 \times 1)$$

$$= 4000 + 200 + 30 + 4 = 4234$$

2.5.2 Binary Number System

- The number system which uses only two digits or symbols, (0 and 1) is called a binary number system.

- Naturally, the base (or radix) in this number system is 2 and numbers used are 0 and 1.

- In binary number system, a binary number is called a bit, instead of binary digit. Incidentally, bit is a contradiction of the words binary digit.

- Digital computers use the binary number system because many simple physical elements can be used for representing and storing binary numbers. For example, the ON or OFF positions of a switch, the presence or absence of hole in a card, set or reset positions of a bistable circuit or device etc. are conveniently used to represent binary numbers.

- Also called base 2 number system.

- From right to left, the successive positions of the binary number are weighted 1, 2, 4, 8, 16, 32, 64 etc. A list of the first several powers of 2 follows :

$$2^0 = 1 \qquad 2^1 = 2 \qquad 2^2 = 4 \qquad 2^3 = 8 \qquad 2^4 = 16 \qquad 2^5 = 32$$
$$2^6 = 64 \qquad 2^7 = 128 \quad 2^8 = 256 \quad 2^9 = 512 \qquad 2^{10} = 1024 \qquad 2^{11} = 2048$$

- For reference, the following table shows the decimal numbers 0 through 31 with their binary equivalents :

Decimal	Binary	Decimal	Binary
0	0	16	10000
1	1	17	10001
2	10	18	10010
3	11	19	10101
4	100	20	10100
5	101	21	10101
6	110	22	10110
7	111	23	10111
8	1000	24	11000
9	1001	25	11001
10	1010	26	11010
11	1011	27	11011
12	1100	28	11100
13	1101	29	11101
14	1110	30	11110
15	1111	31	11111

- For example, value of $(11100)_2$

$$= (1 \times 2^4) + (1 \times 2^3) + (1 \times 2^2) + (0 \times 2^1) + (0 \times 2^0)$$

$$= 16 + 8 + 4 + 0 + 0$$

$$= 28$$

2.5.3 Octal Number System

- The number system which has the base (or radix) 8 and uses only eight digits or symbols, (0, 1, 2, 3, 4, 5, 6 and 7) is called octal number system.

- This system has 8 digits or symbols 0 – 7. Since its base (or radix) is $8 = 2^3$.

- From right to left, the successive positions of the octal number are weighted 1, 8, 64, 512 etc. A list of the first several powers of 8 follows :

$8^0 = 1$ $8^1 = 8$ $8^2 = 64$ $8^3 = 512$ $8^4 = 4096$ $8^5 = 32768$

- For reference, the following table shows the decimal numbers 0 through 31 with their octal equivalents :

Decimal	Octal	Decimal	Octal
0	0	16	20
1	1	17	21
2	2	18	22
3	3	19	23
4	4	20	24
5	5	21	25
6	6	22	26
7	7	23	27
8	10	24	30
9	11	25	31
10	12	26	32
11	13	27	33
12	14	28	34
13	15	29	35
14	16	30	36
15	17	31	37

- For example, $(4131)_8$ is,

$$= (4 \times 8^3) + (1 \times 8^2) + (3 \times 8^1) + (1 \times 8^0)$$

$$= 4 \times 512 + 1 \times 64 + 3 \times 8 + 1 \times 1$$

$$= 2048 + 64 + 24 + 1$$

$$= 2137$$

2.5.4 Hexadecimal Number System

- Hexadecimal means 16. The number system which uses the radix (or base) 16 and 16 digits (or symbols), viz. 0, 1, 2, 3, 4, 5, 6, 7, 8, 9, A, B, C, D, E and F is called Hexadeximal number system.

- It is clear that number of digits corresponding to a given decimal or binary number is much less because the radix is 16. Thus, it is economical to use this system in digital computers and microprocessors.

- Another important point is that in computers the word length is usually provided with 8 bits, 16 bits, 32 bits and so on.

- For reference, the following table shows the decimal numbers 0 through 31 with their hexadecimal equivalents :

Decimal	Hexadecimal	Decimal	Hexadecimal
0	0	16	10
1	1	17	11
2	2	18	12
3	3	19	13
4	4	20	14
5	5	21	15
6	6	22	16
7	7	23	17
8	8	24	18
9	9	25	19
10	A	26	1A
11	B	27	1B
12	C	28	1C
13	D	29	1D
14	E	30	1E
15	F	31	1F

- For example, $(2BD)_{16}$ is equivalent to:

$$= (2 \times 16^2) + (B \times 16^1) + (D \times 16^0)$$

$$= (2 \times 256) + (11 \times 16) + (13 \times 1)$$

$$= 512 + 176 + 13$$

$$= 601$$

Thus, $(2BD)_{16} = (601)_{10}$

2.5.5 Conversions

- The computer system accept data in decimal form, whereas they store and process the data in binary form. Therefore, it becomes necessary to convert a given number system into another number system for the internal processing of a computer system.

1. **Binary to Decimal Conversion:**

- The conversion of the binary number into decimal number is carried out by multiplying each binary bit by its positional weight and then adding all the product of binary bit and positional weight.

- To determine the value of a binary number (1001_2, for example), we can expand the number using the positional weight as follows :

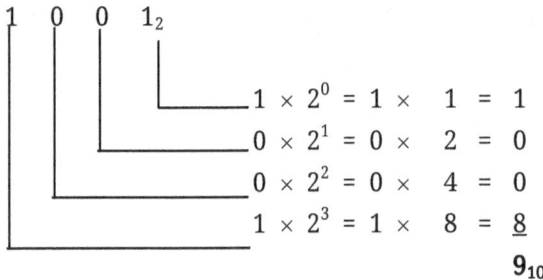

$$1 \times 2^0 = 1 \times 1 = 1$$
$$0 \times 2^1 = 0 \times 2 = 0$$
$$0 \times 2^2 = 0 \times 4 = 0$$
$$1 \times 2^3 = 1 \times 8 = \underline{8}$$
$$9_{10}$$

So, $(1001_2) = 9_{10}$

- Here's another example to determine the value of the binary number 1101010_2.

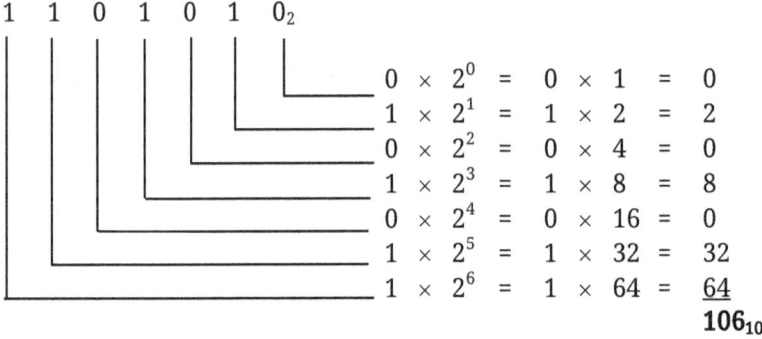

$$0 \times 2^0 = 0 \times 1 = 0$$
$$1 \times 2^1 = 1 \times 2 = 2$$
$$0 \times 2^2 = 0 \times 4 = 0$$
$$1 \times 2^3 = 1 \times 8 = 8$$
$$0 \times 2^4 = 0 \times 16 = 0$$
$$1 \times 2^5 = 1 \times 32 = 32$$
$$1 \times 2^6 = 1 \times 64 = \underline{64}$$
$$106_{10}$$

So, $(1101010_2) = 106_{10}$

- Convert $(0.111)_2 = ()_{10}$

$$\begin{aligned}(0.111)_2 &= 1 \times 2^{-1} + 1 \times 2^{-2} + 1 \times 2^{-3} \\ &= 1/2 + \frac{1}{4} + 1/8 \\ &= 0.5 + 0.25 + 0.125 \\ &= (0.875)_{10} \\ &= 0.875\end{aligned}$$

So, $(0.111)_2 = (0.875)_{10}$

- Convert $(0.1101)_2 = ()_{10}$

$$\begin{aligned}0.1101 &= 1 \times 2^{-1} + 1 \times 2^{-2} + 0 \times 2^{-3} + 1 \times 2^{-4} \\ &= 1 \times 0.5 + 1 \times 0.125 + 1 \times 0.03125 \\ &= 0.65625\end{aligned}$$

So, $(0.1101)_2 = (0.65625)_{10}$

2. Decimal to Binary Conversion:

- To convert a decimal number to its binary equivalent, the remainder method can be used. (This method can be used to convert a decimal number into any other base).

- The remainder method involves the following four steps:
  1. Divide the decimal number by the base (in the case of binary, divide by 2).
  2. Indicate the remainder to the right.
  3. Continue dividing into each quotient (and indicating the remainder) until the divide operation produces a zero quotient.
  4. The base 2 number is the numeric remainder reading from the last division to the first (if you start at the bottom, the answer will read from top to bottom).
- Convert the decimal number 99_{10} to its binary equivalent.

$$\begin{array}{c} 0 \\ 2\overline{)1} \end{array} \quad 1$$
(7) Divide 2 into 1. The quotient is 0 with a remainder of 1, as indicated. Since the quotient is 0, stop here.

$$\begin{array}{c} 1 \\ 2\overline{)3} \end{array} \quad 1$$
(6) Divide 2 into 3. The quotient is 1 with a remainder of 1, as indicated.

$$\begin{array}{c} 3 \\ 2\overline{)6} \end{array} \quad 0$$
(5) Divide 2 into 6. The quotient is 3 with a remainder of 0, as indicated.

$$\begin{array}{c} 6 \\ 2\overline{)12} \end{array} \quad 0$$
(4) Divide 2 into 12. The quotient is 6 with a remainder of 0, as indicated.

$$\begin{array}{c} 12 \\ 2\overline{)24} \end{array} \quad 0$$
(3) Divide 2 into 24. The quotient is 12 with a remainder of 0, as indicated.

$$\begin{array}{c} 24 \\ 2\overline{)49} \end{array} \quad 1$$
(2) Divide 2 into 49 (the quotient from the previous division). The quotient is 24 with a remainder of 1, indicated on the right.

START HERE $\Rightarrow$ $$\begin{array}{c} 49 \\ 2\overline{)99} \end{array} \quad 1$$
(1) Divide 2 into 99. The quotient is 49 with a remainder of 1; indicate the 1 on the right.

- The answer, reading the remainders from top to bottom, is 1100011, so $(99)_{10} = (1100011)_2$.
- Convert the decimal number 13_{10} to its binary equivalent.

$$\begin{array}{c} 0 \\ 2\overline{)1} \end{array} \quad 1$$
(4) Divide 2 into 1. The quotient is 0 with a remainder of 1, as indicated.

$$\begin{array}{c} 1 \\ 2\overline{)3} \end{array} \quad 1$$
(3) Divide 2 into 3. The quotient is 1 with a remainder of 1, as indicated.

$$\begin{array}{c} 3 \\ 2\overline{)6} \end{array} \quad 0$$
(2) Divide 2 into 6. The quotient from the previous division). The quotient is 3 with a remainder of 0, indicated the right.

START HERE $\Rightarrow$ $$\begin{array}{c} 6 \\ 2\overline{)13} \end{array} \quad 1$$
(1) Divide 2 into 13. The quotient is 6 with a remainder of 1; indicate the 1 on the right.

- The answer, reading the remainders from top to bottom, is 1101, so $(13)_{10} = (1101)_2$.

3. Octal to Decimal Conversion:

- The conversion of octal to decimal is simple. It is similar to binary to decimal conversion. The only difference is that the radix (or base) is 8 instead of 2.
- An example will make the procedure more illustrative.
- Convert the octal number $(7204)_8$ to its decimal equivalent.

$$(7204)_8 = 7 \times 8^3 + 2 \times 8^2 + 0 \times 8^1 + 4 \times 8^0$$
$$= 7 \times 512 + 2 \times 64 + 0 \times 8 + 4 \times 1$$
$$= 3584 + 128 + 4 = (3716)_{10}$$

Thus, $(7204)_8 = (3716)_{10}$

- To determine the value of an octal number $(367)_8$, we can expand the number using the positional weight as follows :

$3 \quad 6 \quad 7_8$

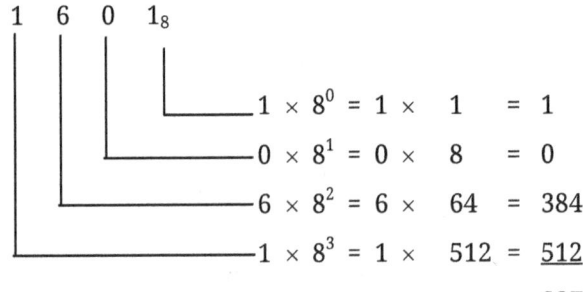

$$\begin{aligned}
7 \times 8^0 &= 7 \times \quad 1 \ = 7 \\
6 \times 8^1 &= 6 \times \quad 8 \ = 48 \\
3 \times 8^2 &= 3 \times \quad 64 = \underline{192} \\
&\qquad\qquad\qquad\quad 247_{10}
\end{aligned}$$

So, $(367_8) = 247_{10}$

- Here's another example to determine the value of the octal number 1601_8.

$1 \quad 6 \quad 0 \quad 1_8$

$$\begin{aligned}
1 \times 8^0 &= 1 \times \quad 1 \quad = 1 \\
0 \times 8^1 &= 0 \times \quad 8 \quad = 0 \\
6 \times 8^2 &= 6 \times \quad 64 \quad = 384 \\
1 \times 8^3 &= 1 \times \quad 512 \quad = \underline{512} \\
&\qquad\qquad\qquad\qquad\quad 897_{10}
\end{aligned}$$

So, $(1601_8) = 897_{10}$

4. Octal to Binary Conversion:

- Converting a binary number to its octal equivalent or vice-versa is a simple matter. Three binary digits are equivalent to one octal digit, as shown in the table below:

Binary	Octal
000	0
001	1
010	2
011	3
100	4
101	5
110	6
111	7

- To convert from binary to octal, divide the binary number into groups of 3 digits starting on the right of the binary number.
- If the leftmost group has less than 3 bits, put in the necessary number of leading zeroes on the left.
- For each group of three bits, write the corresponding single octal digit.

  For examples :

  1. $1101001101110111_2 = ?_8$

      Binary : 001 101 001 101 110 111

      Octal : 1   5   1   5   6   7

      So, $1101001101110111_2 = 151567_8$

  2. $101101111_2 = ?_8$

      Binary : 101 101 111

      Octal : 5   5   7

      So, $101101111_2 = 557_8$

- To convert from octal to binary, write the corresponding group of three binary digits for each octal digit.

  For examples :

  1. $1764_8 = ?_2$

      Binary : 1   7   6   4

      Octal : 001 111 110 100

      So, $1764_8 = 001111110100_2$

  2. $731_8 = ?_2$

      Binary : 7   3   1

      Octal : 111 011 001

      So, $731_8 = 111011001_2$

5. **Decimal to Octal Conversion:**

- To convert a decimal number to its octal equivalent, the remainder method (the same method used in converting a decimal number to its binary equivalent) can be used.
- To review, the remainder method involves the following four steps:
  1. Divide the decimal number by the base (in the case of octal, divide by 8).
  2. Indicate the remainder to the right.
  3. Continue dividing into each quotient (and indicating the remainder) until the divide operation produces a zero quotient.
  4. The base 8 number is the numeric remainder reading from the last division to the first (if you start at the bottom, the answer will read from top to bottom).

Example 1: Convert the decimal number 465_{10} to its octal equivalent:

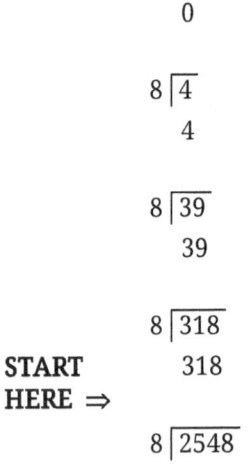

START
HERE ⇒

(3) Divide 8 into 7. The quotient is 0 with a remainder of 7, as indicated. Since, the quotient is 0, stop here.

(2) Divide 8 into 58 (the quotient from the previous division). The quotient is 7 with a remainder of 2, indicated the right.

(1) Divide 8 into 465. The quotient is 58 with a remainder of 1; indicate the 1 on the right.

- The answer, reading the remainders from top to bottom, is 721, **so $465_{10} = 721_8$.**

- Convert the decimal number 1548_{10} to its octal equivalent:

```
       0
      ___
    8 | 4
       4
      ___
    8 | 39
      39
      ___
    8 | 318
     318
      ___
    8 | 2548
```

START
HERE ⇒

(4) Divide 8 into 4. The quotient is 0 with a remainder of 4, as indicated. Since, the quotient is 0, stop here.

(3) Divide 8 into 39. The quotient is 4 with a remainder of 7, indicated on the right.

(2) Divide 8 into 318 (the quotient from the previous division). The quotient is 39 with a remainder of 6, indicated on the right.

(1) Divide 8 into 2548. The quotient is 318 with a remainder of 4; indicate the 4 on the right.

- The answer, reading the remainders from top to bottom, is 4764, **so $2548_{10} = 4764_8$.**

6. Decimal to Hexadecimal Conversion:

- To convert a decimal number to its hexadecimal equivalent, the remainder method (the same method used in converting a decimal number to its binary equivalent) can be used.

- To review, the remainder method involves the following four steps:

   1. Divide the decimal number by the base (in the case of hexadecimal, divide by 16).

   2. Indicate the remainder to the right. If the remainder is between 10 and 15, indicate the corresponding hex digit A through F.

   3. Continue dividing into each quotient (and indicating the remainder) until the divide operation produces a zero quotient.

   4. The base 16 number is the numeric remainder reading from the last division to the first (if you start at the bottom, the answer will read from top to bottom).

- Convert 9263_{10} to its hexadecimal equivalent:

$$\begin{array}{r} 0 \\ \hline 16\overline{)2} \end{array}$$

    2   (4) Divide 16 into 2. The quotient is 0 with a remainder of 2, as indicated. Since, the quotient is 0, stop here.

$$\begin{array}{r} 2 \\ \hline 16\overline{)36} \end{array}$$

    4   (3) Divide 16 into 36. The quotient is 2 with a remainder of 4, indicated on the right.

$$\begin{array}{r} 36 \\ \hline 16\overline{)578} \end{array}$$

    2   (2) Divide 16 into 578 (the quotient from the previous division). The quotient is 36 with a remainder of 2, indicated on the right.

START HERE ⇒

$$\begin{array}{r} 578 \\ \hline 16\overline{)9263} \end{array}$$

    F   (1) Divide 16 into 9263. The quotient is 578 with a remainder of 15; indicate the hex equivalent, "F", on the right.

- The answer, reading the remainders from top to bottom is 242F
  So, 9263_{10} = $242F_{16}$
- Convert 4259_{10} to its hexadecimal equivalent:

$$\begin{array}{r} 0 \\ \hline 16\overline{)1} \end{array}$$

    1   (4) Divide 16 into 1. The quotient is 0 with a remainder of 1, as indicated. Since the quotient is 0, stop here.

$$\begin{array}{r} 1 \\ \hline 16\overline{)16} \end{array}$$

    0   (3) Divide 16 into 16. The quotient is 1 with a remainder of 0, indicated on the right.

$$\begin{array}{r} 16 \\ \hline 16\overline{)266} \end{array}$$

    A   (2) Divide 16 into 266 (the quotient from the previous division). The quotient is 16 with a remainder of 10, so the hex equivalent "A" is indicated on the right.

START HERE ⇒

$$\begin{array}{r} 266 \\ \hline 16\overline{)4259} \end{array}$$

    3   (1) Divide 16 into 4259. The quotient is 266 with a remainder of 3; so indicate 3 on the right.

- The answer, reading the remainders from top to bottom, is 10A3, **So 4259_{10} = $10A3_{16}$.**

7. **Hexadecimal to Decimal Conversion:**

- We can use the same method that we used to convert binary numbers and octal numbers to decimal numbers to convert a hexadecimal number to a decimal number, keeping in mind that we are now dealing with base 16.
- From right to left, we multiply each digit of the hexadecimal number by the value of 16 raised to successive powers, starting with the zero power, then sum the results of the multiplications.
- Remember that if one of the digits of the hexadecimal number happens to be a letter A through F, then the corresponding value of 10 through 15 must be used in the multiplication.

- Convert the hexadecimal number $20B3_{16}$ to its decimal equivalent.

2   0   B 3_{16}

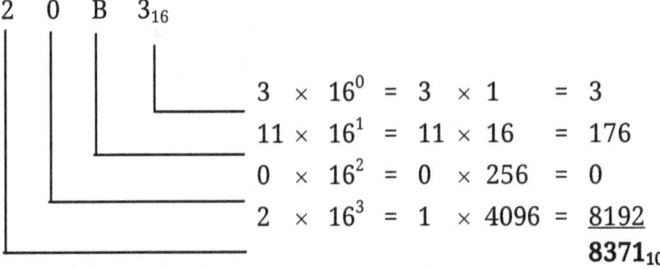

$3 \times 16^0 = 3 \times 1 = 3$
$11 \times 16^1 = 11 \times 16 = 176$
$0 \times 16^2 = 0 \times 256 = 0$
$2 \times 16^3 = 1 \times 4096 = \underline{8192}$
8371_{10}

So, $20B3_{16} = 8371_{10}$

- Convert the hexadecimal number $12AE5_{16}$ to its decimal equivalent.

1   2   A   E 5_{16}

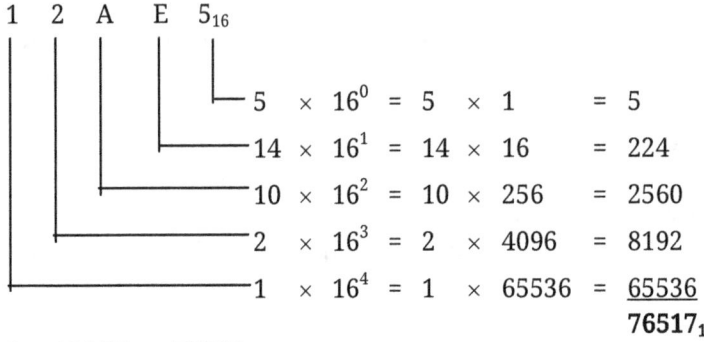

$5 \times 16^0 = 5 \times 1 = 5$
$14 \times 16^1 = 14 \times 16 = 224$
$10 \times 16^2 = 10 \times 256 = 2560$
$2 \times 16^3 = 2 \times 4096 = 8192$
$1 \times 16^4 = 1 \times 65536 = \underline{65536}$
76517_{10}

So, $12AE5_{16} = 76517_{10}$

8. **Binary to Hexadecimal Conversion:**
- Converting a binary number to its hexadecimal equivalent or vice-versa is a simple matter.
- Four binary digits are equivalent to one hexadecimal digit, as shown in the table below:

Binary	Hexadecimal
0000	0
0001	1
0010	2
0011	3
0100	4
0101	5
0110	6
0111	7
1000	8
1001	9
1010	A
1011	B
1100	C
1101	D
1110	E
1111	F

- To convert from binary to hexadecimal, divide the binary number into groups of 4 digits starting on the right of the binary number.
- If the leftmost group has less than 4 bits, put in the necessary number of leading zeroes on the left.
- For each group of four bits, write the corresponding single hex digit.

  For example :

  1. $1101001101110111_2 = ?_{16}$

Binary :	1101	0011	0111	0111
Hexadecimal :	D	3	7	7

     So, $1101001101110111_2 = D377_{16}$

  2. $101101111_2 = ?_{16}$

Binary :	0001	0110	1111
Hexadecimal :	1	6	F

     So, $101101111_2 = 16F_{16}$

- To convert from hexadecimal to binary, write the corresponding group of four binary digits for each hex digit.

  For example :

  1. $1BE9_{16} = ?_2$

Hexadecimal :	1	B	E	9
Binary :	0001	1011	1110	1001

     So, $1BE9_{16} = 0001101111101001_2$

  2. $B0A_{16} = ?_2$

Hexadecimal:	B	0	A
Binary :	1011	0000	1010

     So, $B0A_{16} = 101100001010_2$

9. **Octal to Hexadecimal Conversion:**

- For changing an octal number into a hexadecimal number, the octal number is first changed into a 3 bit binary number.
- Then the 4 bit binary number is converted into a hexadecimal number.
- Convert the following octal numbers to the hexadecimal equivalents :
  (a) 5634, (b) 7431.

  (a)

5	6	3	4	octal
101	110	011	100	binary

  B 9 C — hexadecimal

  Hence, $(5634)_8 = (B9C)_{16}$

(b)   7   4   3   1   octal
       111 100 011 001   binary
                               hexadecimal

        F   1   9

Hence, $(7431)_8 = (F19)_{16}$

2.5.6 Binary Arithmetic

- Binary arithmetic is at the heart of the computer and the majority of arithmetic performed by computers is binary arithmetic, i.e. arithmetic on base two numbers i.e., 0 and 1.

- The computer arithmetic is also referred as binary arithmetic because the computer system stores and processes the data in the binary form only.

- Various binary arithmetic operations can be performed in the same way as the decimal arithmetic operations, but by following a predefined set of rules.

- There are four binary arithmetic operations i.e., Binary Addition, Binary Subtraction, Binary Multiplication, and Binary Division.

- The binary arithmetic operations in computer systems are usually simpler to carry out as compared to the decimal operations because one needs to deal with only two digits i.e., 0 and 1.

1. Binary Addition :

- Binary addition is the simplest arithmetic operation performed in the computer system.

- Operations in binary arithmetic are similar to decimal arithmetic operations. The only difference is that the binary arithmetic involves only two digits i.e., 0 and 1.

- Like decimal system, we can start the addition of two binary-numbers column-wise from the right most bit and move towards the left most bit of the given numbers.

- However, we need to follow certain rules while carrying out the binary addition of the given numbers.

- Following Table lists the rules for binary addition.

X	Y	X + Y	Carry
0	0	0	0
0	1	1	0
1	0	1	0
1	1	0	1

- In the above table, the first three entries do not generate and carry. However, a carry would be generated when both X and Y contain the value, 1. The carry, if it is generated, while performing the binary addition in a column would be forwarded to the next most significant column.

- For example: Add 7 and 2. To add the number 7 + 2 in binary form, note that the binary form 2 is 10, while 7 = 111. The sum 7 + 2 in binary form is shown as follows:

$$10$$
$$+\ 111$$
$$1001$$

- The right-hand column adds up as 1 + 0 = 1. The next column adds up as 1 + 1 = 0 with a carry of 1 to the next column. The left most column again is 1 + 1 = 0 with a carry of 1 to the next column. Therefore, sum of binary numbers 10 + 111 = 1001 = 9.

- Take another example of binary addition:

0011010 + 001100 = 00100110

	1 1	carry
0 0 1 1 0 1 0	=	26_{10}
+ 0 0 0 1 1 0 0	=	12_{10}
0 1 0 0 1 1 0	=	38_{10}

2. Binary Subtraction :

- The binary subtraction is performed in the same way as the decimal subtraction.
- Binary subtraction can be performed using two ways i.e., the easiest way is the borrowing subtraction and the second way is complement technique.
- Like binary addition and binary multiplication, binary subtraction is also associated with a set of rules that need to be followed while carrying out the operation.
- Following Table lists the rules for binary subtraction.

X	Y	X – Y	Borrow
0	0	0	0
0	1	1	1
1	0	1	0
1	1	0	0

- The above table shows that the binary subtraction like the decimal subtraction uses the borrow method to subtract one number from another.
- For example: Subtract 7 from 9. The numbers are converted to their binary equivalents.

$$9\ =\ 1001$$
$$-\ 7\ =\ 0111$$
$$2\ =\ 0010$$

- 1 in the first column is subtracted from 1 and gives 0. Since, 1 in the second column cannot be subtracted from 0 we borrow from the next column. Since, the third column also has only 0, 1 from last column having power 2^4 is borrowed. Therefore, the 1 remains and is hence the output.

- Take another example on Binary Subtraction:

  0011010 – 001100 = 00001110

  $$\begin{array}{rcl}
  1\ 1 & & \text{borrow} \\
  0\ 0\ 1\ 1\ 0\ 1\ 0 & = & 26_{10} \\
  -\ 0\ 0\ 0\ 1\ 1\ 0\ 0 & = & 12_{10} \\
  \hline
  0\ 0\ 0\ 1\ 1\ 1\ 0 & = & 14_{10}
  \end{array}$$

3. Binary Multiplication :

- Binary multiplication is similar to decimal multiplication. However, unlike decimal multiplication, only two values are generated as the outcome of multiplying the multiplicand bit by 0 or 1 in the binary multiplication. These values are either 0 or 1.

- Binary multiplication is much easier compared to the other multiplication forms as only two digits 0 or 1 is used for multiplication.

- While performing binary multiplication, the following rules are to be considered:

X	Y	X × Y
0	0	0
0	1	0
1	0	0
1	1	1

- For example: Multiply 191 (Decimal = 5) with 100 (Decimal 4)

  $$\begin{array}{ll}
  101 & \text{Multiplicand} \\
  \times\ 100 & \text{Multiplier} \\
  \hline
  000 & \\
  000\times & \\
  101\times\times & \\
  \hline
  10100 & \text{(Decimal 20)}
  \end{array}$$

- Take another example on Binary Multiplication:

  0011010 × 001100 = 100111000

  $$\begin{array}{rcl}
  0\ 0\ 1\ 1\ 0\ 1\ 0 & = & 26_{10} \\
  \times\ 0\ 0\ 0\ 1\ 1\ 0\ 0 & = & 12_{10} \\
  \hline
  0\ 0\ 0\ 0\ 0\ 0\ 0 & & \\
  0\ 0\ 0\ 0\ 0\ 0\ 0 & & \\
  0\ 0\ 1\ 1\ 0\ 1\ 0 & & \\
  0\ 0\ 1\ 1\ 0\ 1\ 0 & & \\
  \hline
  0\ 1\ 0\ 0\ 1\ 1\ 1\ 0\ 0\ 0 & = & 312_{10}
  \end{array}$$

4. Binary Division :

- Binary division is also performed in the same way as we perform decimal division. The dividend involved in binary division should be greater than the divisor.

- Binary division can be performed by the technique of long division in decimal division. Binary division however uses only 1's and 0's.
- The following rules are to be taken care while performing binary division:
  1. While performing division, if the divisor is less than or equal to the remainder, then 1 is added to the quotient and subtracted.
  2. When the divisor is greater than the remainder, 0 is written in the quotient and to this the next digit from the dividend is added.
- For example: Divide 111 (Decimal 7) by 10 (Decimal 2). The divisor is 10 and dividend is 111.

$$
\begin{array}{r}
11.1 \\
10 \enclose{longdiv}{111} \\
\underline{10} \\
11 \\
\underline{10} \\
10 \\
\underline{10} \\
0
\end{array}
$$

Answer is 11.1 i.e., 3, 5 indecimal.

- Take another example on Binary Division:

101010 / 000110 = 000111

$$
\begin{array}{r}
1\,1\,1 \quad = 7_{10} \\
000110 \enclose{longdiv}{1\,0\,1\,0\,1\,0} \quad = 42_{10} \\
\underline{-1\,1\,0} \quad\quad = 6_{10} \\
1\,0\,0\,1 \\
\underline{-1\,1\,0} \\
1\,1\,0 \\
\underline{-1\,1\,0} \\
0
\end{array}
$$

PRACTICE QUESTIONS

1. What is meant by storage?
2. Enlist types of storages.
3. What is primary and secondary storage devices?
4. What is RAM? State its advantages.
5. Write short note on: ROM.
6. Compare RAM and ROM.
7. Enlist secondary storage devices.
8. What is CD and HD?

9. With the help of diagram explain HD in detail.
10. Explain pen drive in detail.
11. Describe scanner in detail.
12. What is meant by pointing devices? Enlist two of them.
13. Explain mouse with its types.
14. Describe number system in detail.
15. Writes short note on: (i) Plotters, (ii) Digitizers.
16. Explain working of touch screen with diagram.
17. Convert the following:
    (i) $1AC_{16} = (\quad)_{10}$
    (ii) $2057_8 = (\quad)_{10}$
    (iii) $10101_2 = (\quad)_{10}$
    (iv) $42_{10} = (\quad)_2$
    (v) $211_{10} = (\quad)_{16}$
    (vi) $562_8 = (\quad)_2$

■■■

Concepts of Software

Contents ...

3.1	**INTRODUCTION**

- Knowledge is a familiarity, awareness or understanding of someone or something, such as facts, information, descriptions, or skills, which is acquired through experience or education by perceiving, discovering, or learning.

- Knowledge can be broadly categorized as being one of two types i.e., declarative knowledge, which is knowledge about the world, knowledge that something is the case, and procedural knowledge which is knowledge about how to do things.

- Fig. 3.1 shows declarative to procedural knowledge.

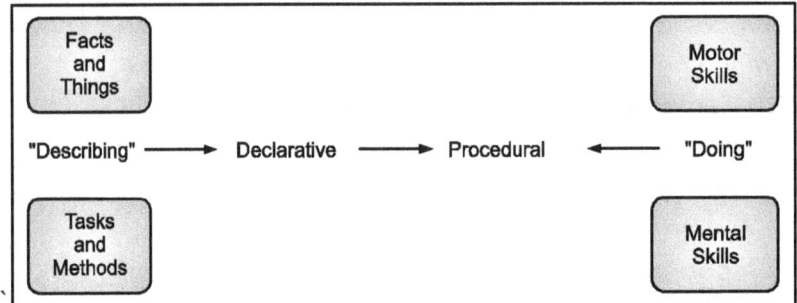

Fig. 3.1: Declarative to Procedural Knowledge

3.2	**DIFFERENCE BETWEEN IMPERATIVE KNOWLEDGE AND DEFINITIONAL KNOWLEDGE**

1. **Imperative Knowledge:**

- Procedural knowledge, also known as imperative knowledge, is the knowledge exercised in the performance of some task.

- Procedural knowledge (knowing "how"), this explains what to do to reach a certain conclusion. For example, to determine if Amar or Kiran is older, first find their ages.

- Procedural knowledge is different from other kinds of knowledge, such as declarative knowledge, in that it can be directly applied to a task. For instance, the procedural knowledge one uses to solve problems differs from the declarative knowledge one possesses about problem solving because this knowledge is formed by doing.

- In some legal systems, such procedural knowledge has been considered the Intellectual Property (IP) of a company, and can be transferred when that company is purchased.

- **Examples of Procedural Knowledge:**
  (i)   Knowing how to use a computer.
  (ii) Knowing how to play basketball.
  (iii) Knowing how to write.
  (iv) Knowing how to look up information in the library.

- One advantage of procedural knowledge is that it can involve more senses, such as hands-on experience, practice at solving problems, understanding of the limitations of a specific solution, etc.

- One limitation of procedural knowledge is its job-dependence; thus it tends to be less general than declarative knowledge.

2. **Definitional Knowledge:**

- Declarative knowledge (knowing "what"), this takes the form of relatively simple and clear statements, which can be added and modified without difficulty.

- It is knowledge of facts and relationships. For example, a car has four tires; Amar is older than Kiran.

- Definitional knowledge consists of concepts, constructs, terminologies, definitions, vocabularies, classifications, taxonomies, and other kinds of conceptual knowledge.

- Definitional knowledge may be formal and precise, such as the basic concepts of relational database theory, which includes relations, attributes, functional dependencies, and multivalued dependencies. Definitional knowledge may also include vague and informal concepts such as the Human Computer Interaction (HCI) notions of usability, affordance, and situatedness.

- Definitional knowledge does not include statements about reality that are claimed to be true. Instead, it is used as a basis for all other types of knowledge in the sense that it provides the basic concepts that are required to express that knowledge. J.G. Bennett in 1985 succinctly phrased this as "We do not know structures, but we know because of structures".

- **Examples of Definitional Knowledge:**

    (i)   A black hole is a region of space from which nothing can escape.

    (ii) A right triangle is a triangle in which one angle is a right angle.

    (iii) A relation is in Third Normal Form (3NF), within relational database theory, if all of its attributes are dependent on the key, the whole key and nothing but the key.

- Above statements only define certain concepts but do not claim that right triangles, black holes, or 3NF really exist; such claims are made by descriptive knowledge.

Comparison between Declarative Knowledge and Procedural Knowledge:

Sr. No.	Declarative Knowledge	Procedural (Imperative) Knowledge
1.	Declarative knowledge refers to factual knowledge and information that a person knows.	Procedural knowledge is knowing how to perform certain activities.

contd. ...

2.	Declarative knowledge answers the question 'What do you know?'	Procedural knowledge answers the question 'What can you do?'
3.	It is your understanding of things, ideas, or concepts.	While declarative knowledge is demonstrated using nouns, procedural knowledge relies on action words, or verbs.
4.	In other words, declarative knowledge can be thought of as the who, what, when and where of information.	It is a person's ability to carry out actions to complete a task.
5.	Declarative knowledge is normally discussed using nouns, like the names of people, places, or things or dates that events occurred.	Imperative knowledge is about how to accomplish something.
6.	Declarative knowledge can be acquired after a single exposure.	Procedural knowledge is often acquired only after extensive practice.
7.	Examples: (i) Knowing what a circle is. (ii) Knowing the names of all the states and their capitals.	Examples: (i) Knowing how to play cricket. (ii) Knowing how to use book.

3.3 DIFFERENCE BETWEEN FIXED PROGRAM AND STORED PROGRAM

- A computer program is a collection of instructions that performs a specific task when executed by a computer.

- Computer program can be divided into stored program and fixed program as discussed below.

1. Stored Program:

- The stored program architecture is the basis on which most of the conventional and today's modern computer works.

- An instruction is a bit string that tells the CPU what to do. An instruction contains an op (operation code) and address information such as where and how to find the operand if there is one.

- In 1946, John Von Neumann and his team members started designing the stored program computer known as the IAS computer, at the Princeton Institute for Advanced Studies.

- A stored program concept is one in which first the program and data are stored in the main memory and then the processor fetches instructions and executes them, one after another, (See Fig. 3.2).

- The stored program concept was conceived by John Von Neumann stating that all instructions and data must be stored in memory before their execution can begin. Thus, instructions are retrieved from memory, one by one in sequence, interpreted, and executed.

- If the operation needs an operand in memory, the CPU issues a memory read request and waits for the arrival of the operand before the operation can start.

- Instructions and data look alike and programmers can modify the address field or the whole instruction by performing arithmetic or logical operations on them in the execution unit.

- John Von Neumann architecture is a computer design that uses a single store for both machine instructions and programs. It is also known as a stored program computer and it is a sequential architecture.

- Fig. 3.2 shows the state in a stored-program digital computer.

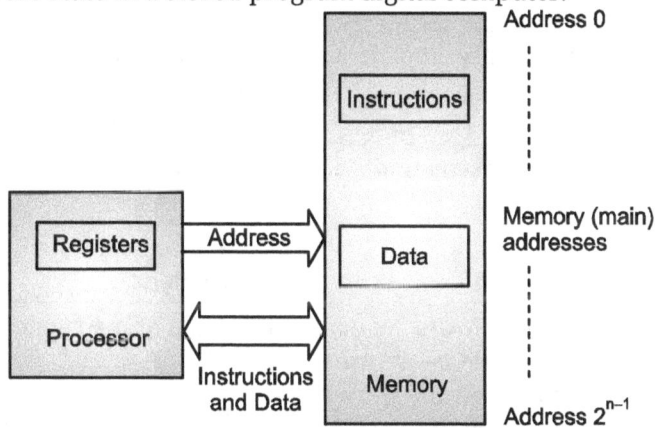

Fig. 3.2: The State in a Stored-program Digital Computer

- The stored program, digital computer keeps its instructions and data in the same memory system, allowing the instructions to be treated as data when necessary. This enables the processor itself to generate instructions which it can subsequently execute.

2. Fixed Program:

- Fixed program in a digital computer in which the sequence of instructions are permanently stored or wired in, and which performs the instruction sequence without change except by rewiring or changing the stored input.

- The earliest computing machines were designed with a fixed-program architecture, designed and programmed to do a specific task or tasks.
- A fixed program architecture implies that the instructions for the computer are built into the actual hardware of the machine itself, and only the data that is processed by the computer is stored in memory.
- These computers were not truly reprogrammable since changing the program required that the machine itself be rebuilt or rewired to follow a new sequence of instructions.
- Certain modern computing systems can be understood as using a fixed program architecture. A basic hand calculator, for example, can perform a small number of arithmetic tasks, but it cannot be programmed for text processing or instant messaging.
- Many elements of a graphics system also follow a fixed program architecture since graphical processing is computationally expensive and can be accelerated by specialized hardware.

Difference between Stored Program and Fixed Program:

Sr. No.	Stored Program	Fixed Program
1.	Data and instructions are kept in the main memory.	They implies that the instructions for the computer are built into the actual hardware of the machine itself.
2.	The sequence of instruction not permanently stored.	The sequence of instruction are permanently stored.
3.	Not time consuming.	Time consuming for rewriting instructions.
4.	In this, instructions from the memory and the programs could be setup or changed from within the memory as well without having to redesign.	Redesign of instruction is complex.

3.4 SYNTAX, SEMANTICS AND STATIC SEMANTICS

- A programming language is a set of rules, symbols, and special words used to construct a program. There are rules for both syntax (grammar) and semantics (meaning).

1. **Syntax:**
- The formal rules governing how valid instructions (constructs) are written in a programming language.

- A programming language's syntax is concerned with the form of programs: how expressions, commands, declarations, and other constructs must he arranged to make a well-formed program.

- Syntax can be defined as, "a formal set of rules that defines exactly what combinations of letters, numbers, and symbols can be used in a programming language."

2. **Semantics:**

- A programming language's semantics is concerned with the meaning of programs: how a well-formed program may be expected to behave when executed on a computer.

- The set of rules that determines the meaning of instructions (constructs) written in a programming language.

- Semantics can be defined as, "the set of rules that determines the meaning of instruction written in a programming language".

3. **Static Semantics:**

- The term semantics refers to the meaning of languages, as opposed to their form (syntax).

- The static semantics defines restrictions on the structure of valid texts that are hard or impossible to express in standard syntactic formalisms.

- For compiled languages, static semantics essentially include those semantic rules that can be checked at compile time.

- Examples include checking that every identifier is declared before it is used or that the labels on the arms of a case statement are distinct.

- Other forms of static analyses like data flow analysis may also be part of static semantics. Newer programming languages like Java and C# have definite assignment analysis, a form of data flow analysis, as part of their static semantics.

4. **Dynamic Semantics:**

- Once, data has been specified, the machine must be instructed to perform operations on the data. For example, the semantics may define the strategy by which expressions are evaluated to values, or the manner in which control structures conditionally execute statements.

- The dynamic semantics (also known as execution semantics) of a language defines how and when the various constructs of a language should produce a program behavior.

3.5 | SOFTWARE

- Software is a generic term for an organized collection of computer data and instructions.

- Software is responsible for controlling, integrating and managing the hardware components of a computer and for accomplishing specific tasks. In other words, software tells the computer what to do and how to do it.

- For example, the software instructs the hardware what to display on the user's screen, what kinds of input to take from the user, and what kinds of output to generate.

- Software set of instructions (computer programs) that when executed provide desired function task.

3.5.1 Definition

- Computer software also called a program or simply software is "a series of instructions that directs a computer to perform specific tasks or operations".

OR

- Definition of Software given by IEEE as "software is the collection of computer programs, procedure rules and associated documentation and data".

- Software can be categorized as system software and application software. **System software** controls and supports the operations of a computer system as it performs various information processing tasks. **Application software** directs the performance of a particular use or application of computers to meet the information processing needs of computers.

- Fig. 3.3 shows relationship between application software and system software.

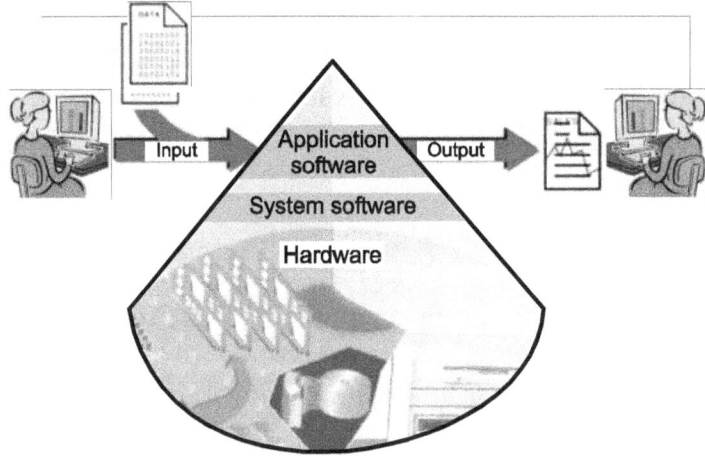

Fig. 3.3: Relationship between Application Software and System Software

3.5.2 System Software

- System software refers to that collection of programs which co-ordinate the activities at hardware and all programs running on the computer system.
- System software is computer software that manages and controls the computer hardware thus allowing it to do useful job. System software is a set of programs which instructs the hardware on what to do.
- The purposes of the system software are listed below:
  1. To control computer hardware,
  2. To provide basic functionality to computer, and
  3. To act as an interface between user; application software and computer hardware.
- The software that controls the execution of an application program is called as system software.
- In simple terms, system software makes the computer functional. It provides basic functionality like file management, visual display and keyboard input and is used by the application software to accomplish these functions.
- Some examples of system software are:
  1. **System Control Program:** They control the execution of programs. Example, Operating System (OS). The OS intermediates between the user of a computer and the computer hardware. Different kinds of application software use specific hardware resources of a computer like CPU, I/O devices and memory, as needed by the application software. OS controls and coordinates the use of hardware among the different application software and the users. It provides an interface that is convenient for the user to use, and facilitates efficient operations of the computer system resources.
  2. **Device Drivers:** Device drivers are system programs, which are responsible for proper functioning of device. A device driver acts as a translator between the hardware and the software that uses the devices. In other words, it intermediates between the device and the software, in order to use the device. Example, device like printer. A user must load the device driver of that particular printer.
  3. **System Support Programs:** They provide routine service function to other computer programs and users. Example, utility programs. Utility programs are a set of programs, which help users in system maintenance tasks, and in performing tasks of routine nature. Some of the tasks commonly performed by utility programs include formatting of hard disks or floppy disks, taking backups of files stored in hard disk on to a tape or floppy disk. The anti-virus utilities detects the virus, identify and prevent it from spreading. Some examples of anti-virus software are Norton's Anti-virus, MCafee etc.

4. **Data Recovery Software:** Sometimes an illegal operation may result in an accidental loss of data which was still to be needed then we used data recovery software. Example, Recycle bin.

5. **Language Translators Programs:** Translator software converts a program written in assembly language, and high level language to a machine-level language program. Some common language translators are compiler, assembler and interpreter.

6. **Communication Software:** In a network environment, communications software enables transfer of data and programs from one computer system to another.

3.5.3 Application Software

- The software that a user uses for accomplishing a specific task is the application software.

- Application software is a general purpose program or a collection of programs written by the users to solve a specific problem.

- Typical applications include industrial automation, business software, educational software, medical software, databases and computer games.

- Application software may consist of a single program, such as Microsoft's Notepad (for writing and editing simple text) or a collection of programs, often called a software package, which work together to accomplish a task, such as database management software.

- Application software may also include a larger collection of related but independent programs and packages (a software suite) that have a common user interface or shared data format, such as Microsoft Office suite.

- Examples of Application Softwares:

    1. **Word Processor:** Word processor is the software used to word processing. There are many word processors available in the market. The common and the popular among are Word Star, MS-Word.

    2. **Spreadsheet:** A spreadsheet contains greed of cells arranged in columns and rows. Data is entered into the cells to represent information. Examples of electronics spreadsheet are Lotus 1, 2, 3 and Excel.

    3. **Presentation Software:** Presentation software is the software which are used to present information. Microsoft PowerPoint is one of the most popular presentation software.

    4. **Desktop Publishing (DTP) Software:** Desktop publishing software are used for type setting and designing purposes. Well know desktop publishing software are Coral Draw, PageMaker etc.

5. **Web Browser Software:** With an Internet connection, this type of software enables a user to visit from one Website to another. Examples are Netscape Communicator, Microsoft Internet Explorer.

6. **Education Software:** Education software allows a computer system to be used as a teaching and learning tool. For example, Pune university software.

7. **Entertainment Software:** Entertainment software allows a computer system to be used as an entertainment tool. For example ganna.com is a music software.

8. **Personal Assistance Software:** A personal assistance software allows us to use personal computers for storing and retrieving our personal information and planning and managing our schedules, contacts, financial and inventory of important items.

9. **Graphics Software:** A graphics software enables user to use a computer system for creating, editing, viewing, storing, retrieving and printing designs, drawings, pictures, graphs and anything else that can be drawn in the traditional manner. For example, ArcGIS.

10. **Special purpose application software:** Application software is created to satisfy specific needs of an organization. Examples are Payroll software, Railway Reservation software etc.

Difference between System Software and Application Software:

Sr. No.	System Software	Application Software
1.	System software is a set of programs that controls operation of a computer system.	Application software is a set of programs that accomplishes user specific tasks.
2.	We can define system software as "it is computer software designed to operate the computer hardware and to provide a platform for running application software."	We can define application software as "it is computer software designed to help the user to perform specific tasks."
3.	System software is written to perform a several task.	Application software is written to perform a specific task.
4.	Generally, users do not interact with system software.	Generally, users interact with application software.
5.	System software runs independently.	Application software can not run without the present of the system software.
6.	Examples: Operating System (OS), Compilers, Assemblers etc.	Examples: MS-Word, MS-Excel etc.

3.5.4 Operating System

- An OS is an intermediary between users and computer hardware. It provides users an environment in which a user can execute programs conveniently and efficiently.
- An operating system is an integrated set of programs that is used to manage various resources and overall operations of a computer system.
- OS is a system software that helps the user in interacting with the resources and executing the user applications.
- OS also manages the other computer system resources that might be shared by different users in multi-user environments.
- Popular modern operating systems include Android, iOS, Unix, Microsoft Windows, Linux, Mac etc.

Functions of OS:

1. OS provides a convenient interface to the user in the form of commands and graphical interface, which facilitates the use of computer.
2. It provides an environment in which users and application software can do work.
3. OS manages different resources of the computer like the CPU time, memory space, file storage, I/O devices etc. During the use of computer by other programs or users, operating system manages various resources and allocates them whenever required, efficiently.
4. It controls the execution of different programs to prevent occurrence of error.

Definition:

- An operating system is a "program that acts as an interface between the user and the computer hardware and controls the execution of all kinds of programs".

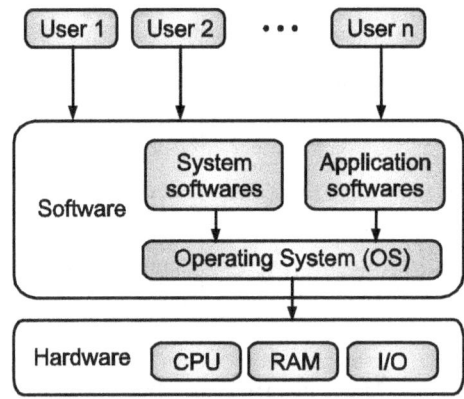

Fig. 3.4: Interaction among Hardware, OS, Software and Users

3.5.4.1 Types of Operating Systems

- There are many types of operating systems, which are categorized based on the types of computers they control and the sort of applications they support.
- The broad categories of OS are:

1. **Real-time Operating System:**
- Real-time operating systems are used to control machinery, scientific instruments and industrial systems.
- Real-time operating system has very little user-interface capability, and no end-user utilities, as the system is a 'sealed box' when delivered for use.
- A very important part of a real-time operating system is managing the resources of the computer so that a particular operation executes in precisely the same amount of time every time it occurs. The response time of a real-time operating system is very quick.
- The operating system which guarantees the maximum time for these operations are commonly referred to as hard real-time, while operating systems that can only guarantee a maximum of the time are referred to as soft real-time.
- Examples of real-time OS are QNX, RTLINUX etc.

2. **Single-user, Single-tasking:**
- As the name implies, this operating system is designed to manage the computer so that one user can effectively do one thing at a time.
- The palm OS for palm handheld computers is a good example of a modern single-user, single-task operating system.

3. **Single-user, Multi-tasking:**
- This type of OS which allows a single user to execute two or more tasks at a time.
- Single-user, multi-tasking is the type of operating system most people use on their desktop and laptop computers today.
- Both Windows 98 and the Macintosh OS are examples of operating systems that will let a single user have several programs in operation at a time.

4. **Multi-user, Multi-tasking:**
- A multi-user operating system allows many different users to take advantage of the computer's resources simultaneously.
- Unix, Linux, VMS and mainframe operating systems (such as MVS), are examples of multi-user operating systems.

5. **Distributed Operating System:**
- Distributed operating system is a type of multi-user operating system, where processing is distributed, i.e. each user workstation is assigned a task to be processed.
- The processed results are later compiled together on a central computer.

Computer Processing Techniques:

- The way in which the programs submitted by the users are executed is called the computer processing techniques.
- Some common computer processing technique are explained below:

1. Time Sharing:

- In time sharing a number of simultaneous users are there.
- Each user is given a trivial amount of time (a quantum/time slice) in which he/she processes interactively or conversationally.

2. Multi-programming:

- Multi-programming is a term given to a system that may have several processes in the 'state of execution' at the same time.
- A process is in a state of execution, if the computation is started but has not been completed or terminated.
- A process may be in a state of execution and not be executing, i.e. some intermediate results may have been completed but the processor is not currently working on the process.

3. Multi-processing:

- In a multi-processing, a single CPU has more than one processor.
- All these processors may or may not be equally powerful and may or may not prefer same operation.

4. Batch-processing:

- In this type of processing, there is no direct interaction between user and the computer. The user has to submit a job (written on cards or tape) to a computer operator. Then computer operator places a batch of several jobs on an input device.
- Jobs are batched together by type of languages and requirement. Then a special program, the monitor, manages the execution of each program in the batch. The monitor is always in the main memory and available for execution.

5. Multi-tasking:

- It allows executing more than one task at the same time. An operating system that is capable of allowing multiple software processes to run at the same time.
- Some examples of multitasking operating systems are Unix and Windows 2000 Windows XP, Windows 7, Windows Vista etc.

6. Multi-threading:

- It allows different parts of a single program to run concurrently.
- Multithreading operating systems allow different parts of a software program to run concurrently.
- Operating systems that would fall into this category are Linux, Unix and Windows 2000.

3.6 | INTRODUCTION TO DOS

- The Disk Operating System (DOS) is a single user operating system released by Microsoft Cor. in the early 1980's.

- DOS also known as MS-DOS, is a command line user interface, which enables users to organise data files, load and execute (run) program files and control the input and output devices attached to the computer.

- It is called DOS because, much of it work deals with managing and handling disk and disk files.

- DOS resides on a disk and is loaded into memory and executed when the computer is switched ON or reset.

- When the PC is switched ON, after performing the self checks, a command prompt character C:\> appears on the monitor. This indicates that DOS is loaded properly in the memory of the PC. The presence of any one of the prompt means that the PC is ready to execute the command given by the user.

- Fig. 3.5 shows DOS window.

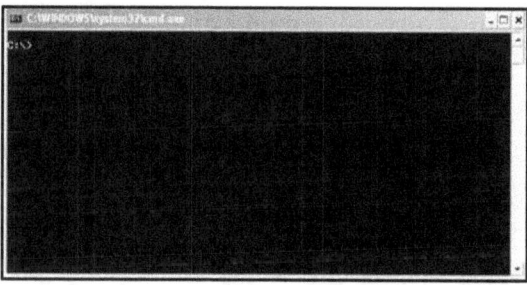

Fig. 3.5

MS-DOS Environment:

- The DOS environment gives the user a quick and direct access to the basic utilities of a computer. All tasks are accomplished by typing commands at a command prompt i.e., at the cursor location.

- A prompt is defined as "a character or string of characters used in the command line interface to indicate that a computer is ready to accept commands from users".

- In DOS, '>' is used as a prompt, which is preceded by other information such as current drive and path of the current working directory.

Working with DOS Files an Directories:

1. File:

- A file is a primary unit of storage in computers. DOS uses a unique filename to describe the content of a file and keep track of the file so that you can use it later.

- In DOS, the name of a file is divided into two parts, the filename itself and an extension. For example, the filename Emp.doc. has two parts, namely, Emp (filename) and .doc (extension). DOS uses different file extensions such as .corn, .exe, .bat, .txt, etc.

- DOS contains following files:

    (i) IO.SYS contains the system initialization code and built-in device drives.

    (ii) MSDOS.SYS contains the DOS kernel.

    (iii) COMMAND.COM is the command interpreter.

    (iv) AUTOEXEC.BAT is run by the default shell to execute commands at startup.

    (v) CONFIG.SYS contains statements to configure DOS and load device drivers.

2. **Directory:**

- Files are organised under different directories. A directory allows users to group files under one category.

- Every disk has one basic directory called the root directory, which is created automatically when the disk is formatted.

- In addition to files, a directory can contain other directories also in itself known as sub-directories.

3. **Pathname:**

- To access a file in DOS, a user may have to traverse through different directories. Thus, a path-name is used to instruct the computer where to look for any particular file.

- A pathname is a sequence of directories separated by a backslash ('\') followed by a filename.

- For example, the pathname for a file named EMP can be C:\Employee\Details\Emp.doc. In this pathname, C drive contains a directory Employee in which Details is a subdirectory where the file Emp.doc is stored.

- A pathname can be either absolute or relative. An absolute pathname mentions the path to a specific file from the root directory while a relative pathname mentions the path to a specific file from the current working directory and does not begin with ' \ '.

3.6.1 DOS Commands

- The command generally means an instruction written in computer acceptable language that user types to execute a specific operation on the DOS prompt.

- In an operating system, a command is defined as "a directive given to the computer to perform of a specific operation".

- In MS-DOS, commands are used to perform different operations such as copying files, deleting files, creating a directory, etc.

- There are two types of DOS command.
  1. **Internal Commands:** These are the command which get loaded in the memory of Computer automatically along with DOS at the time of booting.

     For examples: dir, del, rename, copy, type etc.
  2. **External Command:** These are the short programs or utilities which are available on floppy/hard disk and are loaded in the memory of computer when specially asked for.

     For examples: format, print, chkdsk, discopy etc.

3.6.1.1 Internal Commands

- Internal commands are those commands that are loaded automatically in the memory when DOS is loaded into memory during booting process.
- These commands are easier to learn and use. Internal commands are permanent part of the resident portion of the memory. These commands can be used without the need of any DOS file.
- No external file is required to run these commands. These commands are used for common tasks like creating a file, typing the contents of the file, copying a file, and erasing a file etc.

1. **DIR Command:**
- DIR command displays the list of directories and files on the screen.
- DIR is basically used to display all files and directories on the monitor screen page wise and width wise.

  Syntax: `C:\>DIR\switches`

  Example:

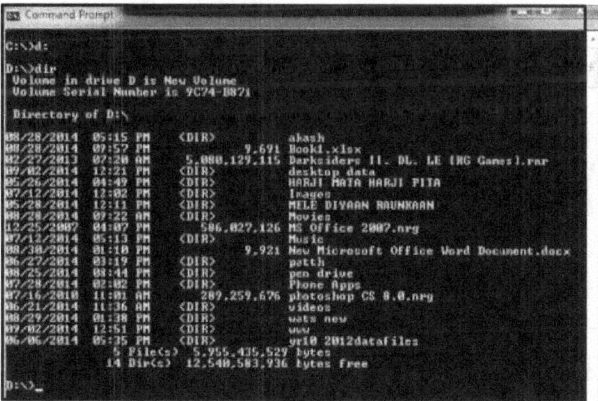

2. **CLS Command:**
- CLS is a command that allows a user to clear the complete contents of the screen and leave only a prompt.

  Syntax: `C:\> CLS`

Example:

```
C:\WINDOWS\system32\cmd.exe                              _ □ ×

C:\>echo Hello
Hello

C:\>time /t
11:41

C:\>date /t
04/06/2010

C:\>cls
```

3. DATE Command:

- This command is used for display the current system's date.

    Syntax: C:\>DATE

    Example:

```
C:\>date
The current date is: Tue 03/29/2011
Enter the new date: (mm-dd-yy)

C:\>date/t
Tue 03/29/2011

C:\>
```

4. TIME Command:

- This command is used for display the current system's time.

    Syntax: C:\>TIME

    Example:

```
C:\>time
The current time is: 13:41:53.99
Enter the new time:

C:\>time/t
01:42 PM

C:\>
```

5. COPY CON Command:

- This command is used to create a file. The file created by this command can not be modified.

    Syntax: C:\>COPY CON Filename

    Example:

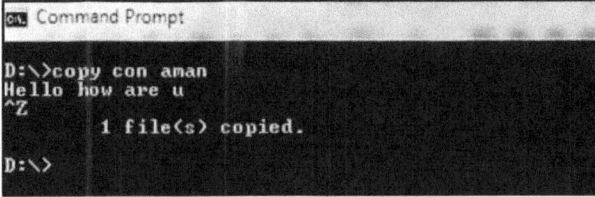

```
Command Prompt

D:\>copy con aman
Hello how are u
^Z
        1 file(s) copied.

D:\>
```

6. TYPE Command:

- TYPE command allows the user to see the contents of a file.

   Syntax: `Type [drive:][path]filename`

   `C:\>TYPE Filename`

   Example:

7. REN or RENAME Command:

- This command is used to **rename** an old filename with new filename.

   Syntax: `C:\>REN Oldfilename Newfilename`

   Example:

8. DEL or DELETE Command:

- This command is used to delete a single file.

   Syntax: `C:\>DEL filename`

   Example:

9. COPY Command:

- This command allows the user to copy one or more files to an alternate location.

   Syntax: `C:\>COPY source path target path`

   Example:

10. MD (Make Directory) or MKDIR Command:

- This command is used to create a new directory or sub directory that is subordinate to the currently logged directory.

  Syntax: C:\>MD Directory name

  C:\>MD Sub Directory name

  Example:

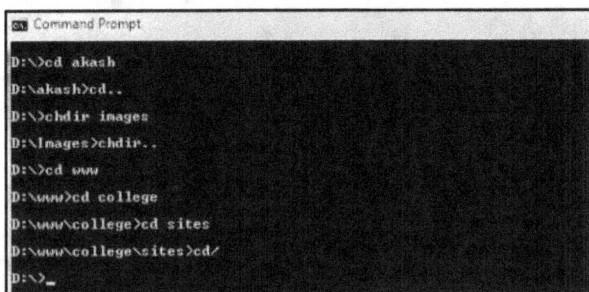

11. CD or CHDIR Command:

- CD (Change Directory) is a command used to switch directories in MS-DOS and the Windows command line.
- This command is used to change from one directory or sub directory to another directory or sub directory.

  Syntax: C:\>CD Directory name

  C:\>CD Sub Directory name

  Example:

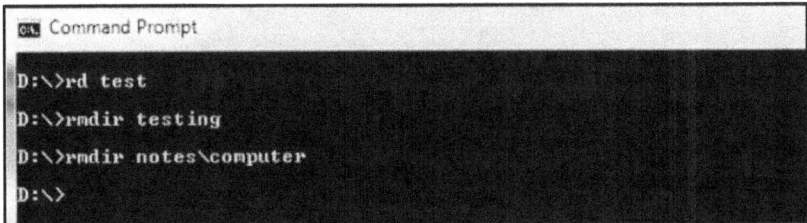

12. RD (Remove Directory) or RMDIR Command:

- This command is used to remove a directory or sub directory. If user wants to remove a directory or sub directory, then first delete all the files and sub directory in it. User can remove only empty directory or subdirectory.

  Syntax: C:\>RD Directory name

  C:\>RD Sub Directory name

  Example:

13. PATH Command:

- This command is used to provide access to files located in other directory paths or other disk.
- User can access only those files that have extension them .EXE, .COM, .BAT. By setting the path to these executable files user can execute them anywhere.
- There are three options for the setting Path to executable files.
  (a) To set the Path
  (b) To remove the Path
  (c) To see the Path

Syntax: `C:\>PATH = Drive name:\Directory name;`

Example:

1. To set the Path

   `C:\>PATH = C:\DOS`

2. To see the Path

   `C:\>PATH`

3. To remove the Path

   `C:\> PATH;`

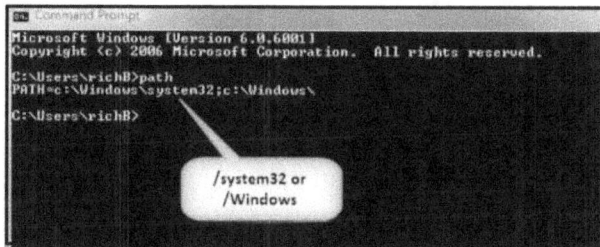

14. Prompt Command:

- This command is used to configure a DOS Prompt.
- User can ON/OFF the prompt by using this command.

  Syntax: `C:\>PROMPT`

  Example:

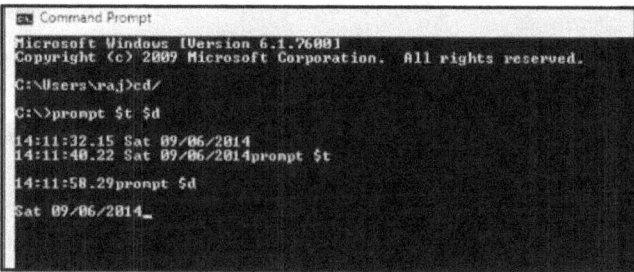

15. ECHO Command:

- It displays messages or turns on or off the display of commands in a batch file.

  ```
  ECHO on|off
  ECHO (message)
  ```

3.6.1.2 External Commands

- External commands are conventional program files. These files can be deleted, copied and even renamed.

1. **EDIT Command:**

- The MS-DOS Editor is a command line text editor that allows you to view, create, or modify any file on your computer.

- Using this command user can display multiple lines and move within displayed text both vertically and horizontally.

- To execute Edit command file is required.

  Syntax:

  ```
  C:\>EDIT Filename
  ```
  　　　　　　or
  ```
  C:\>EDIT [/B] [/H] [/R] [/S] [/<nnn>] [/?] [file(s)]
  ```

  where,

/B	Forces monochrome mode.
/H	Displays the maximum number of lines possible for your hardware.
/R	Load file(s) in read-only mode.
/S	Forces the use of short filenames.
/<nnn>	Load binary file(s), wrapping lines to <nnn> characters wide.
/?	Displays this help screen.
[file]	Specifies initial files(s) to load. Wildcards and multiple file specs can be given.

  Example:

  ```
  C:\>EDIT Aman
  ```
  　　　　　or
  ```
  C:\>edit c:\autoexec.bat
  ```

2. **ATTRIB Command:**

- This command is used to change the attribute of a file i.e. user can use ATTRIB to make a file "read only" which prevents the file from the change of contents.

- User can also hide or unhide a file. Also user can make the file in the "non readable" form. These commands provide a time saving and security during updating of file which user is updating.

  (a) Read-only: Allows the file to be only viewed and not written to or changed.

(b) **Archived:** Allows Microsoft Backup and other backup programs to know what files to back up.

(c) **Hidden:** Makes files invisible to standard users and hidden if show hidden files is enabled.

(d) **System:** Makes the file an important system file.

Syntax:

```
C:\>ATTRIB Filename attributes
```

Examples:

```
Hide the file

    C:\>ATTRIB Gill +h

Unhide the file

    C:\>ATTRIB Gill -h

Read only the file

    C:\>ATTRIB Gill +r
```

3. **SYS Command:**

- This command is used to copy the system files from one drive to another drive, allowing that drive to be bootable.

Syntax:

```
C:\>SYS <Drive name>
```

Example:

```
C:\>SYS A:
```

4. **PRINT Command:**

- This command is used to print the files.
- The files that are to be printed must be standard text file and containing data compatible to the printer.

Syntax:

```
C:\>PRINT <File name>
```

Example:

```
C:\>PRINT testfile.txt
```

5. **SORT Command:**

- This command sorts the data in alphanumeric order which can be ascending or descending.

Syntax:

```
C:\>SORT <File name>
```

Examples:

6. **BACKUP Command:**

- This command is used to store the various important files from the fixed disk to floppy disk as a protect from the various damages or crashes which occurs to the hard disk due to various reasons.

    Syntax:

    ```
    C:\>BACKUP <Source path>/options <Target path>
    ```

    Example:

    ```
    C:\>BACKUP C:\DOS A:/S
    ```

7. **FORMAT Command:**

- This command is used to make a disk usable for operating system by dividing the disk into magnetic tracks and sectors. The number of sectors and tracks depends upon the capacity of the disk and the version of DOS.

- FORMAT command erases all the data from the target disk.

    Syntax:

    ```
    C:\>FORMAT <Drive name>/switches
    ```

    Example:

    ```
    C:\>FORMAT A:
    ```

    Where /s /v /u are switches.

8. **TREE Command:**

- This command displays the list of directories and files on specified path using graphically display.

- It displays directories and files like a tree.

    Syntax:

    ```
    C:\>TREE <Drive name>
    ```

    or

    ```
    C:\>TREE/Swithes
    ```

Example:

9. MOVE Command:

- The MOVE command is used to move files or directories from one folder to another, or from one drive to another.

    Syntax:

    ```
    C:\>MOVE <Source path> <Target path>
    ```

    Examples:

    ```
    C:\>MOVE A:\*.* C:\command
    ```
    ```
    C:\>MOVE SAT GILL
    ```

10. FIND Command:

- This command is used to search files stored on the disk and data stored in the files.

    Syntax:

    ```
    C:\>FIND "text" <File name>
    ```

    Example:

    ```
    C:\>FIND "gill" Satinder
    ```

3.6.2 Batch File

- A special batch file named as AUTOEXEC.BAT file is executed automatically when user boots the computer. A batch file is a collection of DOS commands.

- MS-DOS batch files consist of the normal operating system commands such as DIR, DEL, COPY and MKDIR together with some extra commands such as IF, FOR, GOTO, SHIFT and PAUSE that provide conditional control of execution and enable PARAMETERS to be passed so that the same batch file can be used in many different contexts.

- Batch file is the group of internal and external commands stored in a single file and all commands in batch file are executed automatically with file name only.

- Batch File has extension .BAT.

- Some commonly used batch file commands are:
  1. **REM:** Used for comments.
  2. **PAUSE:** To pause the execution of batch file and waits until user press a key.
  3. **ECHO:** To on/off the text display on the screen.
  4. **CALL:** Calls specified batch file, execute it and returns to the main file.
- **Example of Batch File:**

  ```
  C:\>EDIT SAT.BAT
  ```

3.6.3 Limitations of DOS

- Various limitations of DOS are listed below:
  1. DOS is a single user OS, (one user can work at a time).
  2. DOS is a single tasking OS (One application can run at a time).
  3. It does not supports Graphics.
  4. DOS does not supports Networking.
  5. It is 16-bit and limited to 640k of RAM.
  6. It runs in real mode, so a buggy or malicious program can cause corruption.
  7. DOS has a character-based interface. A Graphical User Interface (GUI) is easier to the users than the character-based interface.

3.7 | MICROSOFT WINDOWS

- Microsoft Windows or simply Windows or MS-Windows is a metafamily of graphical operating systems developed, marketed, and sold by Microsoft.
- Microsoft introduced an operating environment named Windows on November 20, 1985, as a graphical operating system shell for MS-DOS in response to the growing interest in Graphical User Interfaces (GUIs).
- Microsoft Windows came to dominate the world's personal computer market with over 90% market share.
- As of March 2016, the most recent version of Windows for personal computers, tablets, smartphones and embedded devices is Windows 10.

3.7.1 Desktop

- The Desktop is the very first screen you see after Windows starts.
- There you find the folders like Internet Explorer, Computer, Recycle Bin and any shortcuts for applications and files that you have created.

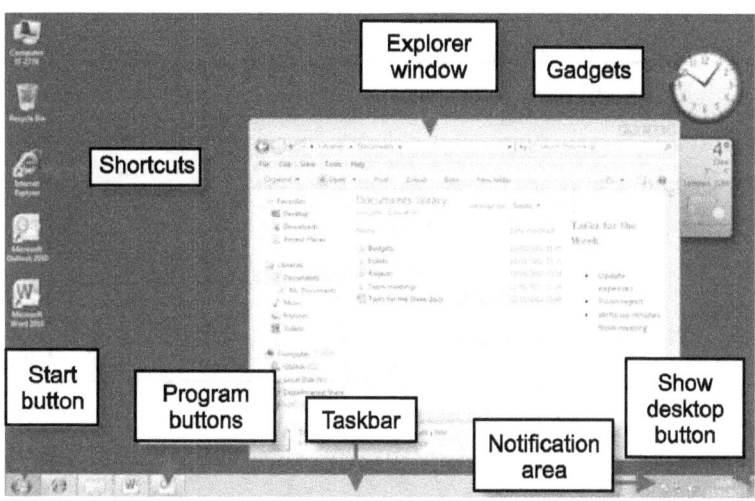

Fig. 3.6: Desktop of Windows 7

• Following table shows features of Windows 7.

Sr. No.	Windows 7 Features	Description
1.	Start Button	The Start Button is located on the taskbar at left down corner of screen.
2.	Program Buttons	Each open program appears as a button - even when multiple items for a program are open - but you can choose to change this view. You can pin programs to the taskbar. Appear Next to Start button.
3.	Taskbar	The horizontal line at the bottom of your screen is the taskbar.
4.	Show Desktop Button	This button will minimise all open windows to display the desktop and located at right down corner of screen.
5.	Explorer Window	In the Explorer Window you can manage your files and folders. You can use the back and forward buttons to navigate around.
6.	Gadgets	Gadgets can be placed anywhere on your desktop. They offer information - such as the time or the weather - at a quick glance.
7.	Notification Area	The notification area displays the time, the date and any program related icons. You can click an icon to display a window of options.
8.	Shortcuts	Shortcuts allow you to open a program without having to search for it in the Start Menu.

3.7.2 Icons

- Icons are small graphical images or pictorial representation of computer programs.
- An icon is a small image displayed on the screen which represent an application program, file or folder and are displayed on the desktop, (See Fig. 3.7).

Fig. 3.7: Icons

- You can simply drag an icon from one place to another on the desktop by keeping the left button of the mouse pressed.
- To open the file/folder that an icon represents, place your mouse pointer over the top of it and double click (two clicks in quick succession) the left mouse button. This will activate the icon and either start a program or open file / folder.
- The icons on the desktop can be renamed by right clicking on them and select Rename, similarly they can be deleted by right clicking and selecting Delete.

Types of Icons:

1. **Disk Drive Icons:**

- These types of icon represent the Drives of the computer, (See Fig 3.8).

Fig. 3.8: Disk Drive Icons

2. **Application Icons:**

- Application icons mean the software package which are used to run various programs, (See Fig. 3.9).

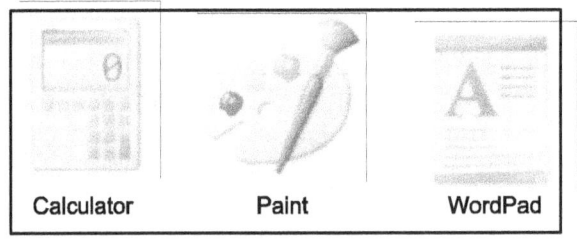

Fig. 3.9: Application Icons

3. Shortcut Icons:

- Shortcut icons are the copy of an application, (See Fig. 3.10).

Fig. 3.10: Shortcut Icons

4. Document Icons:

- These icons represent a document file, (See Fig. 3.11).

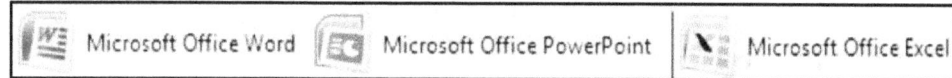

Fig. 3.11

3.7.3 Files and Directories

1. Files:

- A file is a collection of data that is stored on disk and that can be manipulated as a single unit by its name.
- We can define file as "a collection of logically related records".

2. Directories:

- Files (program or data file) are usually stored on disks. DOS organizes these files by grouping related files into lists called directories.
- A directory is a file that acts as a folder for other files. A directory can also contain other directories (sub-directories).
- In addition to directories, DOS use an area called the File Allocation Table (FAT). When a disk is formatted, this table is copied onto the disk and an empty directory, called root directory, is created.
- On every storage disk, files are stored in directories and File Allocation Table keeps the information about their location on the disk surface. The root directory is represented by the backslash character '\'.
- A pathname is a sequence of directory names followed by a filename. Each directory name is separated from the previous one by a backslash.
- A path is similar to pathname except that it does not include a filename. The pathname is specified in the following form:

```
[\dir_name] [\dir_name ...] \filename
```

- For example, the pathname for RAVI's ABC.PAS file is,
  `\STUDENT\RAVI\ABC.PAS`
- Fig. 3.12 shows a bridged version of the directory hierarchy.

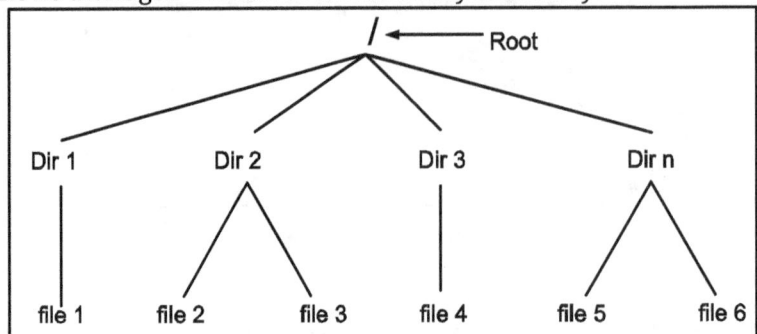

Fig. 3.12: A Bridged Version of the Directory Hierarchy

3.7.4 Control Panel

- The Control Panel is a part of the Microsoft Windows graphical user interface which allows users to view and manipulate basic system settings and controls such as adding hardware, adding and removing software, controlling user accounts, and changing accessibility options.

Fig. 3.13: Control panel icon

- Windows Control Panel provides you with a graphical interface for configuring hardware and customizing Windows.
- Control Panel is a Windows program that provides you with a visual way of modifying your system while working with Windows. Each option that you can change is represented by an icon in the Control Panel window.
- From Control Panel you can do a lot of tasks as given Fig. 3.14.

Fig. 3.14

3.7.5 Menu Items

- When you open a folder or library, you see it in a Window. The various parts of this window are designed to help you navigate around Windows or work with files, folders, and libraries more easily.

- Fig. 3.15 shows a typical window and each of its parts.

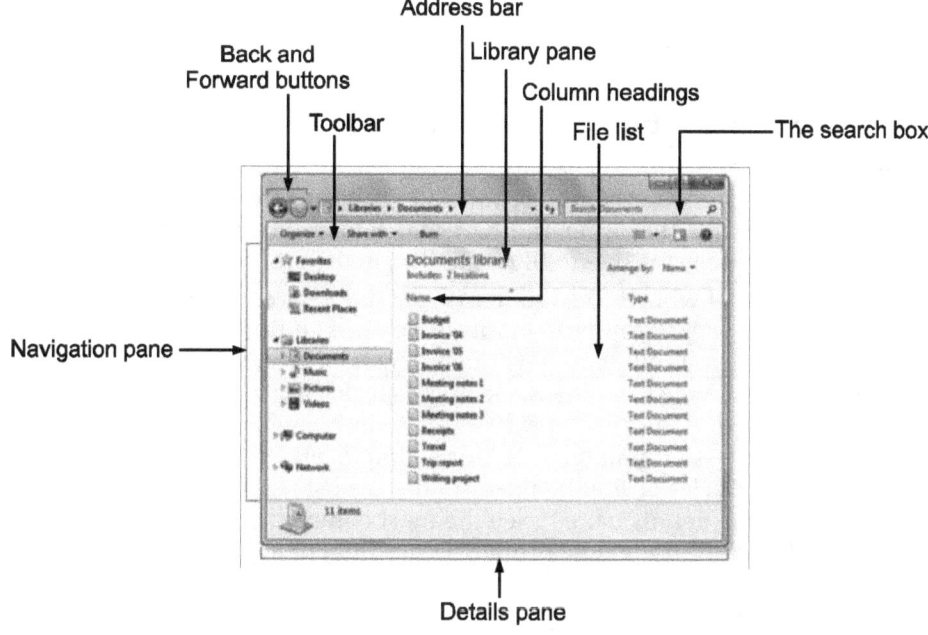

Fig. 3.15

- Various part of Windows are explained below:

Window part	What it's useful for
Navigation pane	Use the navigation pane to access libraries, folders, saved searches, and even entire hard disks. Use the Favorites section to open your most commonly used folders and searches; use the Libraries section to access your libraries. You can also expand Computer to browse folders and subfolders. .
Back and Forward buttons	Use the Back button ⊙ and the Forward button ⊙ to navigate to other folders or libraries you've already opened without closing the current window. These buttons work together with the address bar; after you use the address bar to change folders, for example, you can use the Back button to return to the previous folder.

contd. ...

Toolbar	Use the toolbar to perform common tasks, such as changing the appearance of your files and folders, burning files to a CD, or starting a digital picture slide show. The toolbar's buttons change to show only the tasks that are relevant. For example, if you click a picture file, the toolbar shows different buttons than it would if you clicked a music file.
Address bar	Use the address bar to navigate to a different folder or library or to go back to a previous one.
Library pane	The library pane appears only when you are in a library (such as the Documents library). Use the library pane to customize the library or to arrange the files by different properties.
Column headings	Use the column headings to change how the files in the file list are organized. For example, you can click the left side of a column heading to change the order the files and folders are displayed in, or you can click the right side to filter the files in different ways.
File list	This is where the contents of the current folder or library are displayed. If you type in the search box to find a file, only the files that match your current view (including files in subfolders) will appear.
Search box	Type a word or phrase in the search box to look for an item in the current folder or library. The search begins as soon as you begin typing—so if you type "B," for example, all the files with names starting with the letter B will appear in the file list.
Details pane	Use the details pane to see the most common properties associated with the selected file. File properties are information about a file, such as the author, the date you last changed the file, and any descriptive tags you might have added to the file.
Preview pane	Use the preview pane to see the contents of most files. If you select an e-mail message, text file, or picture, for example, you can see its contents without opening it in a program. If you don't see the preview pane, click the Preview pane button ⊡ in the toolbar to turn it on.

3.7.6 The Search Option

1. **Search for Programs or Applications:**
- If you are not sure where a program is located on the Start menu, begin typing the program name to search for it. Windows will also find programs installed using the Program Installer (link).

Fig. 3.16: Search box

- To search follow the following steps:
  Step 1 : Click the Start menu.
  Step 2 : Click in the search box and start typing.

Step 3 : As you type the Start menu will show possible results.

Step 4 : Results are organised by type with priority given to programs you use most frequently.

- You can also search for files using this search box but for more accurate results see Searching your Files (link).

2. Search for Files and Folders (Directories):

- Search through your files and folders more effectively by refining your search by date, size, file type, tag or search in two or more folders.

- Open Windows Explorer from the Task bar or Documents from the Start menu.

- Select where to search: To search within a specific folder in your Z:\My Documents folder or Shared Departmental X: drive, first navigate to that folder so that the folder shows in the address bar at the top.

Fig. 3.17: Search with 'courses' folder

- To search the whole of your Z:\My Documents folder, select Documents.

Fig. 3.18: Whole search within 'Documents' folder

- **Run the search:**

  1. Type the word or phrase you wish to search for into the Search box in the top right of the window.

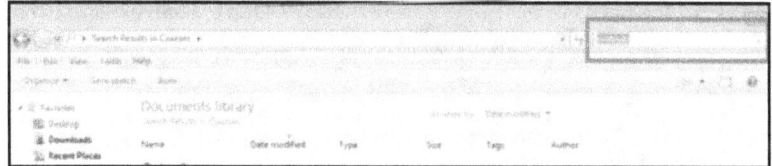

Fig. 3.19: Run the search

  2. The Search will begin immediately and refine the results as you type Only words found in the file name will be returned.

  3. To close the search click ❌ at the right of the search box.

Fig. 3.20: Close the search

3.7.7 Paint

- Paint is a Windows accessory used to create and work with graphics and pictures.
- Paint is a program used for drawing and painting the pictures.
- The pictures in the paint are images in bitmap format.
- A bitmap file is a map of picture created from small dots or pixels.
- The default extension of an image (i.e. paint file) is .bmp.
- To open the paint application follow the following steps:
    1. Open the Start Menu, and click on All Programs, double click on Accessories, and double click on Paint.

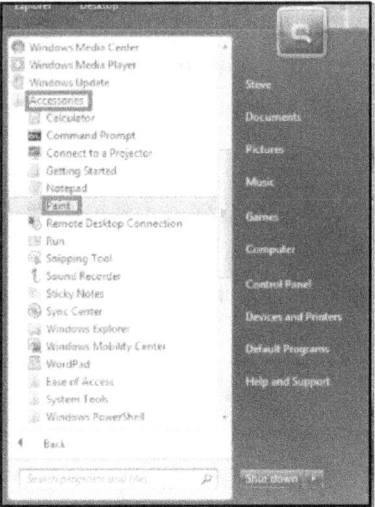

Fig. 3.21: Paint in start menu

- Paint is a feature in Windows that you can use to draw, color, and edit pictures.
- Fig. 3.22 shows Paint Window.

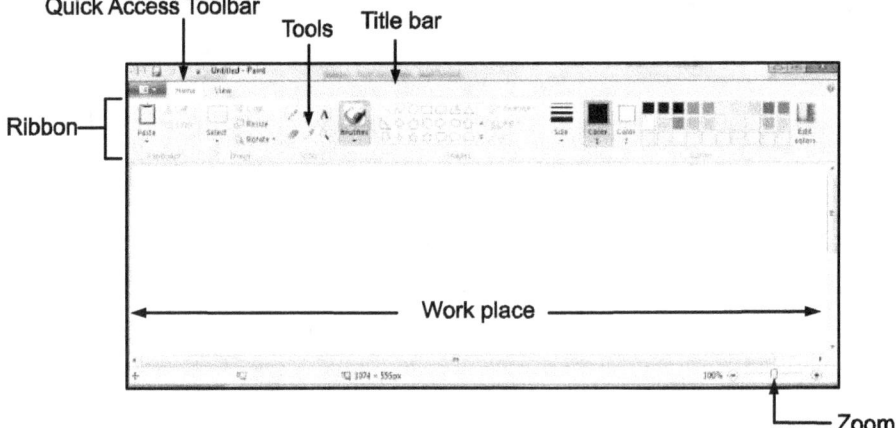

Fig. 3.22: Screen Components of Paint

Working with Tools:

- The ribbon in Paint includes a handy collection of drawing tools. You can use these tools to create freehand drawings and add a variety of shapes to your pictures.

Draw a Line:

- Some tools and shapes, such as the Pencil, Brush, Line, and Curve, let you make a variety of straight, curved, and squiggly lines. What you draw is determined by how you move the mouse as you draw.

- You can use the Line to draw a straight line, for example.

  1. On the Home tab, in the Shapes group, click the Line ＼.
  2. In the Colors group, click Color 1, and then click the color you want to use.
  3. To draw, drag the pointer across the drawing area.

Draw a Squiggly Line:

- Your drawings don't have to be composed of only straight lines. The Pencil and Brushes can be used to make completely random, free-form shapes.

  1. On the Home tab, in the Tools group, click the Pencil tool ✎.
  2. In the Colors group, click Color 1, and then click the color you want to use.
  3. To draw, drag the pointer across the drawing area and make a squiggly line.

Draw a Shape:

- Paint lets you draw many different shapes. For example, you can draw ready-made, defined shapes such as rectangles, circles, squares, triangles, and arrows (to name a few).

- You can also make your own custom shape by using the Polygon shape ◰ to draw a polygon, which is a shape that can have any number of sides.

  1. On the Home tab, in the Shapes group, click a ready-made shape, such as the Rectangle ☐.
  2. To add a ready-made shape, drag the pointer across the drawing area to make the shape.
  3. To change the outline style, in the Shapes group, click Outline, and then click an outline style.
  4. If you don't want your shape to have an outline, click No outline.
  5. In the Colors group, click Color 1, and then click a color for the outline.
  6. In the Colors group, click Color 2, and then click a color to use to fill the shape.
  7. To change the fill style, in the Shapes group, click Fill, and then click a fill style. If you don't want your shape to be filled, click No fill.

Add Text:

- You can also add text to your picture. The Text tool lets you add a simple message or title.

  1. On the Home tab, in the Tools group, click the Text tool $\mathbf{A}$.

  2. Drag the pointer in the drawing area where you want to add text.

  3. Under Text Tools, on the Text tab, click the font face, size, and style in the Font group.

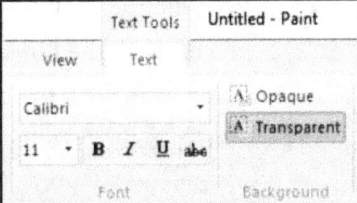

Fig. 3.23

  4. In the Colors group, click Color 1, and then click a color. This is the text color.

  5. Type the text that you want to add.

Erase Part of Your Picture:

- If you make a mistake or need to change part of a picture, use the eraser. By default, the eraser changes any area you erase to white, but you can change the eraser color. For example, if you set the background color to yellow, anything you erase turns to yellow.

  1. On the Home tab, in the Tools group, click the Eraser tool.

  2. In the Colors group, click Color 2, and then click the color that you want to erase with. If you want to erase with white, you don't have to select a color.

  3. Drag the pointer over the area you want to erase.

Saving a Picture:

- Save your picture frequently so you don't accidentally lose your work. To save, click the Paint button, and then click Save. This saves all of the changes made to the picture since the last time you saved.

- The very first time that you save a new picture, you will need to give your picture a file name. Follow following steps:

  1. Click the Paint button, and then click Save.

  2. In the Save as type box, select the file format you want.

  3. In the File name box, type a name, and then click Save.

3.7.8 Notepad

- Notepad is a generic text editor included with Microsoft Windows that enables someone to open and read plaintext files.
- Notepad is a simple and easy to use text editor.
- The default file extension of Notepad file is '.txt'.
- Notepad does not support any text or paragraph formatting i.e., it opens and saves text in the ASCII (American Standard Code for Information Interchange) mode.
- Notepad can also be used to type programs for programming languages or applications like BASIC, dBASE, FoxPro, HTML etc.

How to Open Windows Notepad:

1. Click on the Start button to open the Start menu.

   Click Notepad Icon:

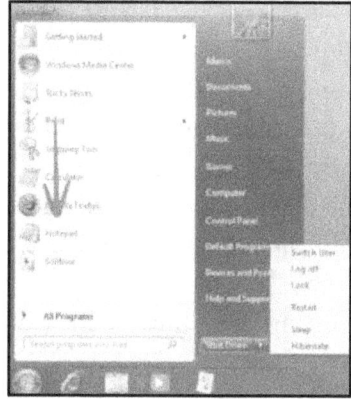

Fig. 3.24: Notepad in Start Menu

2. If you cannot find the notepad on your Start menu, you will have to click on All Programs.

3. A list of programs appears, click on Accessories and then click on Notepad.

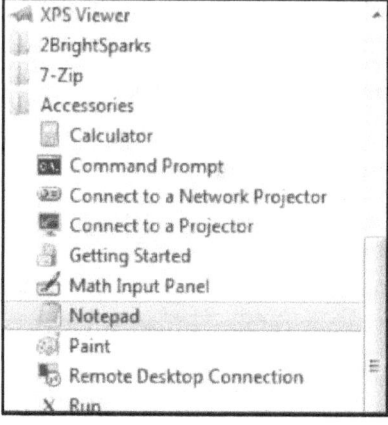

Fig. 3.25: Notepad in Accessories

- After clicking on Notepad the Window of Notepad is open (See Fig. 3.26).

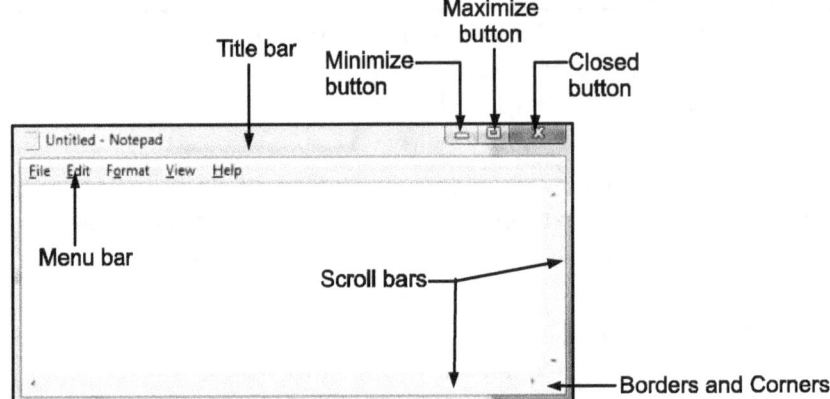

Fig. 3.26: Screen Components of Notepad

- Parts of a Window of Notepad:
    1. **Title bar:** Displays the name of the document.
    2. **Minimize, Maximize, and Close buttons:** These buttons hide the window, enlarge it to fill the whole screen, and close it, respectively.
    3. **Menu bar:** Contains items that you can click to make choices in a program.
    4. **Scroll bar:** Lets you scroll the contents of the window to see information that is currently out of view.
    5. **Borders and Corners:** You can drag these with your mouse pointer to change the size of the window.

3.7.9 Utility Programs

- System utility software is required for the maintenance of computer. System utilities are used for supporting and enhancing the programs and the data in computer.
- Some system utilities may come embedded with OS and others may be added later on.
- The programs that assist in loading and linking the object program/code are called as system utilities.
- Some examples of system utilities are explained below:

1. **Anti-virus Utilities:**

- Anti-virus utilities scan for computer viruses.
- Anti-virus software, as the name suggests, helps to protect a computer system from viruses and other harmful programs.
- A computer virus is a computer program that can cause damage to a computer's software, hardware or data. It is referred to as a virus because it has the capability to replicate itself and hide inside other computer files.
- One of the most common ways to get a virus is to download a file from the Internet. Anti-virus software scans your online activity to make sure you are not downloading

infected files. New viruses are coming out all the time, so anti-virus software needs to be updated very frequently.

- Norton Anti-virus, McAfee Anti-virus, AVG Anti-virus are the example of anti-virus softwares.

2. Disk Cleaning:

- A disk utility is a utility program that allows a user to perform various functions on a computer disk, such as disk partitioning and logical volume management, as well as multiple smaller tasks such as changing drive letters and other mount points, renaming volumes, disk checking, and disk formatting, which are otherwise handled separately by multiple other built-in commands. Types of disk utilities include disk checkers, disk cleaners and disk space analyzers etc.

- Disk cleaners can find files that are unnecessary to computer operation, or take up considerable amounts of space. Disk cleaner helps the user to decide what to delete when their hard disk is full.

- Disk cleaners are computer programs that find and delete potentially unnecessary or potentially unwanted files from a computer. The purpose of such deletion may be to free up disk space, to eliminate clutter or to protect privacy.

- Disk space consuming unnecessary files include temporary files, trash, old backups and web caches made by web browsers. Privacy risks include HTTP cookies, local shared objects, log files or any other trace that may tell which computer program opened which files.

- Disk cleaners must not be mis-taken with anti-virus software (which delete malware), registry cleaners (which clean Windows Registry) or data erasure software (which securely delete files), although multifunction software (such as those included below) may fit into all these categories.

- **Example:** BleachBit is a free and open-source disk space cleaner, privacy manager, and computer system optimizer.

3. File Compression/Decompression:

- File compression is the practice of packaging a file or files to use less disk space.

- The file compression category includes software programs that will archive your files and extract archived files such as ZIP and RAR files.

- Many products in this category let you manage files and protect them with encryption. Notable titles include WinZip, WinRAR, and 7-Zip.

- Uncompressing (or decompressing) is the act of expanding a compression file back into its original form.

- Software that you download from the Internet often comes in a compressed package that can uncompress itself when you click on it. You can also uncompress files using popular tools such as PKZIP in the DOS operating system, WinZip in Windows, and MacZip in Macintosh.

4. Disk Defragmenters:

- In the file systems, defragmentation is a process that reduces the amount of fragmentation. It does this by physically organizing the contents of the mass storage device used to store files into the smallest number of contiguous regions (fragments).

- It also attempts to create larger regions of free space using compaction to impede the return of fragmentation.

- Some defragmentation utilities try to keep smaller files within a single directory together, as they are often accessed in sequence.

- Disk defragmenters can detect computer files whose contents are scattered across several locations on the hard disk, and move the fragments to one location to increase efficiency.

- Fragmentation occurs when the file system cannot or will not allocate enough contiguous space to store a complete file as a unit, but instead puts parts of it in gaps between existing files. Larger files and greater numbers of files also contribute to fragmentation and consequent performance loss. Defragmentation attempts to alleviate these problems.

3.8 EXAMPLES OF COMMERCIAL SOFTWARES

- Commercial software is any software or program that is designed and developed for licensing or sale to end users or that serves a commercial purpose.

- Commercial software is written by software vendors for various markets. Commercial software can usually be customised for an individual or an organisation but are written with a view to meeting the needs of the marketplace.

- Examples of commercial software are explained below:

1. Spreadsheets:

- One of the first commercial uses of computers was in processing payroll and other financial records. So the programs were designed to generate reports in the standard 'spreadsheet' format used by book-keepers and accountants.

- A spreadsheet application is a rectangular grid that allows text, numbers, and complex functions to be entered into a matrix of thousands of individual cells.

- The spreadsheet provides sheets containing cells each of which may contain text and/or numbers. Cells may also contain equations that calculate results from data placed in other cells or series of cells. A simple example might be a column of numbers totalled in a single cell containing an equation relating to that column.

- Microsoft Excel and Lotus 1-2-3 are examples of spreadsheet commercial applications.

2. Image Editors:

- Image editor programs are designed specifically for capturing, creating, editing, and manipulating images. These graphics programs provide a variety of special features for creating and altering (modifying) images.

- In addition to offering a host of filters and image transformation algorithms, some image editors also enable the user to create and superimpose layers.
- Most graphic programs have the ability to import and export one or more graphic file formats. These computer programs enable the user to adjust an image to improve its appearance.
- With image editing software, one can darken or lighten an image, rotate it, adjust its contrast, crop out extraneous detail, and do much more.
- Examples of Image Editor programs are Adobe Photoshop, Adobe Illustrator and CorelDraw.

3. Word Processors:

- A word processor is a software used to compose, format, edit, and print electronic documents.
- Word processing is one of the earliest applications that were used for office productivity and in personal computers.
- Word processing involves not only typing, but also checking the spelling and grammar of the text and arranging it correctly on a page. A variety of different typefaces is available for a variety of effects. It is possible to include pictures, graphs, charts, and many other things within the text of the document. It also allows for changes in margins, fonts, and colour.
- Now-a-days, virtually all personal computers are equipped with a word processing program, which has the same function as a typewriter for writing letters, reports or other documents, and printing.
- Examples of word processors are Microsoft Word and WordPerfect.

4. Presentation Applications:

- A presentation is a means of assessment that requires presentation providers to present their work orally in the presence of an audience. It combines both visual and verbal elements.
- Presentation software allows the user to create presentations by producing slides or handouts for presentation of projects.
- Essentially, such computer programs allow users to create a variety of visually appealing electronic slides for presentations.
- Microsoft PowerPoint is one of the most famous presentation commercial application.

5. DeskTop Publishing (DTP) Software:

- The term desktop publishing is usually used to describe the creation of printed documents using a desktop computer.
- DTP is a technique of using a personal computer to design images and pages, and assemble type and graphics, then using a laser printer or image-setter to output the assembled pages onto paper, film or printing plate.
- DTP software are used for creating magazines, books, newsletters, and so on. Such software assist in creating sophisticated documents including complicated page designs, detailed illustrations, and camera-ready typefaces.
- Quark Express and Adobe PageMaker are examples of commercial desktop publishing softwares.

6. **DataBase Management Systems (DBMS):**

*   Database management software is a collection of computer programs that allow storage, modification, and extraction of information from a database in an efficient manner.
*   It supports the structuring of the database in a standard format and provides tools for data input, verification, storage, retrieval, query, and manipulation. When such software is used, information systems can be changed much more easily as the organization's information requirements change.
*   New categories of data can be added to the database without disrupting the existing system. It also controls the security and integrity of the database from unauthorized access.
*   FoxPro and Oracle are the examples of database management systems.

PRACTICE QUESTIONS

1. What is knowledge? Enlist its types.
2. Explain procedural knowledge and definitional knowledge in detail. Also compare them.
3. What is DOS? Explain its environment.
4. What is fixed and stored 'programs'? Compare them.
5. Define the following terms:
    (i)   Software,
    (ii) OS,
    (iii) Syntax, and
    (iv) Semantic.
6. Enlist commands of DOS?
7. What is Windows OS?
8. Write short notes on:
    (i)   Desktop,
    (ii) Icons,
    (iii) Menu Items, and
    (iv) Files.
9. Describe directories in detail.
10. Enlist internal and external commands of DOS.
11. Explain system software in detail.
12. Describe application software in detail.
13. Differentiate between system and application softwares.
14. Write short notes on:
    (i) Paint
    (ii) Notepad.
15. What are the limitations of DOS?
16. Describe batch file in detail.
17. Explain static and dynamic semantics.
18. Enlist utility programs in computer.

■■■

Editors and Word Processors

Contents ...

4.1 | INTRODUCTION

- Editor is a piece of software which enables the programmer to enter and edit a program.
- Word processors are basically document editors with additional features to produce well formatted hard copy output.
- MS-Word, WordStar are popular editors. In this chapter we study various editors like MS-Word, vi, gedit etc.

4.2 | BASIC CONCEPTS

- Word processing means the process of manipulation of text using computers. It includes entering, editing, formatting and manipulation of text on a computer screen and printing of the processed text.
- The text is saved on the computer as a file for future use. It avoids retyping to correct an error or omission.
- Simply defined, Word-Processing (WP) implies the use of a computer based system for the entering, editing, storing and printing of textual material. These can be in the form of letters, memos, reports, manuals, drafts and almost all documents required by an office.
- A computer program/application/software exclusively used for word-processing is called a Word-processor.

Features of a Word Processor:

1. **Easy to Learn:** To operate word processors, no special skills are required. Most of the word processors are easy to learn and use.

2. **Table and Graphics:** The use of tables, charts and graphics are also supported by the word processors. This helps to increase the visual clarity of the text.

3. **Extensive Built-in Features:** Word processors can be used to make mail merge documents, envelopes and labels etc.

4. **Spelling and Grammar Check:** Word processors help to check and remove spelling and grammatical mistakes. Also, they help in knowing the synonym(s) or the meaning of a particular word.

5. **Foreign Language Features:** Word processors allow documents to be created in different languages other than English. This is helpful for users who do nor know English or require work to be done in some other 'specified' language.

6. **Linking and Embedding:** Word processors allow linking and embedding of objects such as a chart, a video clip, a picture, etc. in a document. This is possible by using Object Linking and Embedding (OLE) technology that can be used to share information between programs.

7. **Easy Formatting:** Word processors help in formatting style, font, and paragraph to increase the readability of the text and to enhance the visual appearance.

8. **Extensive Help:** Word processors include an extensive built-in help feature that can be used to ask queries. This means that the user can easily type in this built-feature to know how to perform an action or set of actions, etc.

4.3 | EXAMPLES

4.3.1 MS-Word 2007

- Microsoft Word is word processing software.

- Word processing software lets you insert and manipulate text and graphics to create all kinds of professional looking documents. A document is written information that can be printed on paper or distributed electronically.

- Microsoft Word is a word processor designed by Microsoft. It was first released in 1983 under the name Multi-Tool Word for Xenix systems.

- Microsoft Word is used to create, format, edit, save and print electronic documents.

Purposes/Uses of Microsoft Word:

1. To create business documents having various graphics including pictures, charts, and diagrams.

2. To store and reuse ready-made content and formatted elements such as cover pages and sidebars.

3. To create letters and letterheads for personal and business purpose.

4. To design different documents such as resumes or invitation cards etc.

5. To create a range of correspondence from a simple office memo to legal copies and reference documents.

- To start MS-Word 2007 follow following steps:

Step 1 : Click the Start button on the Windows taskbar. The Start menu opens.

Step 2 : Click All Programs.

Step 3 : Click the Microsoft Office.

Step 4 : Click Microsoft Office Word 2007. Microsoft Office Word 2007 starts and its program window opens on the desktop with a new, blank document displayed.

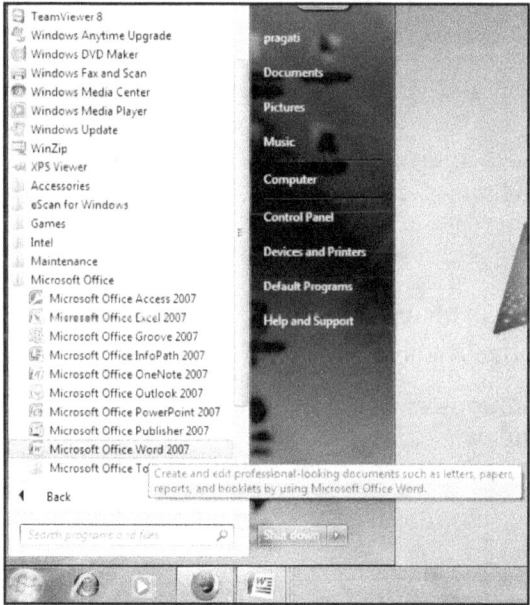

Fig. 4.1

Parts of a Microsoft Word 2007 Window:

- Following (See Fig. 4.2) is the basic window which we get when we start word application. Let us understand various important parts of this window.

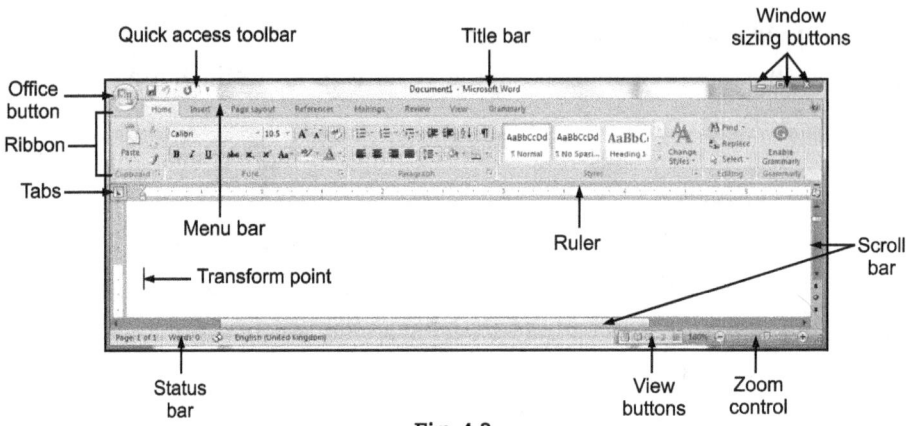

Fig. 4.2

- Fig. 4.2 shows following screen elements of MS-Word 2007 Windows:
    1. **Quick Access Toolbar:** Keeps icons for frequently used commands, such as Save, Undo, and Redo, in a convenient location.
    2. **Ribbon:** Collection of commands organized by tabs and groups.
    3. **Office Button:** Contains common Office 2007 commands, such as New, Open, Save, Save As, and Print.
    4. **Title Bar:** Shows name of active program and file.
    5. **Help Button:** Provides assistance with a program.
    6. **Insertion Point:** Blinking vertical bar indicating where the next character you type will appear.
    7. **Scroll Bar:** Used to adjust view in the document window to view another part of the document.
    8. **Status Bar:** Displays information about current position and settings.
    9. **View Buttons:** Changes the way a document, worksheet, or presentation is displayed on the screen.
    10. **Zoom Controls:** Magnifies or decreases the content currently displayed on the screen.

Creating a New Document in MS-Word 2007:

- To create a new document follow the following steps:

    Step 1 :   Click the Microsoft Office button 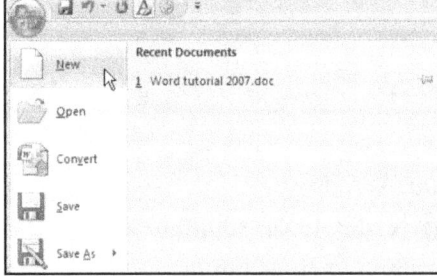 in the top left corner of the Microsoft Word window.

    Step 2 :   In the menu that opens, click New.

Fig. 4.3

- This opens the New Document dialog box as shown in Fig. 4.4.

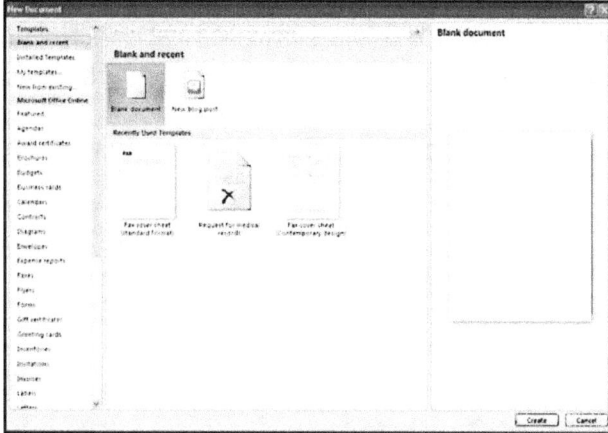

Fig. 4.4

Step 3 : Select Blank document then click Create button in the window.

Saving a Document:

- To save your document, click the Save button on the Quick Access toolbar.

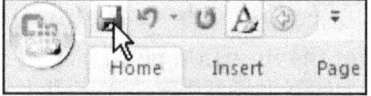

Fig. 4.5

OR

Step 1 : Click the Microsoft Office button.

Step 2 : Click the arrow next to the Save As command.

Step 3 : In the menu that opens, select Word 97-2003 Document.

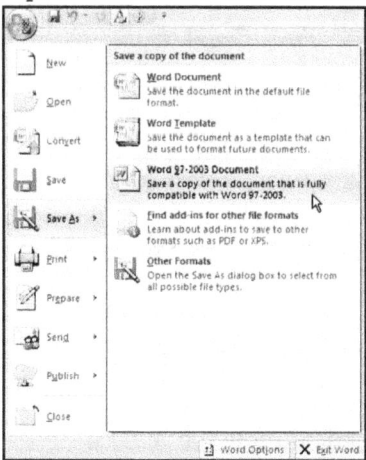

Fig. 4.6

Step 4 : Browse to the location where you want to save the file, enter a file name, and click Save.

Working with Text:

- Document area is the area where where you type your text. The flashing vertical bar is called the insertion point and it represents the location where text will appear when you type.

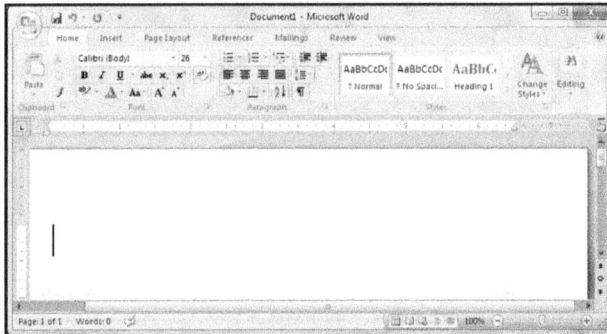

Fig. 4.7

- So just keep your mouse cursor at the text insertion point and start typing whatever text you would like to type. We typed only two word "Hello........." as shown in Fig. 4.8. The text appears to the left of the insertion point as you type.

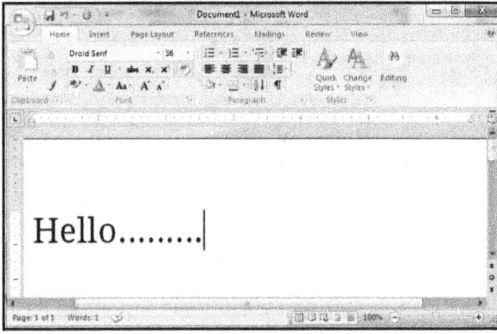

Fig. 4.8

Formatting Text:

- To create and design effective documents, you need to know how to format text.

To Format Font Size:

Step 1 : Select the text you want to modify.

Step 2 : Left-click the drop-down arrow next to the font size box on the Home tab. The font size drop-down menu appears.

Step 3 : Move your cursor over the various font sizes. A live preview of the font size will appear in the document.

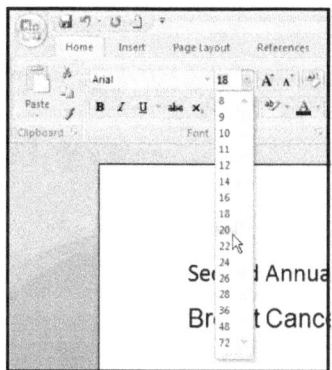

Fig. 4.9

Step 4 : Left-click the font size you want to use. The font size will change in the document.

To Format Font Style:

Step 1 : Select the text you want to modify.

Step 2 : Left-click the drop-down arrow next to the font style box on the Home tab. The font style drop-down menu appears.

Step 3 : Move your cursor over the various font styles. A live preview of the font will appear in the document.

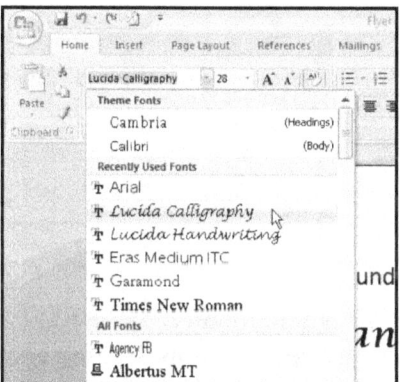

Fig. 4.10

Step 4 : Left-click the font style you want to use. The font style will change in the document.

To Format Font Color:

Step 1 : Select the text you want to modify.

Step 2 : Left-click the drop-down arrow next to the font color box on the Home tab. The font color menu appears.

Step 3 : Move your cursor over the various font colors. A live preview of the color will appear in the document.

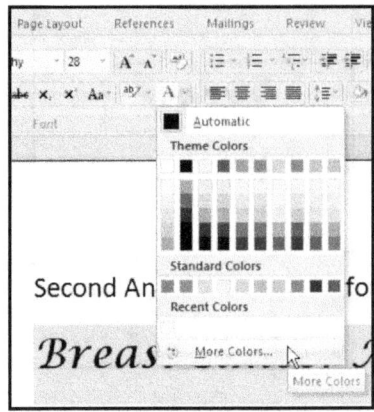

Fig. 4.11

Step 4 : Left-click the font color you want to use. The font color will change in the document.

Use the Bold, Italic, and Underline Commands:

Step 1 : Select the text you want to modify.

Step 2 : Click the bold, italic, or underline command in the Font group on the Home tab.

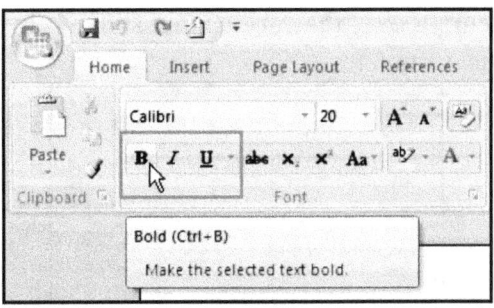

Fig. 4.12

To Change the Text Case:

Step 1 : Select the text you want to modify.

Step 2 : Click the Change Case command in the Font group on the Home tab.

Step 3 : Select one of the case options from the list.

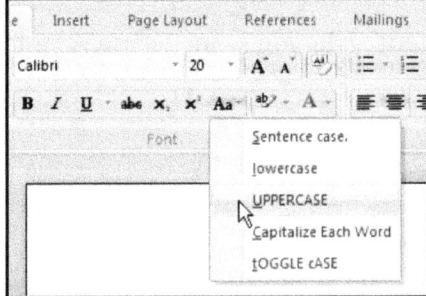

Fig. 4.13

To Change Text Alignment:

Step 1 : Select the text you want to modify.

Step 2 : Select one of the four alignment options from the Paragraph group on the Home tab.

    (i) **Align Text Left:** Aligns all of the selected text to the left margin.

    (ii) **Center:** Aligns text an equal distance from the left and right margins.

    (iii) **Align Text Right:** Aligns all of the selected text to the right margin.

    (iv) **Justify:** Aligns text equally to the right and left margins; used in many books, newsletters, and newspapers.

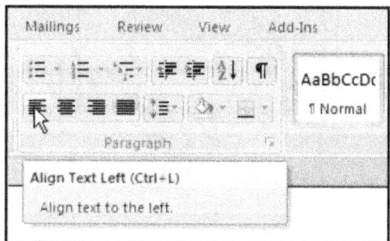

Fig. 4.14

Inserting Clip Art:

• You may want to insert various types of illustrations into your documents to make them more visually appealing. Illustrations include clip art, pictures, SmartArt, and charts.

To Locate Clip Art:

Step 1 : Select the Insert tab.

Step 2 : Click the Clip Art command in the Illustrations group.

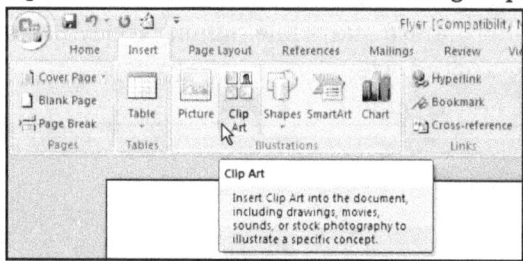

Fig. 4.15

Step 3 : The clip art options appear in the task pane on the right.

Step 4 : Enter keywords in the Search for: field that are related to the image you want to insert.

Step 5 : Click the drop-down arrow next to the Search in: field.

Step 6 : Select Everywhere to ensure Word searches your computer and its online resources for an image that meets your criteria.

Step 7 : Click the drop-down arrow in the Results should be: field.

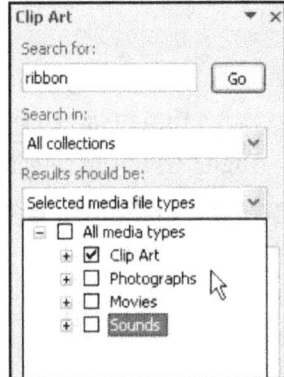

Fig. 4.16

Step 8 : Click Go.

To Insert Clip Art:

Step 1 : Review the results from a clip art search.

Step 2 : Place your insertion point in the document where you want to insert clip art.

Step 3 : Left-click an image in the task pane. It will appear in the document.

Working with Shapes:

• You can add a variety of shapes to your document, including arrows, callouts, squares, stars, and flow chart symbols.

To Insert a Shape:

Step 1 : Select the Insert tab.

Step 2 : Click the Shape command.

Step 3 : Left-click a shape from the menu. Your cursor is now a cross shape.

Step 4 : Left-click your mouse and while holding it down, drag your mouse until the shape is the desired size.

Step 5 : Release the mouse button.

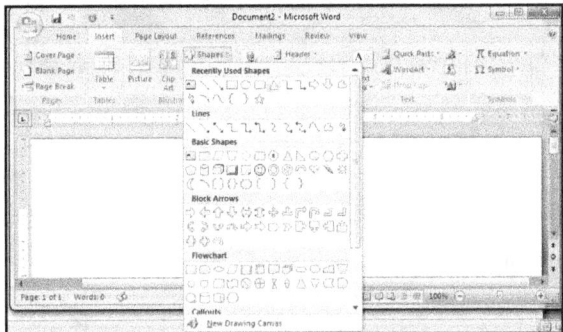

Fig. 4.17

Using a Template:

*   A template is a predesigned document you can use to create new documents with the same formatting.
*   With a template, many of the more important document design decisions such as margin size, font style and size, and spacing are predetermined.

To Insert a Template:

Step 1 : Click the Microsoft Office button.

Step 2 : Select New. The New Document dialog box appears.

Step 3 : Select Installed Templates to choose a template on your computer.

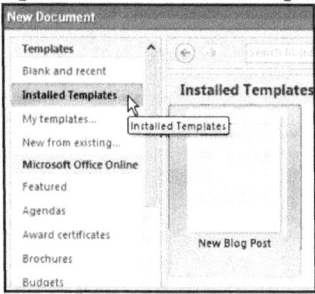

Fig. 4.18

Step 4 : Review the available templates. Left-click a template to select it.

Step 5 : Click Create, and the template opens in a new window.

Fig. 4.19

Lists:

*   Bulleted and numbered lists can be used in your documents to arrange and format text to draw emphasis.

To Insert a New List:

Step 1 : Select the text you want to format as a list.

Step 2 : Click the Bullets or Numbering commands on the Home tab.

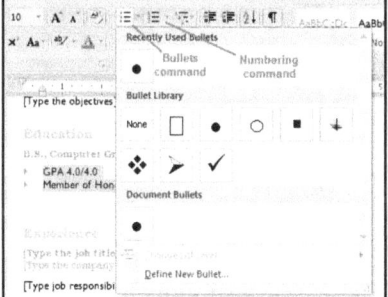

Fig. 4.20

Step 3 : Left-click the bullet or numbering style you want to use. It will appear in the document.

Step 4 : Position your cursor at the end of a list item, and press the Enter key to add an item to the list.

Line and Paragraph Spacing:

• An important part of creating effective documents lies in the document design. As part of designing the document and making formatting decisions, you will need to know how to modify the spacing.

To Format Line Spacing:

Step 1 : Select the text you want to format.

Step 2 : Click the Line spacing command in the Paragraph group on the Home tab.

Step 3 : Select a spacing option.

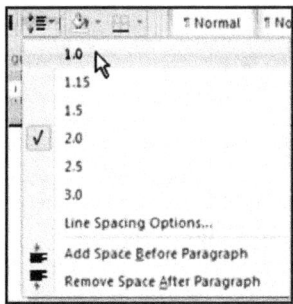

Fig. 4.21

OR

Step 1 : Select Line Spacing options. The Paragraph dialog box appears.

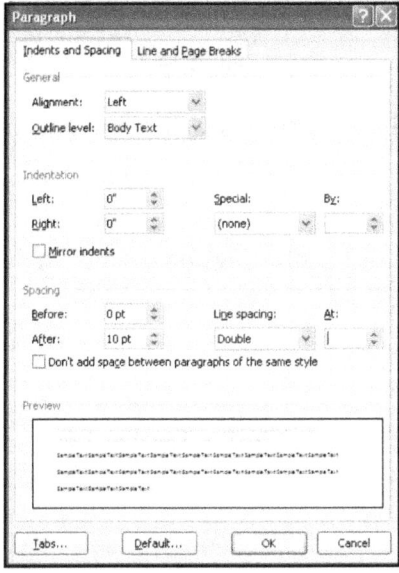

Fig. 4.22

Step 2 : Use the Line spacing drop-down menu to select a spacing option.

Step 3 : Modify the before and after points to adjust line spacing as needed.

Step 4 : Click OK.

Paragraph Spacing:

• Just as you can format spacing between lines in your document, you can choose spacing options between each paragraph. Typically, extra spaces are added between paragraphs, headings, or subheadings. Extra spacing between paragraphs adds emphasis and makes a document easier to read.

To Format Paragraph Spacing:

Step 1 : Click the Line spacing command on the Home tab.

Step 2 : Select Add Space Before Paragraph or Remove Space After Paragraph from the menu. If you don't see the option you want, click Line Spacing Options to manually set the spacing (see below).

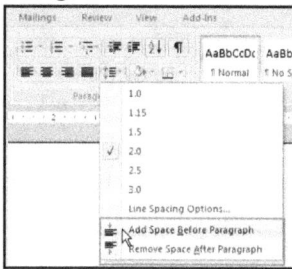

Fig. 4.23

OR

Step 1 : Select Line Spacing options. The Paragraph dialog box appears.

Step 2 : Change the Before and After points in the Paragraph section.

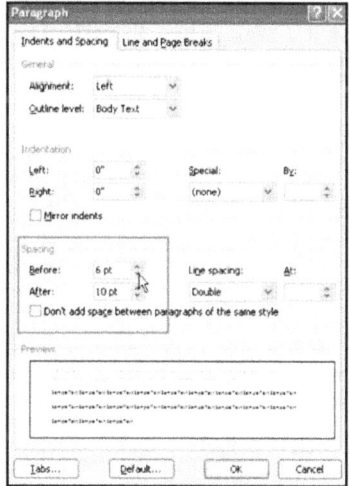

Fig. 4.24

Step 3 : Click OK.

- Line spacing is measured in lines or points, which is referred to as leading. When you reduce the leading, you automatically bring the lines of text closer together. Increasing the leading will space the lines out, allowing for improved readability.

Page Layout:

- You may find that the default page layout settings in Word are not sufficient for the document you want to create, in which case you will want to modify these settings. In addition, you may want to change the page formatting depending on the document you're creating.

To Change Page Orientation:

Step 1 : Select the Page Layout tab.

Step 2 : Click the Orientation command in the Page Setup group.

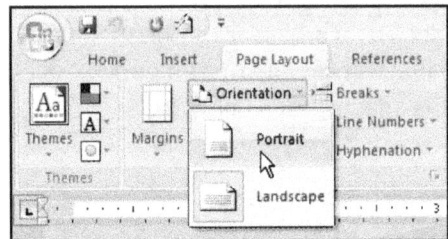

Fig. 4.25

Step 3 : Left-click either Portrait or Landscape to change the page orientation.

- Landscape format means everything on the page is oriented horizontally, while portrait format means everything is oriented vertically.

To Change the Paper Size:

Step 1 : Select the Page Layout tab.

Step 2 : Left-click the Size command, and a drop-down menu will appear. The current paper size is highlighted.

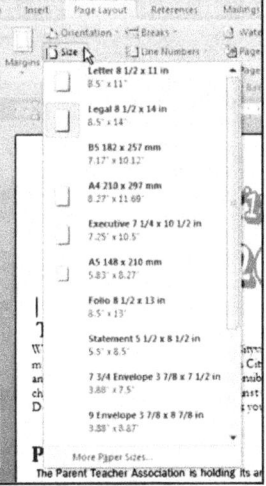

Fig. 4.26

Step 3 : Left-click a size option to select it. The page size of the document changes.

To Format Page Margins:

  Step 1 : Select the Page Layout tab.

  Step 2 : Click the Margins command. A menu of options appears. Normal is selected by default.

  Step 3 : Left-click the predefined margin size you want.

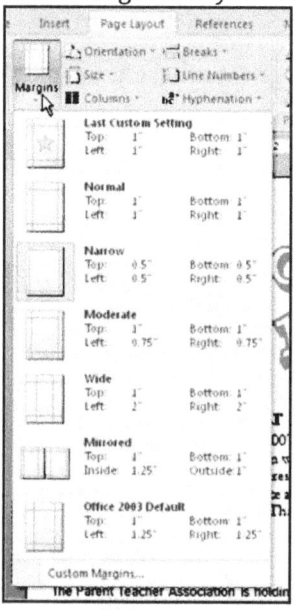

Fig. 4.27

OR

  Step 1 : Select Custom Margins from the menu. The Page Setup dialog box appears.

Fig. 4.28

  Step 2 : Enter the desired margin size in the appropriate fields and click OK.

Working with Pictures:

- Pictures can be added to Word documents and then formatted in various ways.

- The picture tools in Word 2007 make it easy to incorporate images into your documents and modify these images in innovative ways.

To Insert a Picture:

Step 1 : Place your insertion point where you want the image to appear.

Step 2 : Select the Insert tab.

Step 3 : Click the Picture command in the Illustrations group. The Insert Picture dialog box appears.

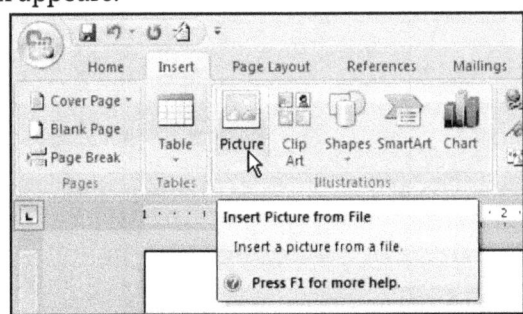

Fig. 4.29

Step 4 : Select the image file on your computer.

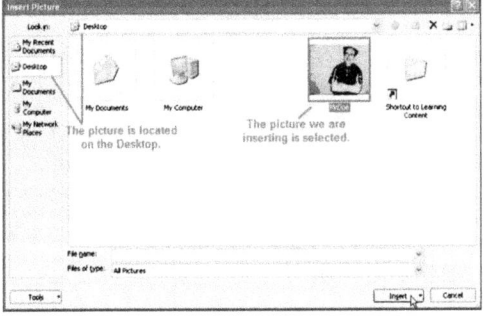

Fig. 4.30

Step 5 : Click Insert, and it will appear in your document.

Tables:

- A table is a grid of cells arranged in rows and columns.

- Tables can be customized and are useful for various tasks such as presenting text information and numerical data.

To Insert a Blank Table:

Step 1 : Place your insertion point in the document where you want the table to appear.

Step 2 : Select the Insert tab.

Step 3 : Click the Table command.

Step 4 : Drag your mouse over the diagram squares to select the number of columns and rows in the table.

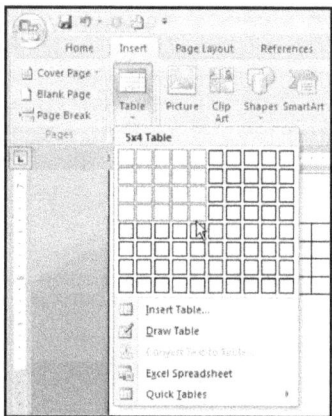

Fig. 4.31

Step 5 : Left-click your mouse, and the table appears in the document. Enter text into the table.

SmartArt Graphics:

• SmartArt allows you to visually communicate information rather than simply using text.

To Insert a SmartArt Illustration:

Step 1 : Place the insertion point in the document where you want the graphic to appear.

Step 2 : Select the Insert tab.

Step 3 : Select the SmartArt command in the Illustrations group. A dialog box appears.

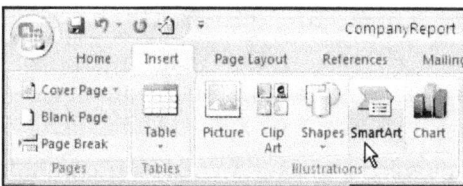

Fig. 4.32

Step 4 : Select a category on the left of the dialog box, and review the SmartArt graphics that appear in the center.

Step 5 : Left-click a graphic to select it.

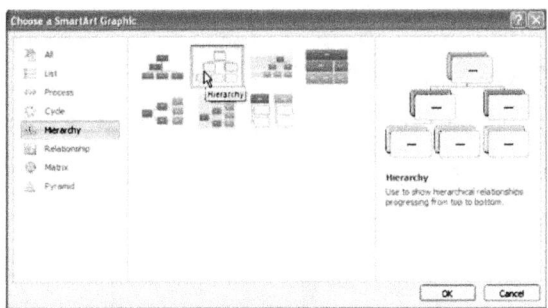

Fig. 4.33

Step 6 : Click OK.

To Use Find and Replace to Replace Existing Text:

Step 1 : Click the Replace command on the Home tab. The Find and Replace dialog box appears.

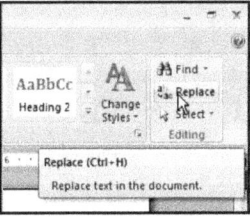

Fig. 4.34

Step 2 : Enter text in the Find field that you want to locate in your document.

Step 3 : Enter text in the Replace field that will replace the text in the Find box.

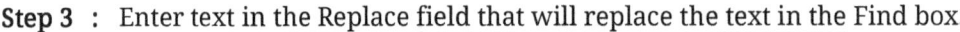
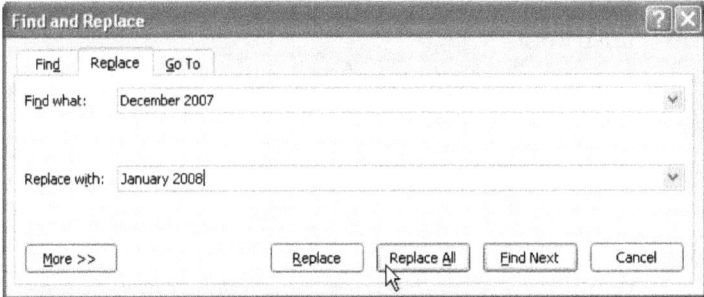

Fig. 4.35

Step 4 : Click OK. The change is made in the document.

Applying Styles and Themes:

- Styles and themes are powerful tools in Word that can help you create professional-looking documents easily.
- A style is a predefined combination of font style, color, and size of text that can be applied to selected text.
- A theme is a set of formatting choices that can be applied to an entire document and includes theme colors, fonts, and effects.

To Select a Style:

Step 1 : Select the text to format. In this example, the title is selected.

Step 2 : In the Style group on the Home tab, hover over each style to see a live preview in the document. Click the More drop-down arrow to see additional styles.

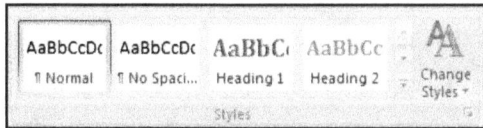

Fig. 4.36

Step 3 : Left-click a style to select it. Now the selected text appears formatted in the style.

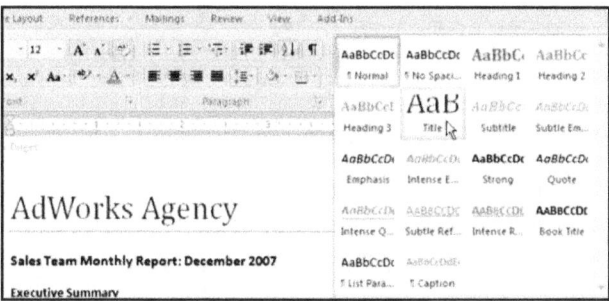

Fig. 4.37

To Apply a Theme:

*   A document theme is a set of formatting choices that includes font styles, sizes, and colors for different parts of the document, as well as a set of theme effects such as lines and fill effects.

Step 1 : Select the Page Layout tab.

Step 2 : Click the Themes command.

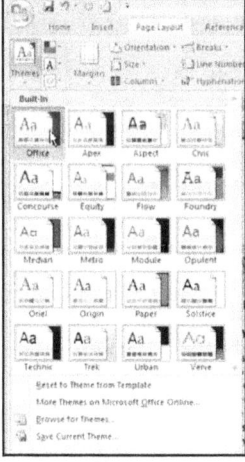

Fig. 4.38

Step 3 : Hover your pointer over a theme to see it displayed in the document.

Step 4 : Left-click a theme to select it.

Mail Merge:

- Mail Merge is a useful tool that will allow you to easily produce multiple letters, labels, envelopes, and more using information stored in a list, database, or spreadsheet.

To Use Mail Merge:

1. Select the Mailings on the Ribbon.
2. Select the Start Mail Merge command.

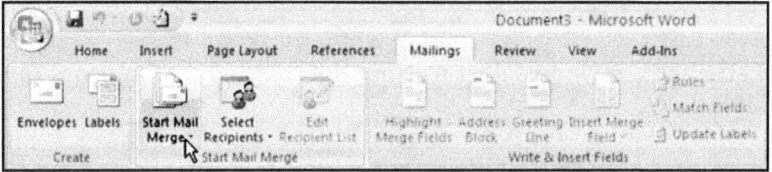

Fig. 4.39

3. Select Step by Step Mail Merge Wizard.

- The Mail Merge task pane appears and will guide you through the six main steps to complete a merge. You will have several decisions to make during the process. The following is an example of how to create a form letter and merge the letter with a data list.

Steps 1-3:

- Choose the type of document you want to create. In this example, select Letters.
- Click Next:Starting document to move to Step 2.
- Select Use the current document.
- Click Next:Select recipients to move to Step 3.
- Select the Type a new list button.
- Click Create to create a data source. The New Address List dialog box appears.
  - Click Customize in the dialog box. The Customize Address List dialog box appears.
  - Select any field you do not need, and click Delete.
  - Click Yes to confirm that you want to delete the field.
  - Continue to delete any unnecessary fields.
  - Click Add. The Add Field dialog box appears.
  - Enter the new field name.
  - Click OK.
  - Continue to add any fields necessary.
  - Click OK to close the Customize Address List dialog box.

To Customize the New Address List:

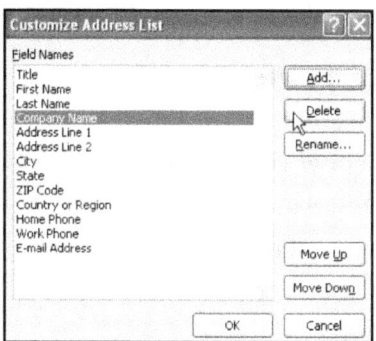

Fig. 4.40

○ Enter the necessary data in the New Address List dialog box.
○ Click New Entry to enter another record.
○ Click Close when you have entered all of your data records.
○ Enter the file name you want to save the data list as.
○ Choose the location where you want to save the file.
○ Click Save. The Mail Merge Recipients dialog box appears and displays all of the data records in the list.
○ Confirm that the data list is correct, and click OK.
○ Click Next:Write your letter to move to Step 4.

Steps 4-6:

• Write a letter in the current Word document, or use an open existing document.

To Insert Recipient Data from the List:

• Place the insertion point in the document where you want the information to appear.
• Select Address block, Greeting line, or Electronic postage from the task pane. A dialog box with options will appear based on your selection.

Fig. 4.41
OR

- ○ Select More Items. The Insert Merge Field dialog box will appear.
- ○ Select the field you want to insert in the document.
- ○ Click Insert. Notice that a placeholder appears where information from the data record will eventually appear.
- ○ Repeat these steps each time you need to enter information from your data record.
- Click Next: Preview your letters in the task pane once you have completed your letter.
- Preview the letters to make sure the information from the data record appears correctly in the letter.
- Click Next: Complete the merge.
- Click Print to print the letters.
- Click All.
- Click OK in the Merge to Printer dialog box.
- Click OK to send the letters to the printer.
- The Mail Merge Wizard allows you to complete the merge process in a variety of ways. The best way to learn how to use the different functions in Mail Merge is to try to develop several of the different documents—letters, labels, and envelopes—using the different types of data sources.

4.3.2 gedit

- Gedit is a lightweight text editor for the GNOME desktop and is found in many Linux distributions, BSD and other Unix systems.
- Designed for the X window system, Gedit uses the GTK+ and GNOME libraries.
- Gedit supports most standard editing features and has a powerful plugin system. This application enables to create and edit text files. Different Gedit plugins help to perform a number of tasks related to text editing from within the Gedit window.
- When launching (opening) the application opens the initial Gedit window as shown in Fig. 4.42. The text editor application window has all the features of any application window and is comprised of title bar, menu bar, tool bar, display area, status bar and so on.
- The title bar displays the title as Unsaved Document 1. Different menu items displayed on the menu bar contain all of the commands to work with files in Gedit.
- Toolbar contains a subset of the commands and these can be accessed from the menu bar.
- The tab appearing at the top of the window, just below the menu bar, displays the name of the file.

- By default, the name of the document is displayed as Unsaved Document 1. Subsequently opened documents are named as Unsaved Document, 2. Unsaved Document 3 and so on.
- Text matter can be typed in the display area or the edit area of the window.
- Status bar displays information about the current Gedit activity and contextual information about the menu items. This bar also displays the cursor position and the mode in which the editor is working, such as Insert mode (INS) or Overwrite mode (OVR).
- While working with the editor, right clicking the mouse provides all major edit options. It is possible for the user to select the required option from the pop-up menu.
- In the opening window, the blinking cursor appears in the first column of the first row of the edit area. When typing the document, the typed matter appears in the edit area.
- The typing of the document can be continued till the document is completed. At the end of each line on the screen, the cursor automatically moves to the next line.
- To start typing on a new line, press the Enter key on the keyboard to move the cursor to the next line. After finishing the typing process, the typed matter can be saved in a file for later use.

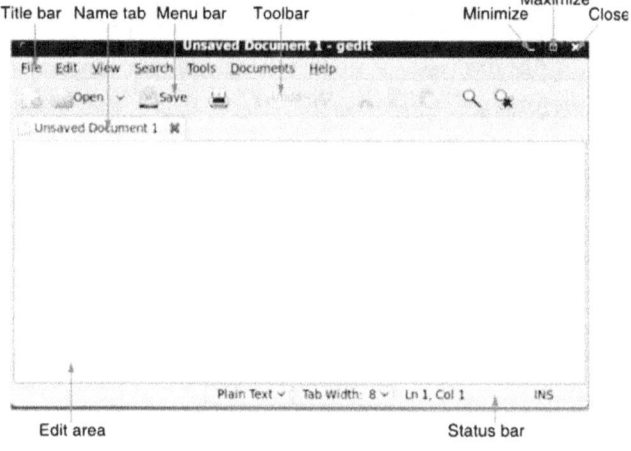

Fig. 4.42

4.3.3 vi

- vi stands for visual editor.
- There are many ways to edit files in Unix and one of the best ways is using screen-oriented text editor vi. This editor enable you to edit lines in context with other lines in the file.
- Now-a-days you would find an improved version of vi editor which is called VIM. Here VIM stands for Vi IMproved.

- The vi is generally considered the de facto standard in Unix editors because;
    1. It's usually available on all the flavors of Unix system.
    2. Its implementations are very similar across the board.
    3. It requires very few resources.
    4. It is more user friendly than any other editors like ed or ex.
- You can use vi editor to edit an existing file or to create a new file from scratch. You can also use this editor to just read a text file.
- vi is a very powerful command-line text editor. It's used for everything from quick fixes in configuration files to professional programming and even for writing large, complex documents.

Starting the vi Editor:

- There are following way you can start using vi editor:

Command	Description
`vi filename`	Creates a new file if it already does not exist, otherwise opens existing file.
`vi -R filename`	Opens an existing file in read only mode.
`view filename`	Opens an existing file in read only mode.

- Following is the example to create a new file testfile if it already does not exist in the current working directory:

    ```
    $vi testfile
    ```

- As a result you would see a screen something like as follows:

```
|
~
~
~
~
~
~
~
~
~
~
~
~
"testfile" [New File]
```

Fig. 4.43

- You will notice a tilde (~) on each line following the cursor. A tilde represents an unused line. If a line does not begin with a tilde and appears to be blank, there is a space, tab, newline, or some other nonviewable character present.

- Basic vi commands are as follows:

  1. Delete character : x

  2. Cursor movement : h, j, k, l (left, down, up and right)

  3. Quit without saving : q!

  4. Mode toggle : Esc, Insert (or i)

  5. Run a shell command : sh (use 'exit' to return)

  6. Quit : q

  7. Delete line : dd

VIM Basic Commands:

- To open Vim and begin creating a new text file, get a command-line open and type:

  ```
  $ vim
  ```

- This presents you with a blank screen, or (if the program running is Vim) a screen of information looking something like this:

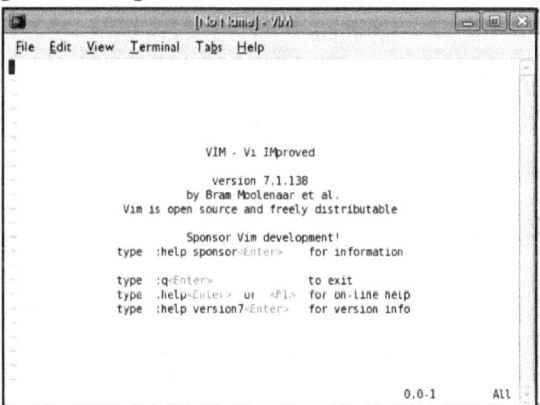

Fig. 4.44

- If you want to open an existing file, just specify it on the command line as an argument. For instance, the following opens a file called /etc/fstab:

  ```
  $ vim /etc/fstab
  ```

- This file already exists on most GNU/Linux systems, but if you open a non-existent file, you'll get a blank screen. The next section shows you how to insert text; when you're finished you can then save the file.

Inserting Text:

*   Whether you have a blank screen or a file with text in it, you can add text by entering what's known as edit mode. Just press i. You should see this on the bottom of the screen:

    `-- INSERT --`

*   Whenever this appears on the bottom of the screen, you are in edit mode. Whatever you type becomes part of the file. For instance, try entering "This is line 1." Then press the Enter key and enter "This is line 2". Here's what this fascinating contribution to literature looks like in Vim:

Fig. 4.45

*   When you are finished inserting text, press the Esc (Escape) key to leave edit mode; that puts you in normal mode.

4.4 | DESKTOP PUBLISHING

*   Desktop publishing (abbreviated DTP) is the creation of documents using page layout skills on a personal computer.

*   Desktop publishing software can generate layouts and produce typographic quality text and images comparable to traditional typography and printing.

*   A desktop publishing package is more powerful than word processor package. The system includes computer and a number of peripherals with powerful software that can produce page layouts complete with pictures and text printed in a variety of attractive ways. Such pages are used in manuals, bulletins, newsletters etc.

*   It contains an art library containing over one thousand pictures which can be used by the programmer in his/her documents. The system contains an output device which can produce text and pictures. Digitizers or scanners are used to convert art, photo and text images into suitable signals to be fed into processors.

*   The screen used is a high resolution screen. Though the package may run on PC, powerful computers are generally used. Photo-typesetter is used which gives better output than dot-matrix or laser printers.

*   The desktop publishing package can accept the text which has already been prepared by word processing package and stored in a file.

- The desktop publishing package includes a program called page layout or page make up or page composition program which permits operators to format pages of the text and merge text and pictures on display screen.
- Examples of desktop publishing softwares are explained below:

1. Corel Ventura/CorelDraw:

- Ventura Publisher, developed by Ventura Software, first released in 1986, was one of the first popular DTP software for IBM compatible PCs running the DOS operating system.
- The capability to import documents from common word processors of 1980s, such as WordStar, WordPerfect and Microsoft Word, made it very popular with book publishers.
- The Ventura Software was later acquired by Xerox Corporation, and then by Corel Corporation in 1994, which has continued its development under the Corel Ventura name.
- The CorelDraw program is developed and marketed by Corel Corporation to create drawings. Besides having page layout facilities, it has excellent capabilities to create graphics and drawings.

2. QuarkXPress:

- QuarkXPress, developed by Quark Inc., and first released in 1987 is one of the most popular DTP software for high-end applications, such as magazines. newspapers, catalogues and flyers that require complex page design.
- Initially released for Apple Macintosh, it is also available for Windows PCs. Though QuarkXPress is mainly used to create complex documents, yet it is very easy to use and learn.
- In QuarkXPress, the document is divided into a number of boxes, which can be of various shapes. Text and graphics are entered and formatted in these boxes.
- The current release of QuarkXPress also has tools to create documents for the Web. Because of the ease of operations, QuarkXPress is also popular with individual users who may not need to design very complex documents.
- QuarkXPress can set up documents in over 30 languages.

3. Adobe PageMaker:

- PageMaker is a popular DTP program for small applications. Launched in 1985 by Aldus Corporation, it was one of the first DTP programs for Apple Macintosh and PCs. Because of its Graphical User Interface (GUI), it soon became very popular for both, Macintosh as well as Windows environment.
- The product was later acquired by Adobe Systems, which continued its development until 2004, though it is still supported by Adobe Systems.

4. Adobe InDesign:

- Adobe InDesign, an alternative to QuarkXPress, is a feature-rich DTP software for high-end applications.

- Adobe InDesign can design complex documents in several languages, including English, Hindi, Arabic, Chinese, Japanese, Korean and Russian. Besides having capabilities to create table of contents and index, it can also do reverse layout (right-to-left).
- It can import document files from Microsoft Word as well as DTP files from QuarkXPress, while retaining layout. Because of all these features, it is a popular DTP software with Designers and Publishers to design and print posters, flyers, brochures, magazines and books.

5. **Microsoft Office Publisher:**
- Microsoft Office Publisher, commonly known as Microsoft Publisher, is an entry-level DTP program developed by Microsoft Corporation.
- First released in early 1990s, Microsoft has continued its development till date, though it commands only a small market share. To some extent, it is similar to Microsoft Word, though Microsoft Publisher gives more emphasis to page layout and design, rather than text entry and editing.

Advantages of DTP:
1. **Complete Control:** Using DTP the user can maintain complete control over the entire production.
2. **More Flexible:** The layout on the computer monitor provides immediate information as to whether a design needs to be changed or not.
3. **Less Errors:** Text is created by the keyboard. So possible sources of introducing new errors are removed.
4. **Simpler and Faster:** Number of columns, size of margins, line spacing type font can be specified or changed by the click of the mouse with DTP and the result is immediately visible on the screen.

Disadvantages of DTP:
1. **Expense:** Additional software and hardware may need to be bought.
2. **Training:** Staff will need to be trained to develop new skills if they are to use the new hardware and software effectively.

PRACTICE QUESTIONS

1. Define the following terms:
   (i) Word processor,
   (ii) Word processing.
2. Enlist features of word processor.
3. Explain desktop publishing in detail.
4. Write short note on: gedit.
5. Describe vi editor in detail.
6. Explain Word in detail.

■■■

Spreadsheets

Contents ...

5.1 | INTRODUCTION

- A spreadsheet is an interactive computer application for organization, analysis and storage of data in tabular form i.e., in table format.

- Spreadsheets are developed as computerized simulations of paper accounting worksheets. The program operates on data entered in cells of an array, organized in rows and columns.

- Each cell of the array may contain either numeric or text data, or the results of formulas that automatically calculate and display a value based on the contents of other cells.

- Modern spreadsheet software can have multiple interacting sheets, and can display data either as text and numerals, or in graphical form.

- LANPAR was the first electronic spreadsheet on mainframe and time sharing computers.

- VisiCalc was the first electronic spreadsheet on a micro computer, and it helped turn the Apple II computer into a popular and widely used system.

- Lotus 1-2-3 was the leading spreadsheet when DOS was the dominant operating system. MS-Excel now has the largest market share on the Windows and Macintosh platforms.

- A spreadsheet program is a standard feature of an office productivity suite; since the advent of web apps, office suites now also exist in web app form.

5.1.1 Purpose

- Spreadsheet is a numerical data analysis tool which allows us to create a computerized ledger.

- A manual ledger is a book having rows and columns that accountants used for keeping record of financial transactions and preparing finance statements. Accountants use pencil, erasure, and hand calculator to prepare financial statements using manual ledger. This is a tedious task and often takes a long time i.e., time consuming to come out with an acceptable and satisfactory financial statement, due to several iterations of formula calculations.

- An electronic spreadsheet offers considerable ease of performing such tasks by automating all arithmetic calculations and making it easier to change certain numerical values and seeing the effect of these changes across the worksheet (ledger) immediately.

- With the availability of spreadsheet package in computer, we are no longer required to use pencils, erasers and hand calculators for dealing with tasks that require numerical data analysis.

- Accounting remains a popular use of spreadsheets, since they are well suited to presenting balance sheet, budget and other accounting information in an organized format.

- In its simplest form, a spreadsheet is a table of rows and columns that contains data, both text and numbers, on which you perform actions, such as sorting and calculations, both simple and complex.

- In business, spreadsheets are especially useful any time you have numerical data to store, organize, calculate and present in easily understood formats.

- Spreadsheets allow the business person to accomplish tasks as diverse as keeping track of receipts and financial forecasting and planning.

5.1.2 Uses

- Spreadsheets are tools for anyone who needs to record, organize, or analyze numbers as rows and columns of data.

- Some typical uses of spreadsheets are given below:

  1. Spreadsheets are used for maintaining and analyzing inventory, payroll and other accounting records by accountants.

  2. Spreadsheets are used for recording grades of students and carrying out various types of analysis of grades by educators.

  3. Spreadsheets are used for tracking stocks and keeping records of investor accounts by stockbrokers.

4.   Spreadsheets are used for preparing budgets and bid comparisons by business analysts.

5.   Spreadsheets are used for creating and tracking personal budgets, loan payments, etc. by individuals.

6.   Spreadsheets are used for anlaysing experimental results by scientists and researchers.

• In this chapter we study Microsoft Excel 2007 spreadsheet application software.

5.2 | MICROSOFT EXCEL 2007

• MS-Excel is a commercial spreadsheet application written and distributed by Microsoft for Microsoft Windows and Mac OS X.

• MS-Excel is a spreadsheet program that enables us to store and manipulate data in a tabular form. Spreadsheets, also called worksheets are made up of columns and rows. Rows are numbered numerically and columns are labeled alphabetically.

• The intersection of rows and columns is called a cell, which can store text, number data, and mathematical formulas.

• MS-Excel contains a group of worksheets, which is known as a workbook.

• MS-Excel is the most commonly used spreadsheet application in the Windows platform. The files created in MS-Excel are characterized by the .xls extension.

• **Applications of MS Excel:**

1.   Businessmen use MS-Excel for automated report generation.

2.   MS-Excel is used in statistical science to collect data for designing sample surveys and analyzing the data for theory inferences.

3.   MS-Excel is used for rapid analysis of data by means of charts.

4.   MS-Excel acts as a data source for other applications, such as M:Access and MS-Word.

5.   MS-Excel is used in research work because it allows us to create survey data and data forms, validate the data entered in a worksheet, and link the data to other applications.

6.   MS-Excel is used in engineering for problem optimization.

To Start Excel 2007 from the Start Menu:

• Click on the Start button, point to All Programs then Microsoft Office and click on Microsoft Office Excel 2007, (See Fig. 5.1).

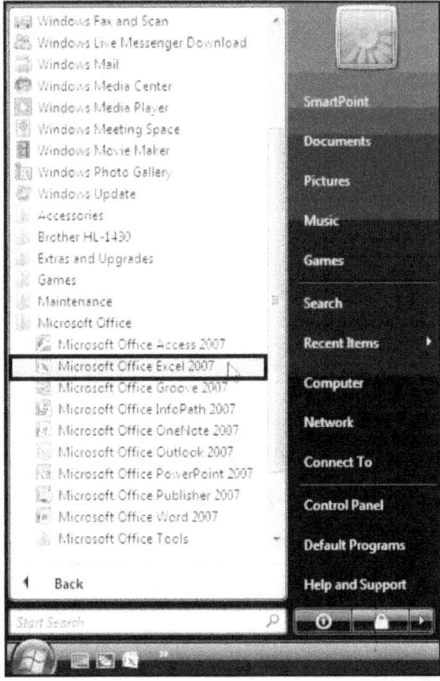

Fig. 5.1

- The first screen you will see a new blank worksheet that contains grid of cells, (See Fig. 5.2). This grid is the most important part of the Excel window. It's where you will perform all your work, such as entering data, writing formulas, and reviewing the results.

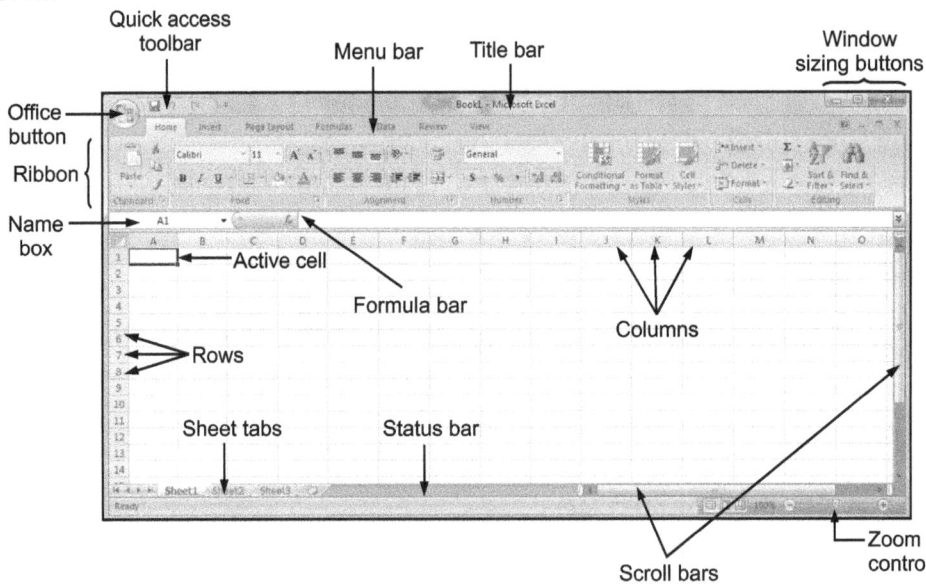

Fig. 5.2: Screen component of MS-Excel 2007

- Fig. 5.2 shows following screen parts or components or elements of MS-Excel 2007:

    1. **Office Button:** When clicked, this button opens the Office menu, from which you can open, save, print, and exit as well as the Excel Options button that enables you to change Excel's default settings.

    2. **Quick Access Toolbar:** A small toolbar next to the Office button contains shortcuts for some of the most common commands such as Save, Undo, and Redo buttons. You also can customize quick access toolbar.

    3. **Ribbon:** A combination of old versions menu bar and toolbar, arranged into a series of tabs ranging from Home through View. Each tab contains buttons, lists, and commands.

    4. **Name Box:** Displays the address of the current active cell where you work in the worksheet.

    5. **Formula Bar:** Displays the address of the active cell on the left edge, and it also shows you the current cell's contents.

    6. **Worksheet Area:** This area contains all the cells of the current worksheet identified by column headings, using letters along the top, and row headings, using numbers along the left edge with tabs for selecting new worksheets.

    7. **Sheet Tabs:** Excel 2007 contains 3 blank worksheet tabs by default. Click on the intended tab will go to the particular worksheet.

    8. **Status Bar:** Reports information about the worksheet and provides shortcuts for changing the view and the zoom.

    9. **Zoom Control:** Use to zoom the Excel screen in or out by dragging the slider.

    10. **Active Cell:** The active cell is recognized by its black outline. Data is always entered into the active cell. Different cells can be made active by clicking on them with the mouse or by using the arrow keys on the keyboard.

    11. **Column Letters:** Columns run vertically on a worksheet and each one is identified by a letter in the column header.

    12. **Row Numbers:** Rows run horizontally in a worksheet and are identified by a number in the row header. Together a column letter and a row number create a cell reference. Each cell in the worksheet can be identified by this combination of letters and numbers such as A1, F456, or AA34.

5.2.1 Creation of Files

To Create a New Blank Workbook:

    Step 1 :   Click Start button of Windows 7.

    Step 2 :   Click All Programs.

Step 3 : Click Microsoft Office.

Step 4 : Click Microsoft Office Excel 2007, which display Excel 2007 Windows.

Step 5 : Select New. The New Workbook dialog box opens, and Blank Workbook is highlighted by default (See Fig. 5.4).

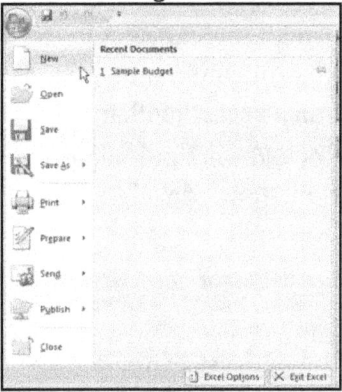

Fig. 5.3

Step 6 : Click Create. A new blank workbook appears in the window.

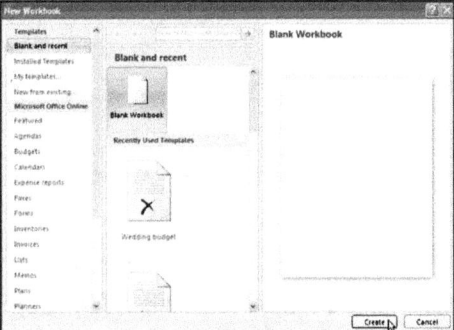

Fig. 5.4

• When you first open Excel, the software opens to a new blank workbook.

To Insert Text:

Step 1 : Each rectangle in the worksheet is called a cell. As you select a cell, the cell address appears in the Name Box.

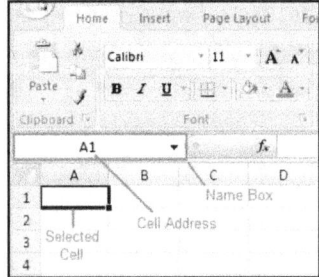

Fig. 5.5

Step 2 : Enter text into the cell using your keyboard. The text appears in the cell and in the formula bar.

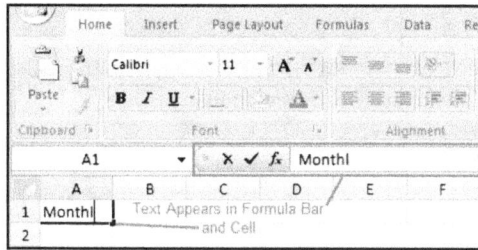

Fig. 5.6

Cell Addresses:

- Each cell has a name, or a cell address, based on the column and row where it is located.

- For example, this cell is C3 because it is where column C and row 3 intersect, (See Fig. 5.7).

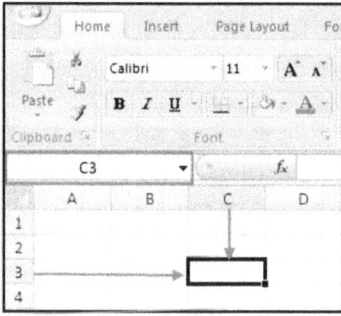

Fig. 5.7

- You can also select multiple cells at the same time. A group of cells is known as a cell range. Rather than a single cell address, you will refer to a cell range using the cell addresses of the first and last cells in the cell range, separated by a colon. For example, a cell range that included cells A1, A2, A3, A4, and A5 would be written as A1:A5.

To Save the Workbook:

- You can save a workbook in many ways, but the two most common ones are as an Excel Workbook, which saves it with a 2007 file extension, and as an Excel 97-2003 Workbook, which saves the file in a compatible format so people who have earlier versions of Excel can open the file.

Step 1 : CLICK the Microsoft Office button.

Step 2 : Select Save or Save As.

o Save As allows you to name the file and choose a location to save the spreadsheet.

o Select Save if the file has already been named.

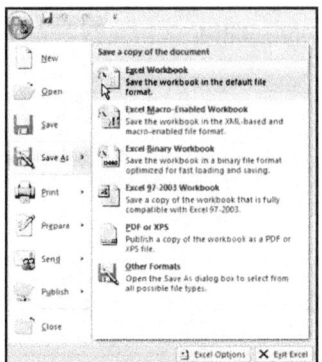

Fig. 5.8

To Modify Column Width:

Step 1 : Position the cursor over the column line in the column heading, and a double arrow will appear.

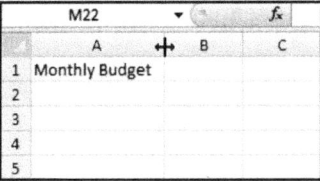

Fig. 5.9

Step 2 : Left-click the mouse, then drag the cursor to the right to increase the column width or to the left to decrease the column width.

Step 3 : Release the mouse button.

OR

Step 1 : Left-click the column heading of a column you'd like to modify. The entire column will appear highlighted.

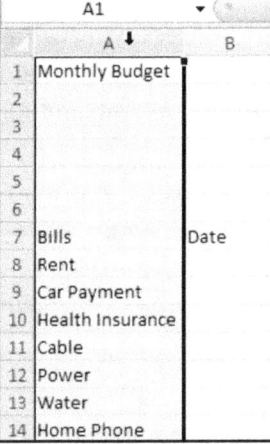

Fig. 5.10

Step 2 : Click the Format command in the Cells group on the Home tab. A menu will appear.

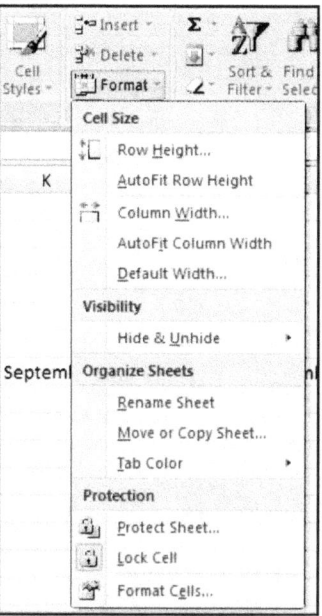

Fig. 5.11

Step 3 : Select Column Width to enter a specific column measurement.

Step 4 : Select AutoFit Column Width to adjust the column so all of the text will fit.

To Modify the Row Height:

Step 1 : Position the cursor over the row line you want to modify, and a double arrow will appear.

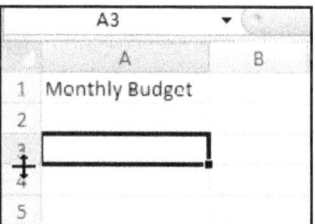

Fig. 5.12

Step 2 : Left-click the mouse, then drag the cursor upward to decrease the row height or downward to increase the row height.

Step 3 : Release the mouse button.

OR

Step 1 : Click the Format command in the Cells group on the Home tab. A menu will appear.

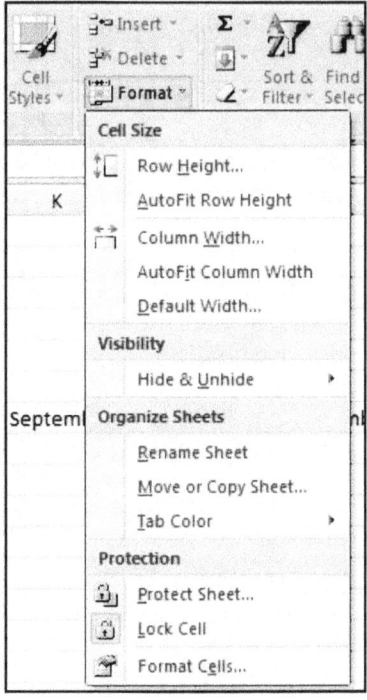

Fig. 5.13

Step 2 :   Select Row Height to enter a specific row measurement.

Step 3 :   Select AutoFit Row Height to adjust the row so all of the text will fit.

To Insert Rows:

Step 1 :   Select the row below where you want the new row to appear.

Step 2 :   Click the Insert command in the Cells group on the Home tab. The row will appear.

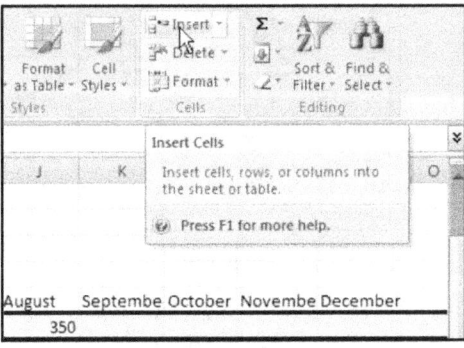

Fig. 5.14

Step 3 :   The new row always appears above the selected row.

Step 4 :   Make sure you select the entire row below where you want the new row to appear and not just the cell. If you select just the cell and then click Insert, only a new cell will appear.

To Insert Columns:

Step 1 : Select the column to the right of where you want the column to appear.

Step 2 : Click the Insert command in the Cells group on the Home tab. The column will appear.

• The new column always appears to the left of the selected column. For example, if you want to insert a column between September and October, select the October column, then click the Insert command.

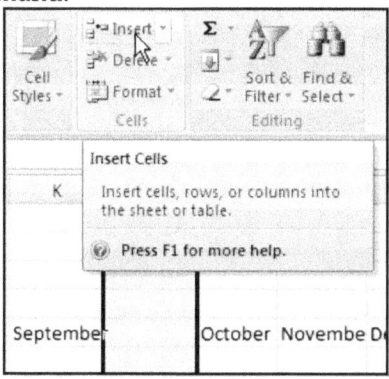

Fig. 5.15

• Make sure you select the entire column to the right of where you want the new column to appear and not just the cell. If you select just the cell and then click Insert, only a new cell will appear.

To Delete Rows and Columns:

Step 1 : Select the row or column you'd like to delete.

Step 2 : Click the Delete command in the Cells group on the Home tab.

Formatting:

• Once, you have entered information into a spreadsheet, you will need to be able to format it.

To Format Text in Bold or Italics:

Step 1 : Left click a cell to select it, or drag your cursor over the text in the formula bar to select it.

Step 2 : Click the Bold or Italics command.

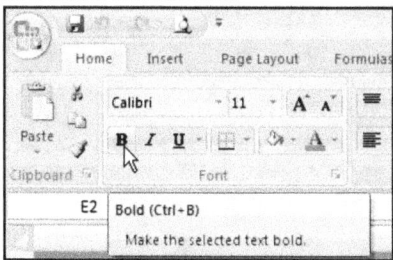

Fig. 5.16

To Format Text as Underlined:

Step 1 :   Select the cell or cells you want to format.

Step 2 :   Click the drop-down arrow next to the Underline command.

Step 3 :   Select the Single Underline or Double Underline option.

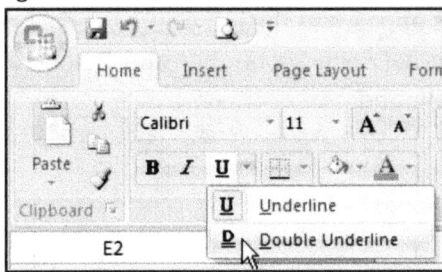

Fig. 5.17

To Change the Font Style:

Step 1 :   Select the cell or cells you want to format.

Step 2 :   Click the drop-down arrow next to the Font Style box on the Home tab.

Step 3 :   Select a font style from the list.

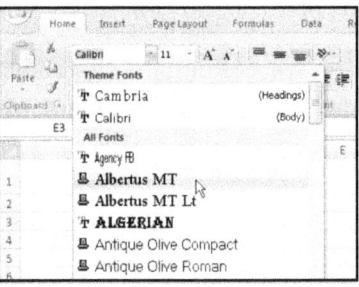

Fig. 5.18

Step 4 :   As you move over the font list, the Live Preview feature previews the font for you in the spreadsheet.

To Change the Font Size:

Step 1 :   Select the cell or cells you want to format.

Step 2 :   Click the drop-down arrow next to the Font Size box on the Home tab.

Step 3 :   Select a font size from the list.

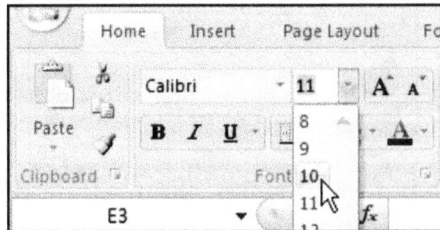

Fig. 5.19

To Change the Text Color:

Step 1 :   Select the cell or cells you want to format.

Step 2 :   Left-click the drop-down arrow next to the Text Color command. A color palette will appear.

Step 3 :   Select a color from the palette.

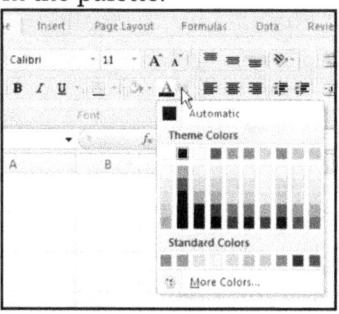

Fig. 5.20

To Add a Border:

Step 1 :   Select the cell or cells you want to format.

Step 2 :   Click the drop-down arrow next to the Borders command on the Home tab. A menu will appear with border options.

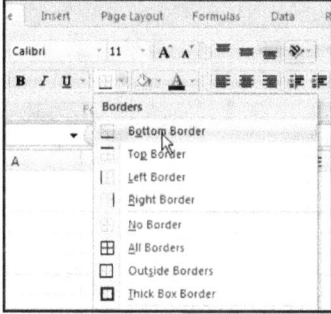

Fig. 5.21

Aligning Text:

- Excel 2007 left-aligns text (labels) and right-aligns numbers (values). This makes data easier to read, but you do not have to use these defaults. Text and numbers can be defined as left-aligned, right-aligned, or centered in Excel.

To Align Text or Numbers in a Cell:

Step 1 :   Select a cell or range of cells.

Step 2 :   Click on either the Align Left, Center, or Align Right commands on the Home tab.

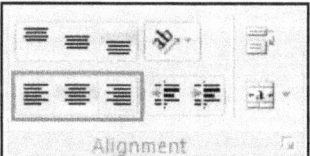

Fig. 5.22

Working With Cell:

- Cells hold all of the data that is being used to create the spreadsheet or workbook.
- To enter data into a cell you simply click once inside of the desired cell, a black border will appear around the cell (Fig. 5.23). This border indicates that it is a selected cell. You may then begin typing in the data for that cell.

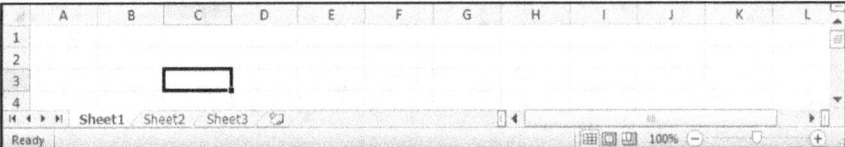

Fig. 5.23

To Copy and Paste Cell Contents:

Step 1 : Select the cell or cells you wish to copy.

Step 2 : Click the Copy command in the Clipboard group on the Home tab. The border of the selected cells will change appearance.

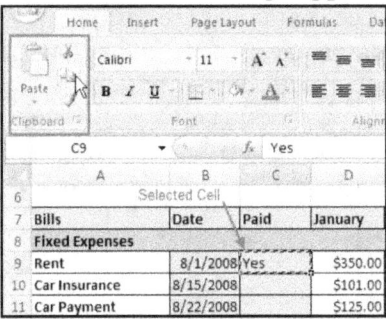

Fig. 5.24

Step 3 : Select the cell or cells where you want to paste the information.

Step 4 : Click the Paste command. The copied information will now appear in the new cells.

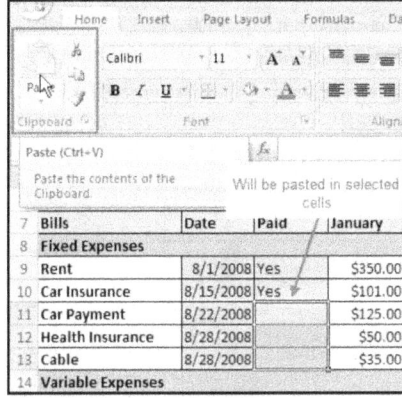

Fig. 5.25

To Cut and Paste Cell Contents:

Step 1 :   Select the cell or cells you wish to cut.

Step 2 :   Click the Cut command in the Clipboard group on the Home tab. The border of the selected cells will change appearance.

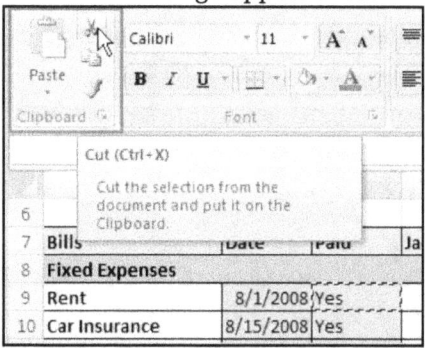

Fig. 5.26

Step 3 :   Select the cell or cells where you want to paste the information.

Step 4 :   Click the Paste command. The cut information will be removed from the original cells and now appear in the new cells.

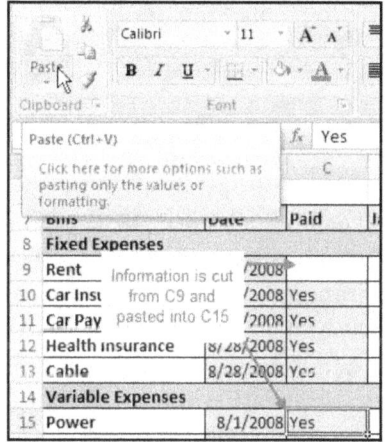

Fig. 5.27

Formatting Cells:

- There are various different options that can be changed to format the spreadsheets cells differently.
- When changing the format within cells you must select the cells that you wish to format.
- To get to the Format Cells dialog box select the cells you wish to change then go to Home Tab → Format → Format Cells. A box will appear on the screen with six different tab options, (Fig. 5.28).

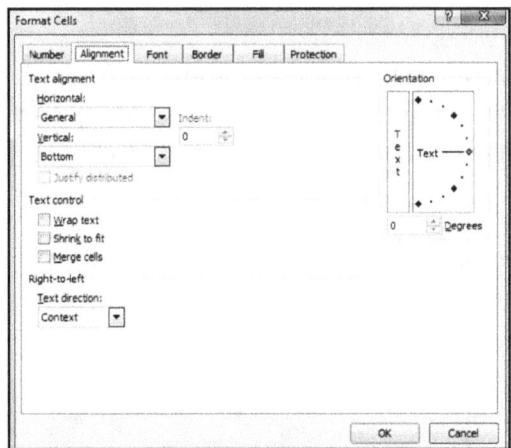

Fig. 5.28

(i) **Number:** Allows you to change the measurement in which your data is used.

(ii) **Alignment:** This allows you to change the horizontal and vertical alignment of your text within each cell. You can also change the orientation of the text within the cells and the control of the text within the cells as well.

(iii) **Font:** Gives the option to change the size, style, color, and effects.

(iv) **Border:** Gives the option to change the design of the border around or through the cells.

Formulas and Functions:

- In MS-Excel, formulas are equations that are used for manipulating the data of the worksheet.
- To write a formula in a cell, first insert the 'equal to' sign (=) and then enter the value, otherwise the content of the cell is considered as simple text.
- A formula may simply contain numbers and operators or a predefined expression to perform a particular computation.
- In general, a formula consists of the following parts:

    1. **Operators:** It includes symbols that represent the type of operations, such as addition, subtraction, multiplication, and division to be performed on the data. Thus, the symbols that constitute operators are +, –, *, and /.

    2. **Reference:** It indicates the address of a cell or a range of cells in a worksheet. It helps to refer the values in different parts of a worksheet in a formula. Using references, we can also refer cells in different worksheets in the same or a different workbook.

    3. **Constants:** It includes simple numbers and texts that are not subjected to change, i.e. their values do not depend upon any formula. For example, the numbers '24', '892' and '1000', and texts 'sum of numbers' and 'product of quotient' are constants.

    4. **Functions:** It includes predefined expressions that accept a set of data and return a set of values after performing a particular operation. Examples of functions are SUM, COUNT, MAX, and so on.

- To write the formula for computing number of working hours, we need to perform the following steps:

  Step 1 : Select the cell that should contain the result of the formula.

  Step 2 : Type the = (equal to) symbol in the selected cell.

  Step 3 : Enter the values and operators to build an expression for the formula, say 8×6.

  Step 4 : Press Enter to display the result.

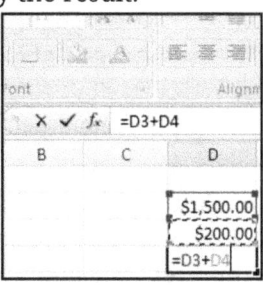

Fig. 5.29

To Create a Simple Formula that Adds Two Numbers:

Step 1 : Click the cell where the formula will be defined (C5, for example).

Step 2 : Type the equals sign (=) to let Excel know a formula is being defined.

Step 3 : Type the first number to be added (e.g., 1500).

Step 4 : Type the addition sign (+) to let Excel know that an add operation is to be performed.

Step 5 : Type the second number to be added (e.g., 200).

Step 6 : Press Enter, or click the Enter button on the Formula bar to complete the formula.

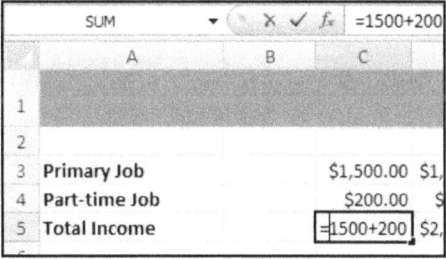

Fig. 5.30

To Create a Simple Formula that Adds the Contents of Two Cells:

Step 1 : Click the cell where the answer will appear (C5, for example).

Step 2 : Type the equals sign (=) to let Excel know a formula is being defined.

Step 3 : Type the cell number that contains the first number to be added (C3, for example).

Step 4 : Type the addition sign (+) to let Excel know that an add operation is to be performed.

Step 5 : Type the cell address that contains the second number to be added (C4, for example).

Step 6 : Press Enter, or click the Enter button on the Formula bar to complete the formula.

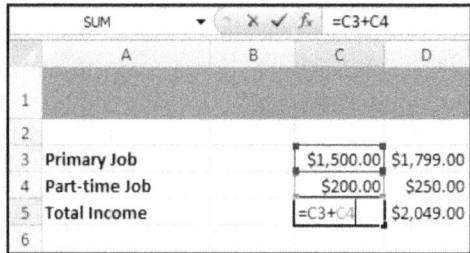

Fig. 5.31

To Create a Simple Formula using the Point-And-Click Method:

Step 1 : Click the cell where the answer will appear (C30, for example).

Step 2 : Type the equals sign (=) to let Excel know a formula is being defined.

Step 3 : Click on the first cell to be included in the formula (C5, for example).

Step 4 : Type the subtraction sign (-) to let Excel know that a subtraction operation is to be performed.

Step 5 : Click on the next cell in the formula (C29, for example).

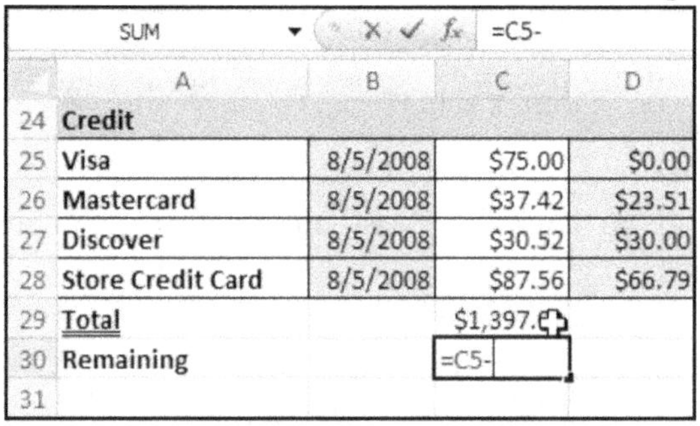

	A	B	C	D
	SUM		✗ ✓ fx =C5-	
24	Credit			
25	Visa	8/5/2008	$75.00	$0.00
26	Mastercard	8/5/2008	$37.42	$23.51
27	Discover	8/5/2008	$30.52	$30.00
28	Store Credit Card	8/5/2008	$87.56	$66.79
29	Total		$1,397.0	
30	Remaining		=C5-	
31				

Fig. 5.32

Step 6 : Press Enter, or click the Enter button on the Formula bar to complete the formula.

	A	B	C	D
	SUM		✗ ✓ fx =C5-C29	
24	Credit			
25	Visa	8/5/2008	$75.00	$0.00
26	Mastercard	8/5/2008	$37.42	$23.51
27	Discover	8/5/2008	$30.52	$30.00
28	Store Credit Card	8/5/2008	$87.56	$66.79
29	Total		$1,397.09	
30	Remaining		=C5-C29	
31				

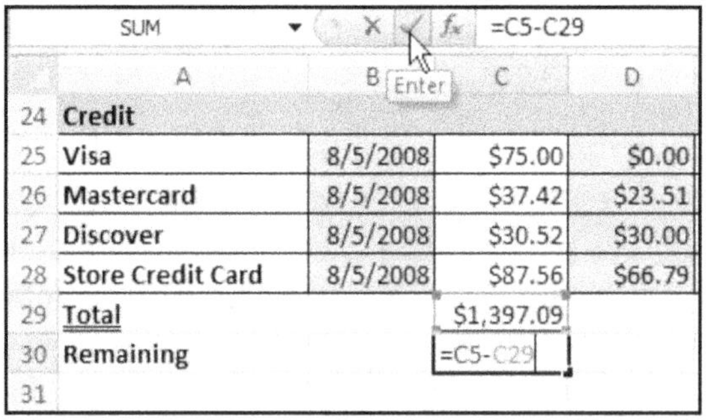

Fig. 5.33

Functions:

- A function is a predefined formula that performs calculations using specific values in a particular order.

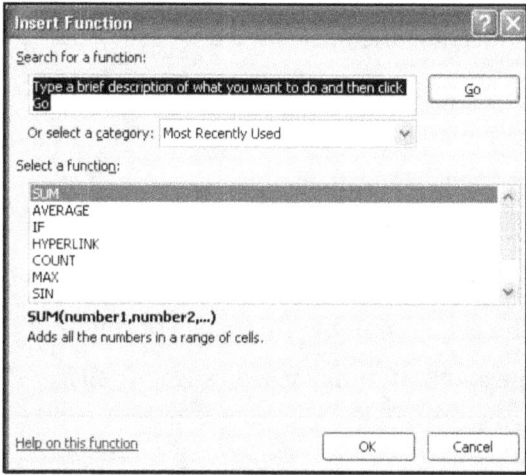

Fig. 5.34

The Parts of a Function:

- Each function has a specific order, called syntax, which must be strictly followed for the function to work correctly.

  Syntax order: All functions begin with the = sign.

  After the = sign, define the function name (e.g., Sum).

- Then there will be an argument. An argument is the cell range or cell references that are enclosed by parentheses. If there is more than one argument, separate each by a comma.

- An example of a function with one argument that adds a range of cells, A3 through A9:

Fig. 5.35

- An example of a function with more than one argument that calculates the sum of two cell ranges:

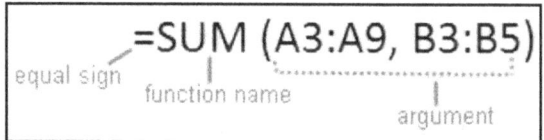

Fig. 5.36

- Excel literally has hundreds of different functions to assist with your calculations. Building formulas can be difficult and time consuming. Excel's functions can save you a lot of time and headaches.

- There are many different functions in Excel 2007. Some of the more common functions include:

Statistical Functions:

1. **SUM:** Adds a range of cells together.

2. **AVERAGE:** Calculates the average of a range of cells.

3. **COUNT:** Counts the number of chosen data in a range of cells.

4. **MAX:** Identifies the largest number in a range of cells.

5. **MIN:** Identifies the smallest number in a range of cells.

Date and Time Functions:

1. **DATE:** Converts a serial number to a day of the month.

2. **TIME:** Returns the serial number of a particular time.

3. **HOUR:** Converts a serial number to an hour.

4. **MINUTE:** Converts a serial number to a minute.

5. **TODAY:** Returns the serial number of today's date.

6. **MONTH:** Converts a serial number to a month.

7. **YEAR:** Converts a serial number to a year.

To Calculate the Sum of a Range of Data Using AutoSum:

Step 1 : Select the Formulas tab.

Step 2 : Locate the Function Library group. From here, you can access all available functions.

Step 3 : Select the cell where you want the function to appear. In this example, select G42.

Step 4 : Select the drop-down arrow next to the AutoSum command.

Step 5 : Select Sum. A formula will appear in the selected cell, G42.

Step 6 : This formula, =SUM(G2:G41), is called a function. The AutoSum command automatically selects the range of cells from G2 to G41, based on where you inserted the function. You can alter the cell range if necessary.

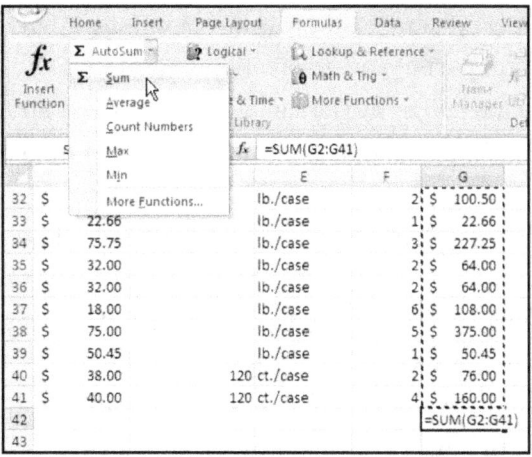

Fig. 5.37

Step 7 : Press the Enter key or Enter button on the formula bar. The total will appear.

Sorting:

• Sorting lists is a common spreadsheet task that allows you to easily reorder your data. The most common type of sorting is alphabetical ordering, which you can do in ascending or descending order.

To Sort in Alphabetical Order:

Step 1 : Select a cell in the column you want to sort (In this example, we choose a cell in column A).

Step 2 : Click the Sort & Filter command in the Editing group on the Home tab.

Step 3 : Select Sort A to Z. Now the information in the Category column is organized in alphabetical order.

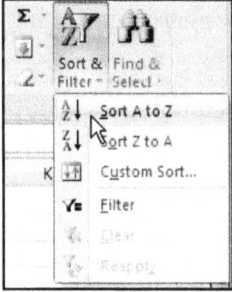

Fig. 5.38

• You can Sort in reverse alphabetical order by choosing Sort Z to A in the list.

Working with Charts:

• A chart is a tool you can use in Excel to communicate your data graphically.

• Charts allow your audience to more easily see the meaning behind the numbers in the spreadsheet, and to make showing comparisons and trends much easier.

- A chart is a visual representation of numeric values. Charts (also known as graphs) have been an integral part of spreadsheets.
- There are various chart types available in MS-Excel as given below:
  1. **Column chart** shows data changes over a period of time or illustrates comparisons among items.
  2. A **bar chart** illustrates comparisons among individual items.
  3. A **pie chart** shows the size of items that make up a data series, proportional to the sum of the items. It always shows only one data series and is useful when you want to emphasize a significant element in the data.
  4. A **line chart** shows trends in data at equal intervals.
  5. An **area chart** emphasizes the magnitude of change over time.
  6. An **xy (scatter) chart** shows the relationships among the numeric values in several data series, or plots two groups of numbers as one series of xy coordinates.
  7. **Stock chart** is most often used for stock price data, but can also be used for scientific data (for example, to indicate temperature changes).
  8. A **surface chart** is useful when you want to find optimum combinations between two sets of data. As in a topographic map, colors and patterns indicate areas that are in the same range of values.
  9. A **doughnut chart** shows the relationship of parts to a whole; however, it can contain more than one data series.
  10. Data that is arranged in columns on a worksheet so that x values are listed in the first column and corresponding y values and bubble size values are listed in adjacent columns, can be plotted in a **bubble chart**.
  11. A **radar chart** compares the aggregate values of a number of data series.

Creating a Chart:

- Charts can be a useful way to communicate data. When you insert a chart in Excel, it appears in the selected worksheet with the source data by default.
- To create a chart follow the following steps:

  Step 1 :   Select the worksheet you want to work with.

  Step 2 :   Select the cells you want to chart, including the column titles and row labels.

  Step 3 :   Click the Insert tab.

  Step 4 :   Hover over each Chart option in the Charts group to learn more about it.

  Step 5 :   Select one of the Chart options. In this example, we'll use the Columns command.

Step 6 : Select a type of chart from the list that appears. For this example, we'll use a 2-D Clustered Column. The chart appears in the worksheet.

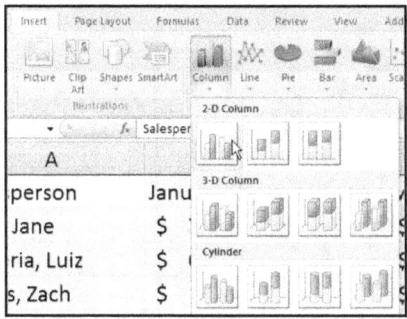

Fig. 5.39

Creating an Excel 2007 Chart from Data in a Worksheet:

- Once, you have entered the data you want to display as a chart into a worksheet and decided which type of chart you require, you can create it with just a few mouse clicks.

- Open Excel 2007 and create a worksheet as illustrated in Fig. 5.40.

	A	B	C	D
1		Mark Scores		
2		Mathematics	History	English
3	Jimmy	67	59	80
4	Saravanan	80	70	72
5	Fiona Wong	86	66	71
6	Tompson	57	75	90
7				

Fig. 5.40

- Click on any cell within the data containing the information that you wish to display as a chart, or highlight the exact data area that you wish to display as a chart.

- On the Insert menu, in the Charts group, click the chart type you require. A gallery of thumbnail images for the related chart subtypes will appear.

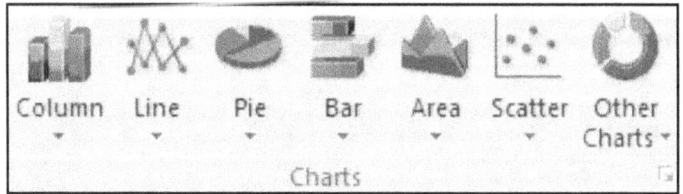

Fig. 5.41

- Click the required chart subtype to create the chart, or click All Chart Types to open the Insert Chart dialog box and choose from all available chart types.

- When you have selected a subtype, a chart will be created as an object in the worksheet and Chart Tools will appear on the Ribbon incorporating Design, Layout, and Format tabs.

- For example, when choose the '3-D Clustered Column' subtype, the chart created as shown in Fig. 5.42.

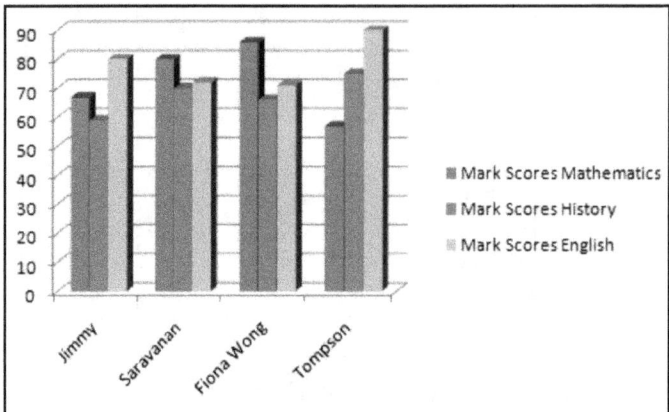

Fig. 5.42

PRACTICE QUESTIONS

1. What is spreadsheet?
2. Explain the uses of spreadsheet?
3. What is the purpose of spreadsheet.
4. Explain MS-Excel screen compounds in detail.
5. What are the applications of MS-Excel?
6. How to aligning text in Excel?
7. What is meant by charts? Enlist its types.
8. Describe formulas and functions in Excel.
9. How to change font and font size in Excel.
10. How to create new spreadsheet? Explain with steps.

■■■

Presentation Tool

Contents ...

6.1 | INTRODUCTION

- Presentation is the process of presenting a topic to an audience, for example, presenting a lesson to students about global warming. Many people make use of presentation software to support them when they have to give a presentation to others.

- Presentation software is a tool used to display information, normally in the form of a slide show. It generally includes three major functions: an editor that allows text to be inserted and formatted, a method for inserting and manipulating graphic images and a slide-show system to display the contents.

- Microsoft PowerPoint is a presentation software that allows users to create presentations and slide shows using a variety of media, including images, video and music.

- The user compiles information regarding his/her topic presentation in any or all of these media formats and then applies effects to enhance the presentation.

- PowerPoint is often used for business presentations.

MS-PowerPoint 2007:

- By default, documents saved in PowerPoint 2007 are saved with the .pptx extension where as the file extension of the prior PowerPoint versions is .ppt.

Opening MS-PowerPoint 2007:

- One way you can open Microsoft PowerPoint by: Clicking Start → (All) Programs → Microsoft Office → Microsoft Office PowerPoint 2007.

- The PowerPoint windows appears as shown in Fig. 6.1.

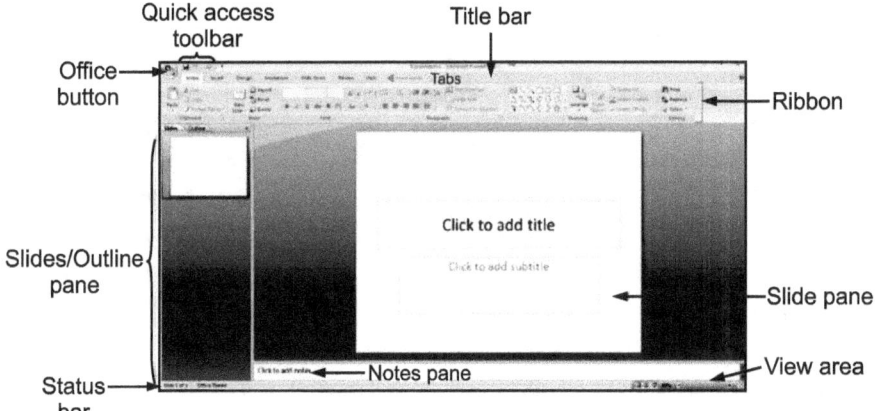

Fig. 6.1

- Fig. 6.1 shows following parts or component or elements of MS-PowerPoint Window:

  1. **Office Button:** The Office 2007 Button is located in the top left hand corner of the screen. The Office Button allows you to open, save, and print documents etc.

  2. **The Ribbon:** The traditional drop-down menus and toolbars of earlier Microsoft releases have been replaced by the more intuitive and graphical Ribbon. Click on the ⎣⌐⎤ arrow to open a dialogue box with more options.

  3. **Command Tabs:** Office 2007 applications automatically open to the Home command tab, which contains formatting options needed to create a basic document, such as font and paragraph settings. Specialized features can be accessed from other command tabs.

  4. **Slide and Outline Tabs:** The Slides tab shows thumbnail images of your slides, allowing you to rearrange and hide slides and view set transitions as you work. The Outline tab shows the content of your slides, making it easy to rearrange your text.

  5. **Slide Pane:** This panel is where you enter the content of your slides.

  6. **Notes Pane:** This is where you can enter notes. If you wish to enter longer notes, you can go to the View tab and select Notes Page.

7. **View Buttons:** These three buttons include the Normal view, shown here, the Slide Sorter, which allows you to shuffle your slides, and the Slide Show, which shows the slides as if you were presenting.

8. **Zoom Slider:** This allows you to zoom in and out on the Slide Panel.

Creating New Presentations:

• When you open PowerPoint from the Start menu or from an icon on your desktop, a new presentation with one slide appears by default. You can also create a new presentation while PowerPoint is already open.

Step 1 : Click the Microsoft Office button, and choose New from the menu.

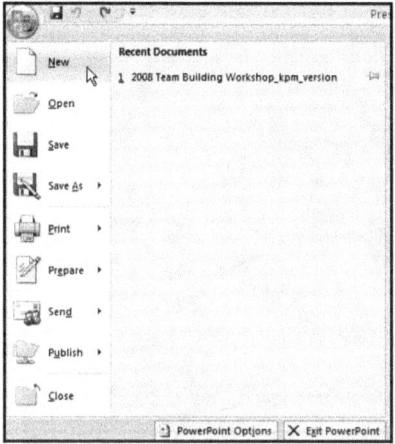

Fig. 6.2

Step 2 : The New Presentation dialog box will appear. Blank Presentation is selected by default.

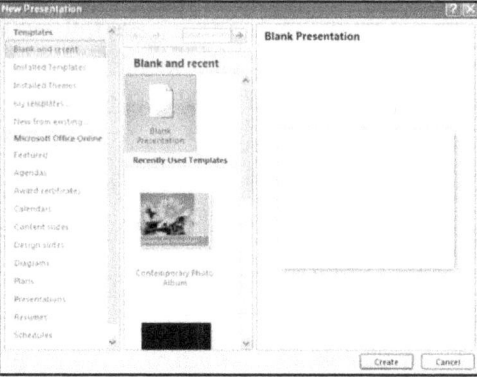

Fig. 6.3

Step 3 : Click Create, and a new presentation will open in the PowerPoint window. The default slide that appears when you create a new presentation is a Title Slide layout.

6.2 | DESIGN SLIDES

- When you create a PowerPoint presentation, it is made up of a series of slides. The slides contain the information you want to communicate with your audience. This information can include text, pictures, charts, video, sound, and more.

- Slides contain placeholders, or areas on a slide that are enclosed by dotted borders. Placeholders can contain many different items, including text, pictures, and charts.

- Some placeholders have placeholder text—or text you can replace—and thumbnail-sized icons that represent specific commands such as Insert Picture, Insert Chart, and Insert Clip Art. However each icon to see the type of information you can insert.

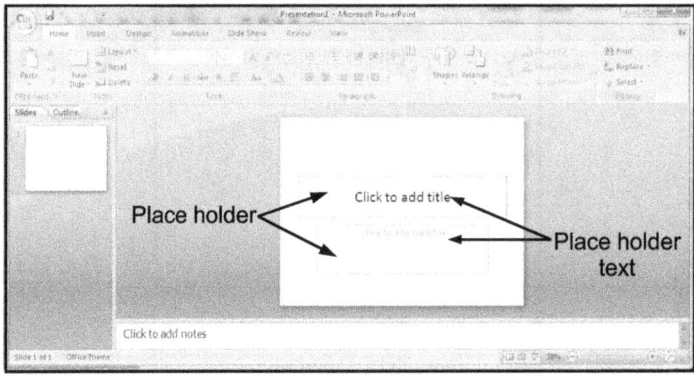

Fig. 6.4

About Slide Layouts:

- The placeholders are arranged in different layouts you can select when you insert a new slide or that can be applied to existing slides.

- A slide layout arranges your slide content. Layouts contain different types of placeholders you can use, depending on what information you want to include in your presentation. Each layout has a descriptive name, but the image of the layout shows you how the placeholders are arranged on the slide.

To Insert Text into a Placeholder:

Step 1 : Click inside the placeholder. The placeholder text will disappear, and the insertion point will appear.

Step 2 : Type your text once the insertion point is visible.

Step 3 : Click outside the placeholder when you have entered all of your text into the placeholder.

To Insert a New Slide:

Step 1 : Click the New Slide command in the Slides group on the Home tab. A menu will appear with your slide layout options.

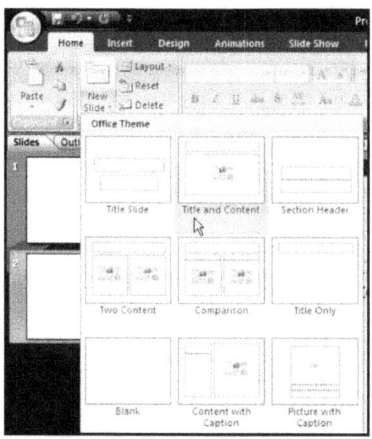

Fig. 6.5

Step 2 : Click the slide you want to insert. A new slide with the chosen layout will appear in the center of the PowerPoint window and in the pane on the left.

To Copy and Paste a Slide:

Step 1 : Select the slide you want to copy.

Step 2 : Click the Copy command on the Home tab.

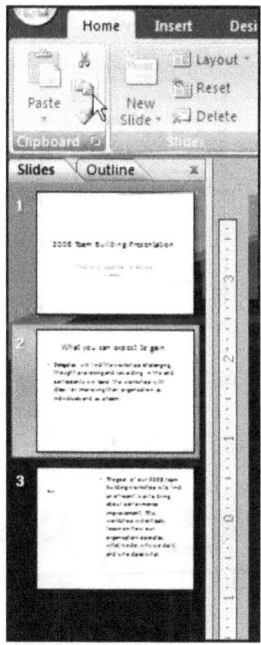

Fig. 6.6

Step 3 : Click inside the Slides tab on the left task pane. A horizontal insertion point will appear.

Step 4 : Move the insertion point to the location where you want the copy of the slide to appear.

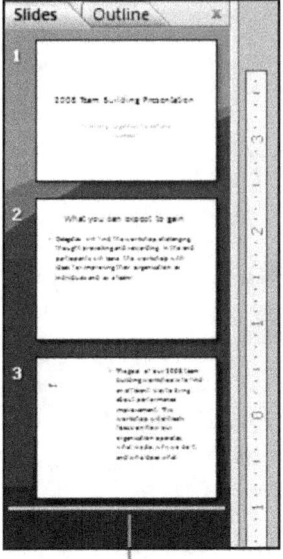

Insertion point

Fig. 6.7

Step 5 : Click the Paste command on the Home tab. The copied slide will appear.

Fig. 6.8

To Delete a Slide:

Step 1 : Select the slide you want to delete.

Step 2 : Click the Delete command in the Slides group on the Home tab.

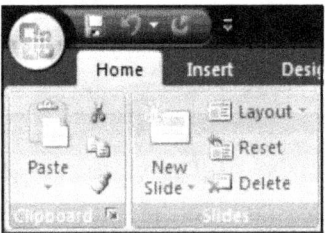

Fig. 6.9

Using different Views from the PowerPoint Window:

- In the bottom-right corner of the PowerPoint window are three view commands. From here, you can change the view to Normal, Slide Sorter, or Slide Show view by clicking a command.

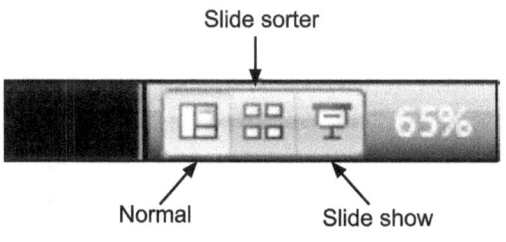

Fig. 6.10

1. **Normal** is the default view and where you will create and edit your slides in the center slide pane, and all of the slides will appear on the Slides tab in the left task pane.

2. **Slide Sorter** is a view of your slides in thumbnail form. The slides are presented horizontally, which allows you to see more slides at the same time.

3. **Slide Show** view fills the computer screen with your presentation so you can see how the presentation will appear to an audience.

Saving Presentation:

- If you are saving a document for the first time, you will need to use the Save As command; however, if you have already saved a presentation, you can use the Save command.

To Use the Save As Command:

Step 1 : Click the Microsoft Office button.

Step 2 : Select Save As. A menu will appear.

Step 3 : Select the type of file you want to save the presentation as. The two most commonly used file types are:

   ➢ **PowerPoint Presentation:** This saves the presentation as a 2007 PowerPoint file. Only users with PowerPoint 2007 or the compatibility pack can view the file without possibly losing some of the formatting.

   ➢ **PowerPoint 97-2003 Presentation:** This saves the presentation so it is compatible with some previous versions of PowerPoint. If you will be sending the presentation to someone who does not have Office 2007, you should use this file type.

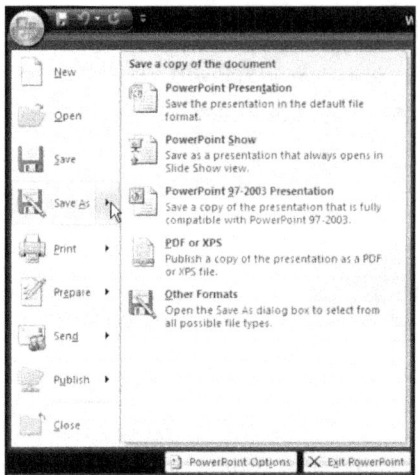

Fig. 6.11

Step 4 : The Save As dialog box will appear. Select the location where you want to save the document using the drop-down menu.

Step 5 : Enter a name for the document.

Step 6 : Click the Save button.

To Use the Save Command:

- Using the Save command saves the document in its current location using the same file name.

Step 1 : Click the Microsoft Office button.

Step 2 : Select Save from the menu.

6.2.1 Using Text

- PowerPoint allows users to add text to the slide in a well-defined manner to ensure the content is well distributed and easy to read. The procedure to add the text in a PowerPoint slide is always the same - just click in the text box and start typing.

- The text will follow the default formatting set for the text box, although this formatting can be changed later as required. What changes is the different kinds of content boxes that support text in a PowerPoint slide.

- In PowerPoint, you can insert text into placeholders or text boxes. Text in both can be formatted using the same commands.

  Title Box: This is typically found on slides with title layout and in all the slides that have a title box in them. This box is indicated by "Click to add title"

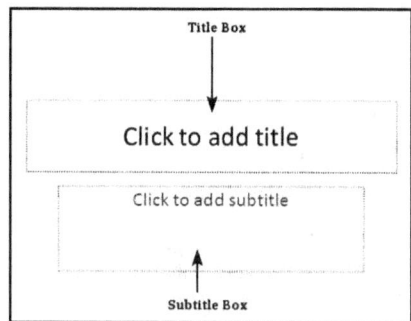

Fig. 6.12

Subtitle Box: This is found only in slides with Title layout. This is indicated by "Click to add subtitle".

To Delete Text:

Step 1 : Place your cursor next to the text you want to delete.

Step 2 : Press the Backspace key on your keyboard to delete text to the left of the cursor.

To Select Text:

Step 1 : Place the insertion point next to the text you want to select.

Step 2 : Click and drag your mouse over the text to select it.

Step 3 : Release the mouse button. You have selected the text. A highlighted box will appear over the selected text.

To Format Font Size:

Step 1 : Select the text you want to modify.

Step 2 : Click the drop-down arrow next to the font size box on the Home tab. The font size drop-down menu appears.

Step 3 : Move your cursor over the various font sizes. A live preview of the font size will appear in the document.

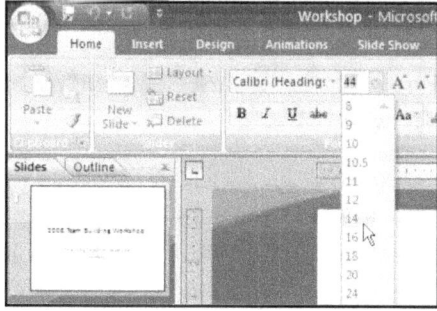

Fig. 6.13

Step 4 : Click the font size you want to use. The font size will change in the document.

To Format Font Style:

Step 1 : Select the text you want to modify.

Step 2 : Click the drop-down arrow next to the font style box on the Home tab. The font style drop-down menu appears.

Step 3 : Move your cursor over the various font styles. A live preview of the font will appear in the document.

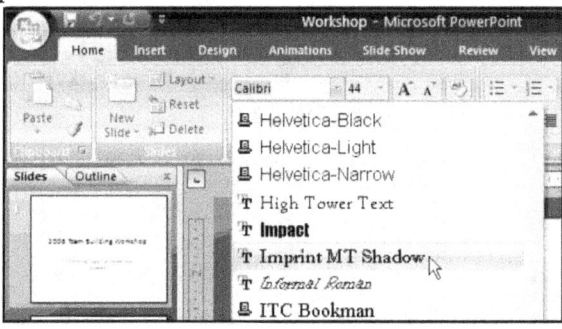

Fig. 6.14

Step 4 : Click the font style you want to use. The font style will change in the document.

To Format Font Color:

Step 1 : Select the text you want to modify.

Step 2 : Click the drop-down arrow next to the font color box on the Home tab. The font color menu appears.

Step 3 : Move your cursor over the various font colors. A live preview of the color will appear in the document.

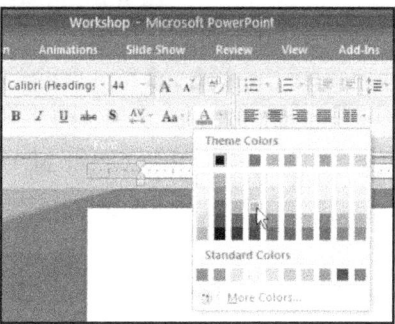

Fig. 6.15

Step 4 : Click the font color you want to use. The font color will change in the slide.

To Use the Bold, Italic, and Underline Commands:

Step 1 : Select the text you want to modify.

Step 2 : Click the Bold, Italic, or Underline command in the Font group on the Home tab.

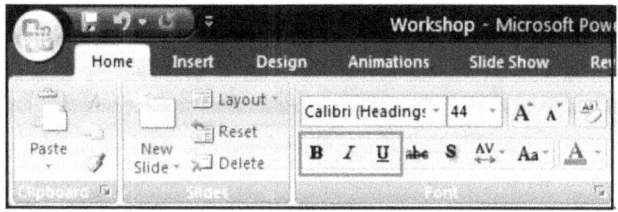

Fig. 6.16

Step 3 : Click the command again to remove the formatting.

Other Font Commands: Fig. 6.17 shows other font commands.

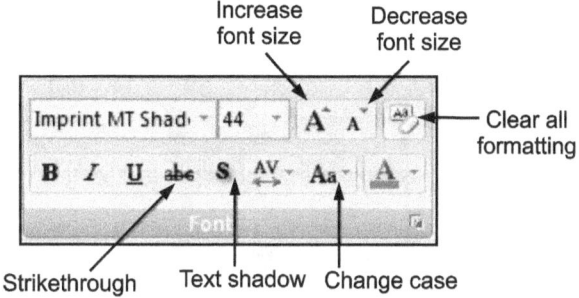

Fig. 6.17

1. **Increase Font Size:** Increases font size of selected text to the next standard font size.
2. **Decrease Font Size:** Decreases font size of selected text to the next standard font size.
3. **Clear All Formatting:** Removes recent formatting changes.
4. **Strikethrough:** Makes a line through text.
5. **Text Shadow:** Adds a drop shadow to text.
6. **Change Case:** Lets you try different capitalization options without having to delete and retype letters or words.

To Change Text Alignment:
• The alignment commands align text within the placeholder or text box where it is located rather than across the slide.

    Step 1 : Select the text you want to modify.

    Step 2 : Select one of the four alignment options from the Paragraph group on the Home tab.

        ➢ **Align Text Left:** Aligns selected text to the left margin.

        ➢ **Center:** Aligns text an equal distance from the left and right margins.

        ➢ **Align Text Right:** Aligns selected text to the right margin.

        ➢ **Justify:** Lines up equally to the right and left margins.

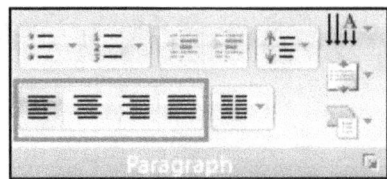

Fig. 6.18

To Copy and Paste Text:

Step 1 : Select the text you want to copy.

Step 2 : Click the Copy command on the Home tab.

Step 3 : Place your insertion point where you want the text to appear.

Step 4 : Click the Paste command on the Home tab. The text will appear.

Fig. 6.19

To Cut and Paste Text:

Step 1 : Select the text you want to cut.

Step 2 : Click the Cut command on the Home tab.

Step 3 : Place your insertion point where you want the text to appear.

Step 4 : Click the Paste command on the Home tab. The text will appear.

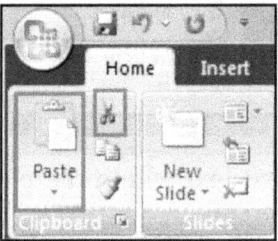

Fig. 6.20

6.2.2 Using Images, Pictures and Clip Art

- PowerPoint supports multiple content types including images or pictures.
- With regards to pictures PowerPoint classifies them into two categories:
    1. **Picture:** Images and photos that are available on your computer or hard drive.
    2. **Clip Art:** Picture collection that you can search from the clip art sidebar.

Inserting Pictures/Images:

- Among the many file types that PowerPoint supports are a set of extensions for image files. The image file extensions supported by PowerPoint include JPEG (.jpg), GIF (.gif), TIFF (.tiff) and Bitmap (.bmp).

- Pictures and clip art can be inserted from the Ribbon, as well as by using the commands that appear in certain placeholders. In both methods, the image is centered in the middle of any selected slide placeholders.

To Insert a Picture From the Ribbon:

Step 1 : Select the Insert tab.

Step 2 : Click the Insert Picture command in the Illustrations group. The Insert Picture dialog box will appear.

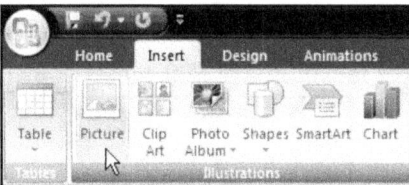

Fig. 6.21

Step 3 : Locate and select the picture you want to use.

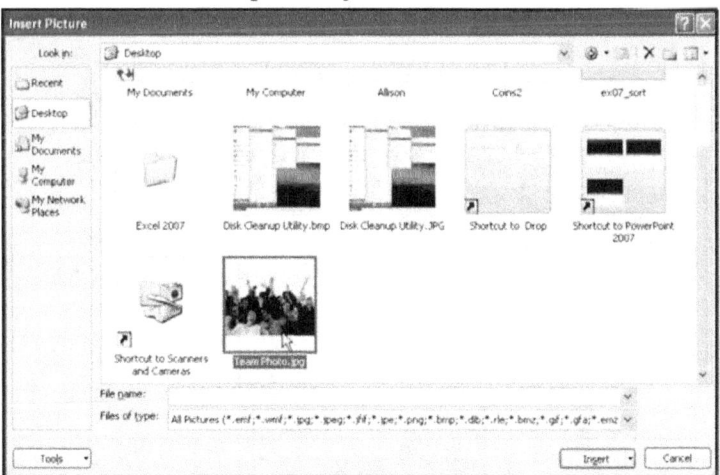

Fig. 6.22

Step 4 : Click Insert, and it will appear on the slide.

To Insert Clip Art:

Step 1 : Select the Insert tab.

Step 2 : Click the Clip Art command in the Illustrations group. The Clip Art task pane will appear on the right.

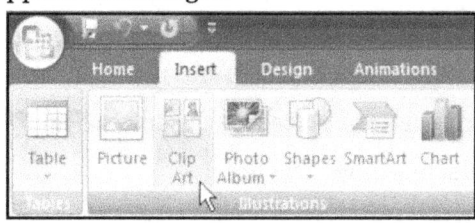

Fig. 6.23

Step 3 : Enter keywords in the Search field that are related to the image you want to insert.

Step 4 : Click the drop-down arrow next to the collections field.

Step 5 : Select Everywhere to make sure PowerPoint searches your computer and online resources for an image that meets your criteria.

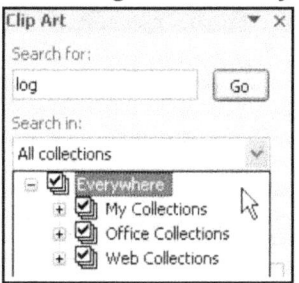

Fig. 6.24

Step 6 : Click the drop-down arrow in the media file types field.

Step 7 : De-select any file types you do not want to see. In this example, we only want photographs, so we'll deselect the other options.

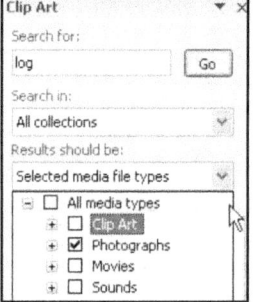

Fig. 6.25

Step 8 : Click Go. A list of clip art images related to the search terms is displayed.

Fig. 6.26

Step 9 : Click a clip art image to insert it, or click the drop-down arrow next to the clip art and select Insert from the menu. The clip art will appear in the slide.

Working with Tables:

- One of the most powerful data representation techniques is the use of tables. Tables allow information to be segregated making them easy to read.

- The goal of most PowerPoint presentations is to communicate information to a person or group of people. The information can be communicated in various ways, such as through pictures, lists, or paragraphs of text. Another way is to use a table to organize the information. A table is a grid of cells arranged in rows and columns.

- To insert a Table follow the following steps:

Step 1 : Click on Insert Tab.

Step 2 : Select Table.

Step 3 : Using mouse select rows and columns.

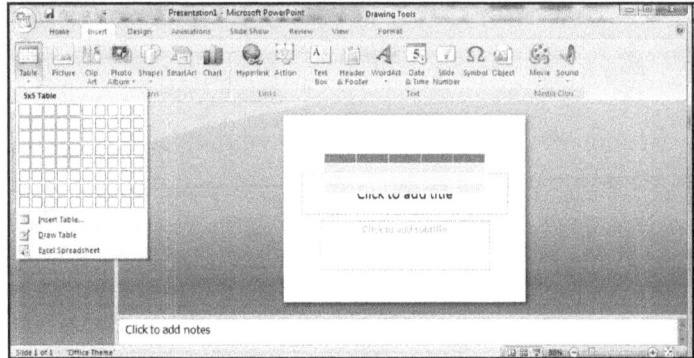

Fig. 6.27

WordArt and Shapes:

- There are many features and commands, we can use in PowerPoint to create visually appealing slides. Two of these features are WordArt and Shapes.
- WordArt allows you to create stylized text with textures, shadows, and outlines. It can be applied to text on any slide.
- Additionally, in PowerPoint we can insert a variety of shapes such as lines, arrows, callouts, stars, and basic shapes, including rectangles and circles.

Insert WordArt:

Step 1 : Go to the Insert Tab.

Step 2 : Click on the WordArt command.

Step 3 : A drop down menu of text options will appear.

Step 4 : Click on the text design you prefer and a text box will appear on your slide.

Step 5 : Click in the text box to modify the text.

Step 6 : Move the WordArt to any area of the slide by clicking on the edge of the text and dragging it. Expand or shrink the WordArt by clicking on the circles surrounding the text and drag.

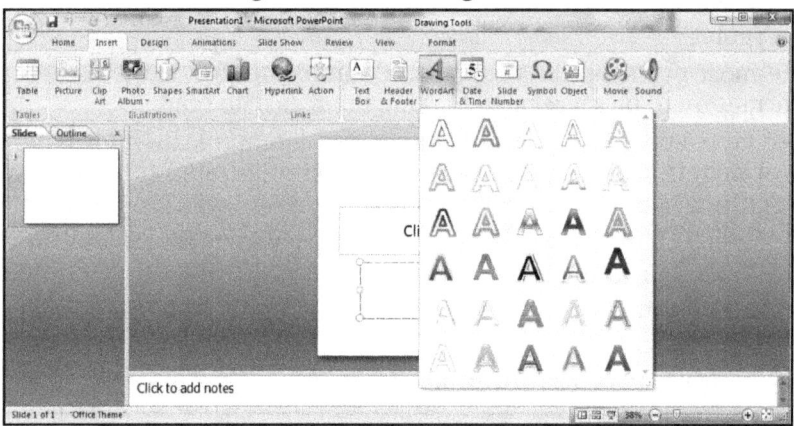

Fig. 6.28

To Insert Shapes:

- Shapes can be used in PowerPoint as a graphic to enhance the presentation or to insert text into to add visual appeal to a slide.

Step 1 : Go to the Insert Tab.

Step 2 : Click on Shapes command.

Step 3 : A large selection of shapes will appear in a drop down menu.

Step 4 : Double click on the shape you want to insert then the shape will appear on the slide.

Step 5 : Move the shape to any area of the slide by clicking on the edge of the shape and dragging it. Expand or shrink the shape by clicking on the circles surrounding the shape and drag.

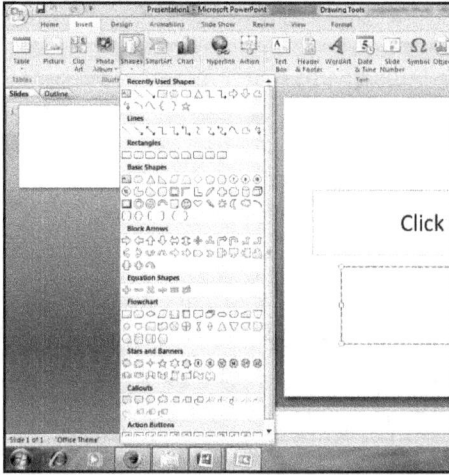

Fig. 6.29

6.3 | THEMES

- A theme is a predefined combination of colors, fonts, and effects that can be applied to your presentation.
- PowerPoint includes built-in themes that allow you to easily create professional-looking presentations without spending a lot of time in formatting. Each theme has additional background styles associated with it that can be applied to the slides to modify the theme.
- A theme is automatically applied when you create a new presentation in PowerPoint, even though the slide background is white. This default theme is called the Office Theme.
- The Office Theme consists of a white background and Calibri font of various sizes for titles and body text.

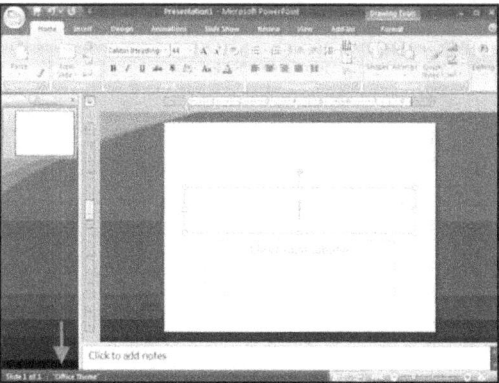

Fig. 6.30

- You can apply a different theme to your slides before adding text or making changes to the default slide. An advantage of doing this is that the location of the text will not move. If you apply the theme after entering text on the slides, the text boxes and placeholders may move, depending on the theme you choose.

To Apply a Theme:

Step 1 : Select the Design tab.

Step 2 : Locate the Themes group. Each image represents a theme.

Fig. 6.31

Step 3 : Click the drop-down arrow to access more themes.

Step 4 : However a theme to see a live preview of it in the presentation. The name of the theme will appear as you hover over it.

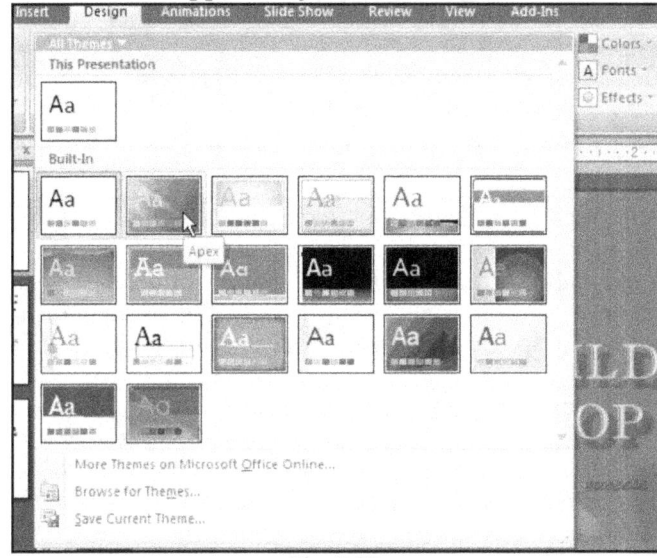

Fig. 6.32

Step 5 : Click a theme to apply it to the slides.

6.4 CHARTS

- Charts are an effective way of representing data. Long list of confusing numbers can instantly become trends which can be spotted when they are captured as charts. PowerPoint supports addition and formatting of charts.
- A chart is a tool you can use to communicate your data graphically.
- Charts often help an audience to see the meaning behind numbers and make showing comparisons and trends easy.

To Insert a Chart:

Step 1 : Select the Insert tab.

Step 2 : Click the Insert Chart command. The Insert Chart dialog box appears.

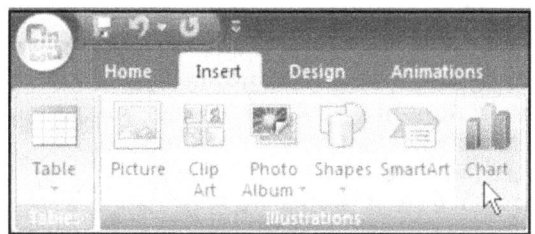

Fig. 6.33

Step 3 : Click and drag the scroll bar to view the chart types, or click a label on the left of the dialog box to see a specific chart style.

Step 4 : Click a chart to select it.

Step 5 : Click OK.

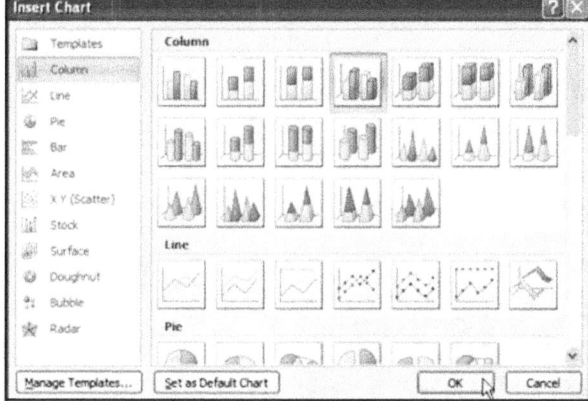

Fig. 6.34

To Enter Chart Data:

• The data that appears in the Excel spreadsheet is placeholder source data you'll replace with your own information. The Excel source data is used to create the PowerPoint chart.

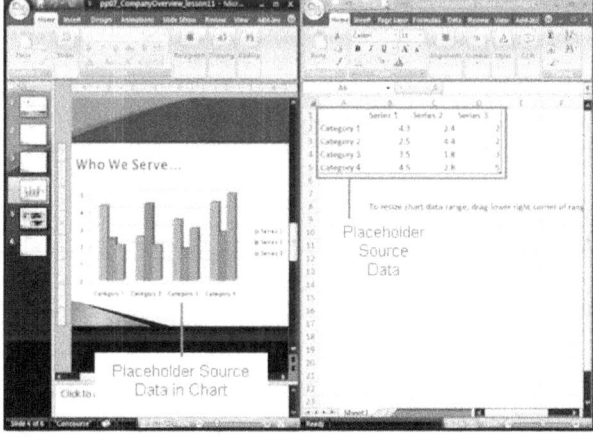

Fig. 6.35

To Enter Chart Data:

Step 1 : Select a cell in the Excel spreadsheet.

Step 2 : Enter your data in the cell. If the cell contains placeholder data, the placeholder data will disappear. As you enter your data, it will appear in the Excel spreadsheet and the PowerPoint chart.

Step 3 : Move to another cell.

Step 4 : Repeat the above steps until all of your data is entered.

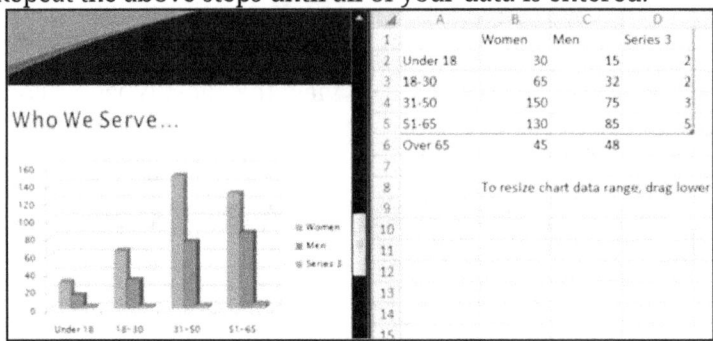

Fig. 6.36

Step 5 : Click and drag the lower-right corner of the blue line to increase or decrease the data range for columns. The data enclosed by the blue lines will appear in the chart.

Step 6 : Click and drag the lower-right corner of the blue line to increase or decrease the data range for rows.

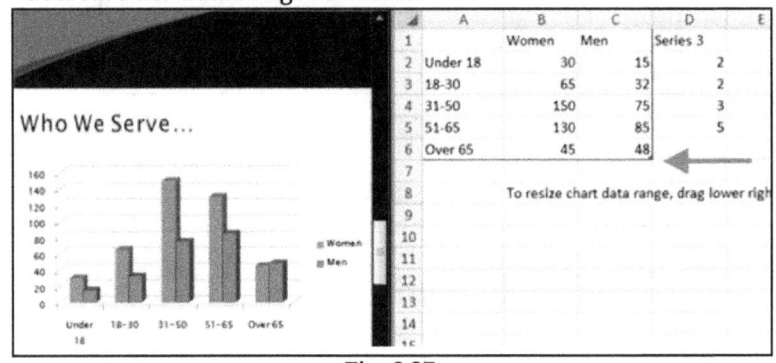

Fig. 6.37

Step 7 : Select any cells with placeholder data remaining. In the example, the column with Series 3 data was not needed.

	A	B	C	D
1		Women	Men	Series 3
2	Under 18	30	15	2
3	18-30	65	32	2
4	31-50	150	75	3
5	51-65	130	85	5
6	Over 65	45	48	
7				

Fig. 6.38

Step 8 : Press the Delete key to delete the remaining placeholder data.

Step 9 : Close Excel. You do not need to save the spreadsheet. The new Excel source data appears in the PowerPoint chart.

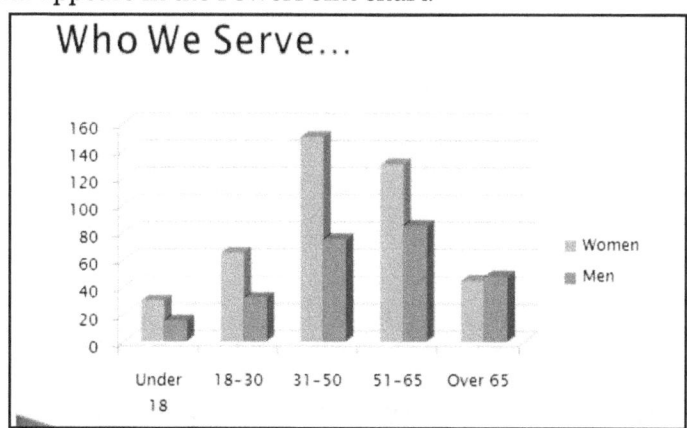

Fig. 6.39

6.5 | SLIDE ANIMATIONS

- Slide animations create animated effects to text and graphics during a slide show.
- There are a variety of animations that can be applied to text or graphics in multiple ways from a single word to all of the text on a slide.
- In PowerPoint, you can animate text and objects such as clip art, shapes, and pictures on the slide. Animation—or movement—on the slide can be used to draw the audience's attention to specific content or to make the slide easier to read.

To **Apply a Default Animation Effect:**

Step 1 : Select the text or object on the slide you want to animate.

Step 2 : Select the Animations tab.

Step 3 : Click the Animate drop-down menu in the Animations group to see the animation options for the selection. The options change based on the selected item.

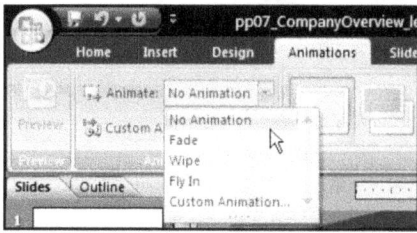

Fig. 6.40

Step 4 : Move your cursor over each option to see a live preview of the animation on the slide.

Step 5 : Click an option to select it.

To Apply a Custom Animation Effect:

Step 1 : Select the text or object on the slide you want to animate.

Step 2 : Select the Animations tab.

Step 3 : Click Custom Animation in the Animations group. The Custom Animation task pane will appear on the right.

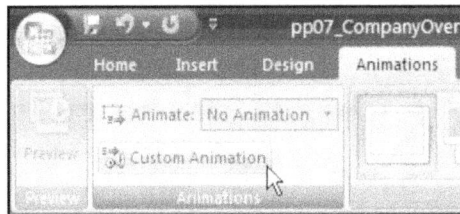

Fig. 6.41

Step 4 : Click Add Effect in the task pane to add an animation effect to the selected text or object.

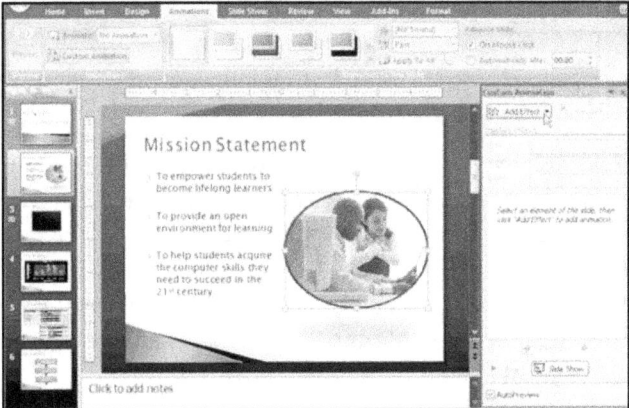

Fig. 6.42

Step 5 : Select Entrance, Emphasis, Exit, or Motion Path to display a submenu of animation effects for the category.

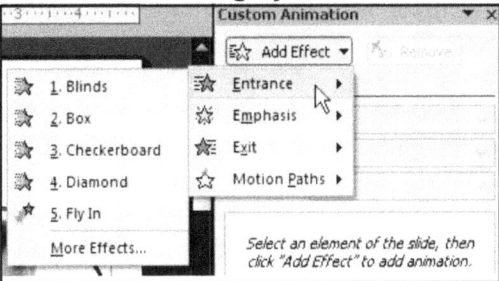

Fig. 6.43

o **Entrance:** Changes how the selected item appears on the page.

o **Emphasis:** Draws attention to the selected item while the slide is displayed.

      o **Exit:** Changes the way the selected item disappears from the slide.

      o **Motion Path:** Animates the selected item so it moves to a specific place on the screen.

Step 6 : Select an animation effect to apply it.

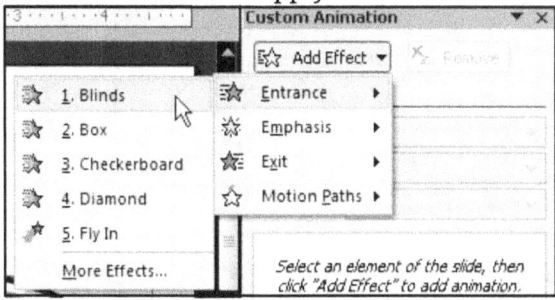

Fig. 6.44

- The animation will display on the selected item on the slide and will appear listed in the Custom Animation task pane.

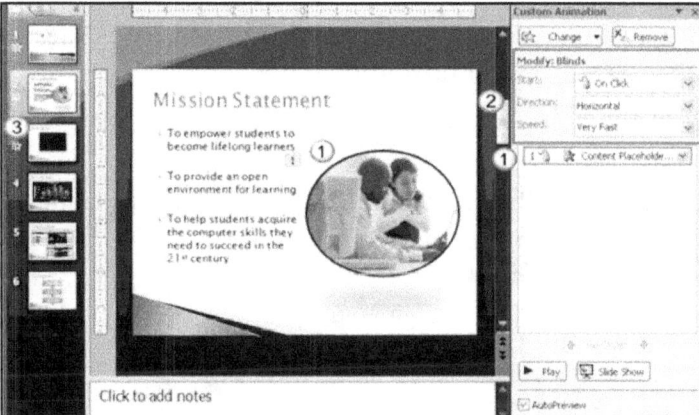

Fig. 6.45

1. A number label appears on the slide next to the animated object. A matching number label also appears next to the animation in the Custom Animation task pane list.

2. Drop-down menus appear at the top of the Custom Animation task pane. You can define the animation effect in greater detail here.

3. The star Play Animations icon appears beneath the slide on the Slides tab in the task pane on the left. It indicates that the slide has an animation effect.

Working with Animation Effects:

To Modify a Default or Custom Animation Effect:

Step 1 : After you apply an animation effect, drop-down menus will appear at the top of the Custom Animation task pane. The menus vary based on the animation effect.

Step 2 : Select an option from a drop-down menu to change the default setting.

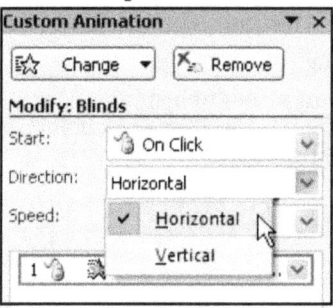

Fig. 6.46

Step 3 : Repeat until all menu options are at desired settings.

To Remove an Animation Effect:

Step 1 : Select the text or object on the slide you want to modify.

Step 2 : Select the Animations tab.

Step 3 : Click Custom Animation in the Animations group. The Custom Animation task pane will appear on the right.

Step 4 : Select the animation in the Custom Animation task pane list, if it is not already selected.

Step 5 : Click Remove. The animation label will disappear from the slide and from the Custom Animation task pane list.

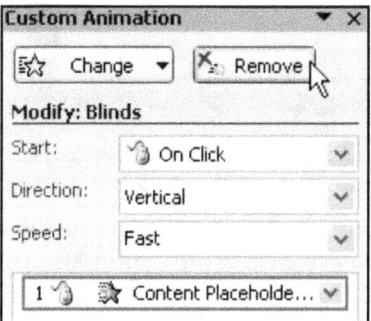

Fig. 6.47

To Apply a Different Animation Effect:

Step 1 : Select the text or object on the slide you want to modify.

Step 2 : Select the Animations tab.

Step 3 : Click Custom Animation in the Animations group. The Custom Animation task pane will appear on the right.

Step 4 : Select the animation in the Custom Animation task pane, if it is not already selected.

Step 5 : Click Change.

Step 6 : Select an Entrance, Emphasis, Exit, or Motion Path animation effect.

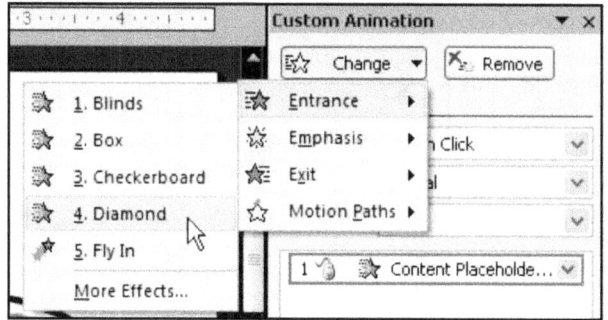

Fig. 6.48

Step 7 : New drop-down menus with default settings will appear at the top of the Custom Animation task pane.

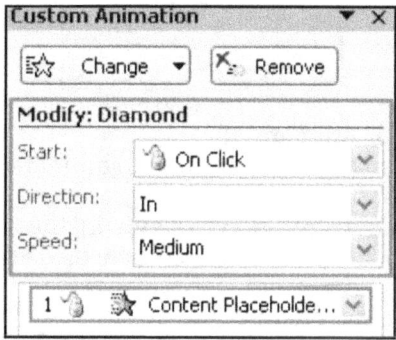

Fig. 6.49

To Preview an Animation Effect:

Step 1 : Select the text or object you want to modify on the slide.

Step 2 : Select the Animations tab.

Step 3 : Click Custom Animation in the Animations group. The Custom Animation task pane will appear on the right.

Step 4 : Select the animation in the Custom Animation task pane list.

Step 5 : Click Play bottom of the task pane to see a preview of the animation in Normal view.

OR

- Click Slide Show to see the animation in Slide Show view. Press the Esc key to return to Normal view.

Fig. 6.50

To Animate Text With a Default Animation:

Step 1 : Select the text box or text you want to animate on the slide.

Step 2 : Select the Animations tab.

Step 3 : Click the Animate drop-down menu in the Animations group to see the animation effects for the selected text. The effects vary based on the selected item.

Step 4 : Select an animation effect.

Fig. 6.51

- **All At Once:** The selected text appears all at once. The entire text is labeled with one number on the slide. Click the drop-down arrow in the task pane to expand the contents and see that the text is labeled with one number.

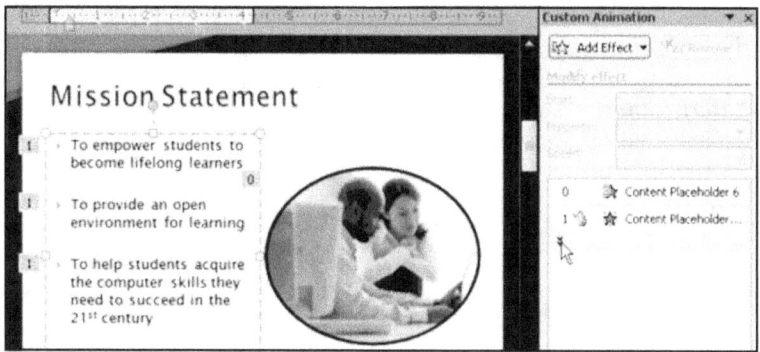

Fig. 6.52

- **By 1st Level Paragraphs:** The text will appear bullet by bullet, or paragraph by paragraph. Each level of text is labeled with a different number on the slide. Click the drop-down arrow in the task pane to expand the contents and see that the text is labeled with multiple numbers.

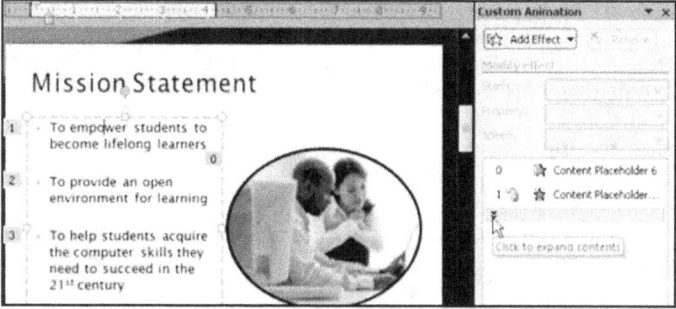

Fig. 6.53

To Modify an Animation Effect in Other Ways:

Step 1 : Select an animation effect in the Custom Animation task pane list.

Step 2 : Click the arrow to display a drop-down menu.

Fig. 6.54

Step 3 : Select Effects Options or Timing. A dialog box will appear.

Step 4 : In the dialog box, add enhancements such as sounds, and define what happens after the animation effect is applied to the selected item.

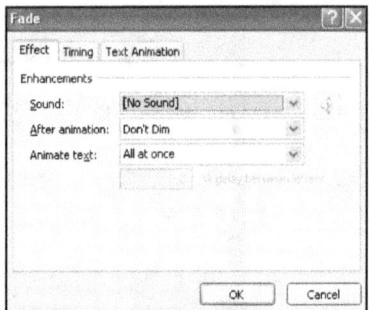

Fig. 6.55

* The dialog box name is based on the animation effect name. In the example above, the animation effect is Fade. The tabs and options on the tabs will vary based on the animation effect that is being modified.

Using Transitions:

* Transition effects—or transitions as they are often called—are the movements you see when one slide changes to another in Slide Show view.
* Transition effects are different from animation effects.
* The term animation in PowerPoint refers to the movements of text and objects on the slide, while transitions refer to the movement of the slide as it changes to another slide.

To Apply a Transition to One Slide:

Step 1 : Select the slide you want to modify.

Step 2 : Select the Animations tab.

Step 3 : Locate the Transition to This Slide group. By default, No Transition is applied to each slide.

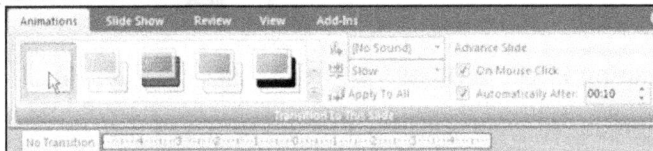

Fig. 6.56

Step 4 : Click the More drop-down arrow to display all available transition effects.

Fig. 6.57

Step 5 : Click a slide transition effect to apply it to the selected slide. However a slide transition effect to see a live preview of the effect on the slide.

To Apply a Slide Transition to All Slides:

Step 1 : Select the slide you want to modify.

Step 2 : Select the Animations tab.

Step 3 : Locate the Transition to This Slide group. By default, No Transition is applied to each slide.

Step 4 : Click the More drop-down arrow to display all transition effects.

Step 5 : Click a slide transition effect to apply it to the selected slide.

Step 6 : Click Apply To All to apply the transition to all slides in the presentation.

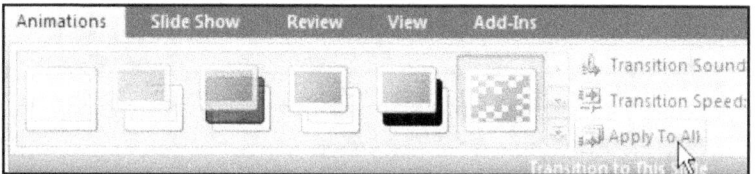

Fig. 6.58

6.6 | TEMPLATES

- A Microsoft Office PowerPoint 2007 template is a pattern or blueprint of a slide or group of slides.
- Templates can contain layouts, theme colors, theme fonts, theme effects, background styles, and even content.
- You can create your own custom templates and store them, reuse them, and share them with others. You can also find hundreds of different types of free templates on Office Online and on other partner Web sites that you can apply to your presentation.

Creating Templates:

Step 1 : Click the Microsoft Office Button , and then click New.

Step 2 : In the New Presentation dialog box, do one of the following:

- To apply a template that you've recently used, click Blank and recent, click the template that you want, and then click Create.

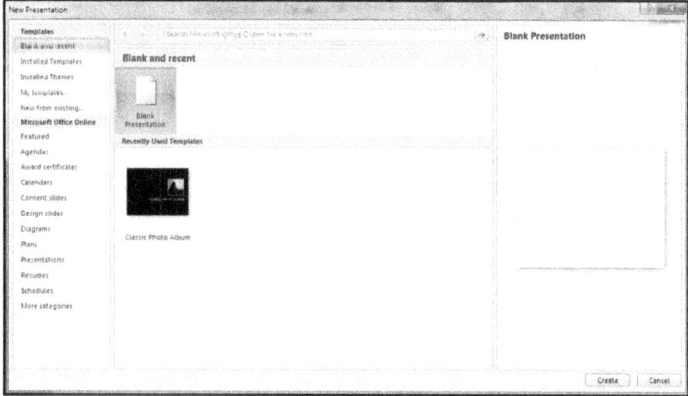

Fig. 6.59

- To apply a template that you've installed to your local hard drive, click Installed Templates, and then click Create.

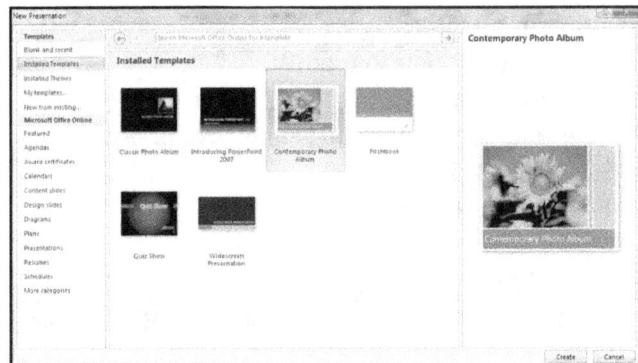

Fig. 6.60

Fig. 6.61

PRACTICE QUESTIONS

1. What is PowerPoint?
2. What is meant by presentation and presentation software?
3. Describe slides in detail.
4. Write short note on:
   (i) Text
   (ii) Images
   (iii) Charts
5. Explain slide animation in detail.
6. Describe slide transition in detail.
7. What is template?
8. Explain theme concept of PowerPoint in detail.
9. How to create charts in PowerPoint? Explain with example.

■■■

PC Hardware

Contents ...

7.1	INTRODUCTION

- A computer system consists of two major elements i.e., hardware and software.
- Hardware and software are mutually dependent. Software cannot be utilized without supporting hardware and hardware without set of program to operate upon is useless. To get a particular job done on the computer, a relevant software should be loaded into the hardware.
- A software acts as an interface between the user and the hardware. It helps the user interact with the particular hardware.
- If hardware is the 'heart' of a computer system, then software is its 'soul'. Both are complimentary to each other.

7.2	COMPUTER HARDWARE

- The physical parts or components, which you can see and touch, are collectively called hardware.

- Computer hardware can be defined as, "all the physical equipments and devices of a computer system, such as keyboard, monitor, printer etc., are called its hardware".
- In other words, hardware is a collective term used for all the components that make up for a computer system.
- PC Hardware contains:
  1. Input devices such as keyboard, mouse etc.
  2. Output devices such as printer, monitor etc.
  3. Secondary storage devices such as Hard disk, CD, DVD etc.
  4. Internal components such as CPU, Motherboard, RAM etc.

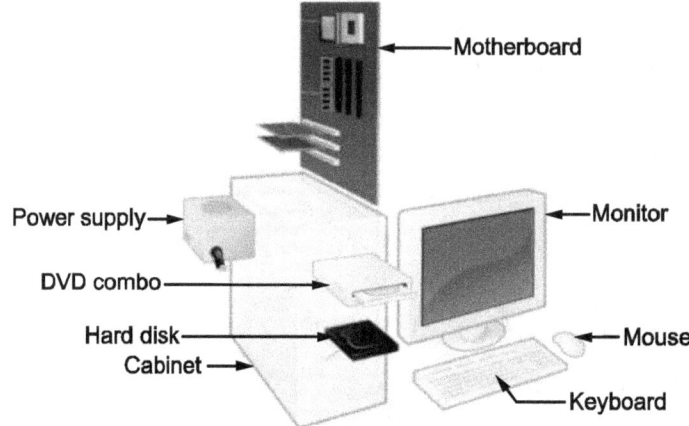

Fig. 7.1: Hardware in Computer

| 7.3 | TYPE AND WORKING OF HARDWARE PARTS |

7.3.1 Ports

- The computer has several components, which are used as pathway for flow of data. A port on a computer is a location or point for passing data in and out of a computer.
- A port is a socket or plug-in on your system case that allows you to attach an external device (mouse, keyboard, printer, etc.) by connecting its cable.
- Today's computers have several types of ports to connect different types of hardware devices for specific purpose. You can see these ports on both the front and back of the computer. Each port has its own interface to connect a particular device.
- A port has the following characteristics:
  1. External devices are connected to a computer using cables and ports.
  2. Ports are slots on the motherboard into which a cable of external device is plugged in.

- Fig. 7.2 shows ports in computer.

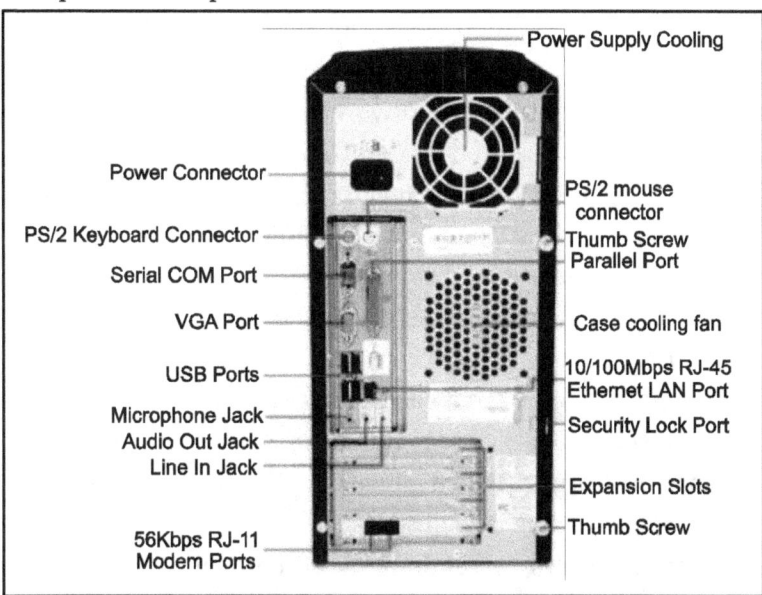

Fig. 7.2: Ports in Cabinet of Computer

- There are many types of ports in a PC. A serial port transmits one bit of data at a time. A parallel port transmits 8 bits or a byte at a time. Therefore, a parallel port transmits more data as compared to a serial port.

- Fig. 7.3 shows various ports symbols in computer.

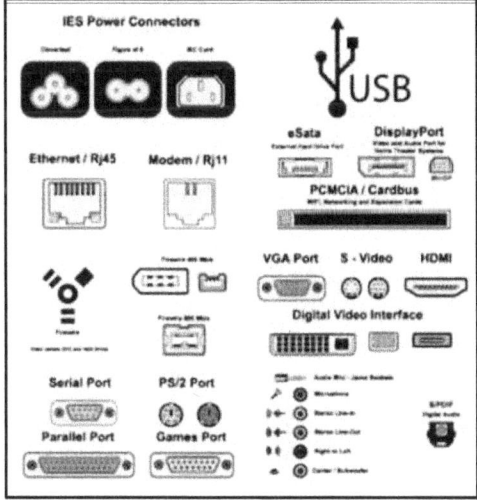

Fig. 7.3

- Following are few important types of ports:

    1. **Serial Port:** Used for external modems and older computer mouse. Two versions : 9 pin, 25 pin model. Data travels at 115 kilobits per second.

2. **Parallel Port:** Used for scanners and printers. It is also called printer port. 25 pin model and also known as IEEE 1284-compliant Centronics port.

3. **PS/2 Port:** Used for old computer keyboard and mouse. Also called mouse port. Most of the old computers provide two PS/2 port, each for mouse and keyboard. Also known as IEEE 1284-compliant Centronics port.

4. **Universal Serial Bus (or USB) Port:** It can connect all kinds of external USB devices such as external hard disk, printer, scanner, mouse, keyboard etc. It was introduced in 1997. Most of the computers provide two USB ports as minimum. Data travels at 12 megabits per seconds. USB compliant devices can get power from a USB port.

5. **VGA Port:** Connects monitor to a computer's video card. It has 15 holes. Similar to serial port connector but serial port connector has pins, it has holes.

6. **Power Connector:** Three-pronged plug. Connects to the computer's power cable that plugs into a power bar or wall socket.

7. **Firewire Port:** Transfers large amount of data at very fast speed. Connects camcorders and video equipments to the computer. Data travels at 400 to 800 megabits per seconds. It is invented by Apple. Three variants i.e., 4-Pin FireWire 400 connector, 6-Pin FireWire 400 connector and 9-Pin FireWire 800 connector.

8. **Modem Port:** Connects a PC's modem to the telephone network.

9. **Ethernet Port:** Connects to a network and high speed Internet. Connect network cable to a computer. This port resides on an Ethernet Card. Data travels at 10 megabits to 1000 megabits per seconds depending upon the network bandwidth.

10. **Game Port:** Connect a joystick to a PC. Now replaced by USB.

11. **Digital Video Interface (DVI) Port:** Connects flat panel LCD monitor to the computer's high end video graphic cards. Very popular among video card manufacturers.

12. **Sockets:** Connect microphone, speakers to sound card of the computer.

7.3.2 Motherboard

- A motherboard is one of the most essential parts of a computer system. It holds together many of the crucial components of a computer, including the Central Processing Unit (CPU), memory and connectors for input and output devices.

- Motherboard, also called as System Board.

- Motherboard is so called as all the other boards (printed circuit boards having chips or other electronic components) of the computer are connected to this board, hence it is like the mother of all other boards.

- The base of a motherboard consists of a very firm sheet of non-conductive material, typically some sort of rigid plastic. Thin layers of copper or aluminum foil, referred to as traces, are printed onto this sheet. These traces are very narrow and form the circuits between the various components. In addition to circuits, a motherboard contains a number of sockets and slots to connect the other components.

- Popular manufacturers of motherboards are Intel, ASUS, AOpen, ABIT, Biostar, and so on.

Parts of Motherboard:

- To understand how computers work you don't need to know every single part of the motherboard. However, it is good to know some of the most important parts and how the motherboard connects the various parts of a computer system together.

- Some of the typical parts are described below and shown in Fig. 7.4.

  o A CPU socket - the actual CPU is directly soldered onto this socket. Since high speed CPUs generate a lot of heat, there are heat sinks and mounting points for fans right next to the CPU socket.

  o A power connector to distribute power to the CPU and other components.

  o Slots for the system's main memory, typically in the form of DRAM chips.

  o A chip forms an interface between the CPU, the main memory and other components. On many types of motherboards this is referred to as the Northbridge. This chip also contains a large heat sink.

  o A second chip controls the input and output (I/O) functions. It is not connected directly to the CPU but to the Northbridge. This I/O controller is referred to as the Southbridge. The Northbridge and Southbridge combined are referred to as the chipset.

  o Several connectors, which provide the physical interface between input and output devices and the motherboard. The Southbridge handles these connections.

  o Slots for one or more hard drives to store files. The most common types of connections are Integrated Drive Electronics (IDE) and Serial Advanced Technology Attachment (SATA).

  o A Read Only Memory (ROM) chip, which contains the firmware, or startup instructions for the computer system. This is also called the BIOS.

  o A slot for a video or graphics card. There are a number of different types of slots, including Accelerated Graphics Port (AGP) and Peripheral Component Interconnect Express (PCIe).

  o Additional slots to connect hardware in the form of Peripheral Component Interconnect (PCI) slots.

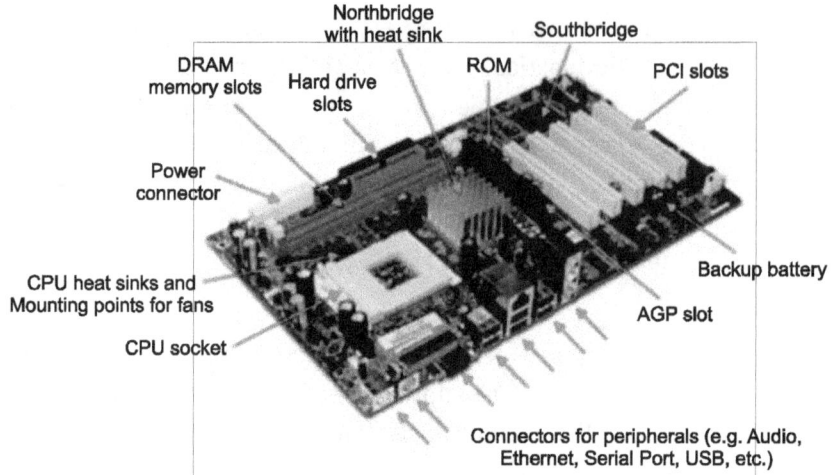

Fig. 7.4: Parts of Motherboard

7.3.3 CPU

*   The system unit is the box-like case that contains major computer's electronic components which many people erroneously refer to the CPU.

*   The system unit is sometimes called computer chassis, cabinet, box, tower, enclosure, housing, system unit or simply case.

*   The computer cabinet encloses the components that are required for the running of the computer. The components inside a computer cabinet include the power supply, motherboard, memory chips, expansion slots, ports and interface, processor, cables and storage devices, (See Fig. 7.5).

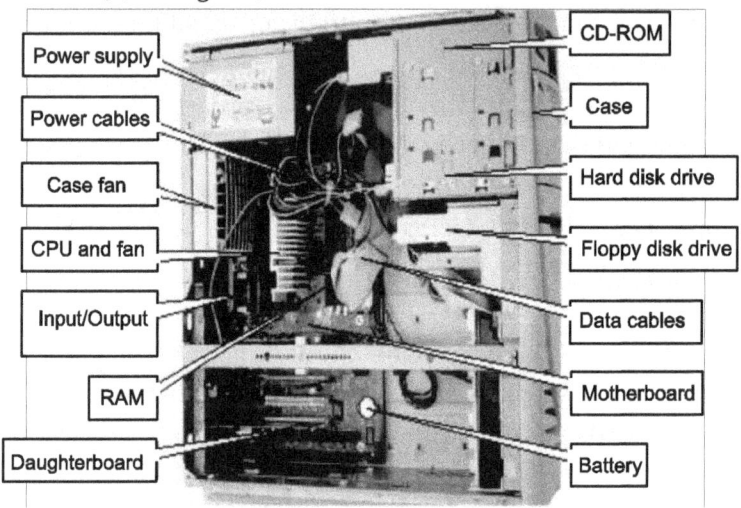

Fig. 7.5: Parts of CPU

- Fig. 7.5 shows following parts of CPU:

1. **Motherboard:**

- The motherboard is sometimes called the system board or main board. It is the main circuit board of a micro computer.

- Typically, the motherboard contains the CPU, BIOS, memory, mass storage interfaces, serial and parallel ports, expansion slots, and all the controllers required to control standard peripheral devices, such as the display screen, keyboard, and disk drive.

2. **Storage Devices:**

- The disk drives are present inside the machine. The common disk drives in a machine are hard disk drive, floppy drive and CD drive or DVD drive.

- High-storage devices like hard disk, floppy disk and CDs are inserted into the hard disk drive, floppy drive and CD drive, respectively. These storage devices can store large amount of data, permanently.

(i) **Hard Disk Drive (HDD):**

- A HDD is a high capacity non-volatile magnetic data storage media with a volume (disk) which is usually non-removable.

- Data is magnetically read and written on the platter by read/write heads that float on a cushion of air above the platters.

(ii) **Floppy Disk Drive (FDD):**

- FDD it is a disk drive that can read and write floppy disks although they are obsolete now-a-days.

- Floppy disk drives have been replaced by the USB flash disk drives.

(iii) **CD-ROM Drive:**

- It is a high capacity optical data storage device with a removable disk, it writes data onto or reads data from a storage medium.

- A CD-ROM drive may be connected to the computer via an IDE (ATA), SCSI, S-ATA, Firewire, or USB interface or a proprietary interface.

3. **Power Supply Unit (PSU):**

- The PSU is used to convert AC current from the mains supply to the different DC voltages required by various computer components.

- Standard power supplies turn the incoming 110V or 220V AC (Alternating Current) into various DC (Direct Current) voltages suitable for powering the computer's components.

- Power supplies are quoted as having a certain power output specified in Watts, a standard power supply would typically be able to deliver around 350 Watts.

4. **BIOS:**
- It is the basic program used as an interface between the operating system and the motherboard.
- BIOS contain the instructions for the starting up of the computer. The BIOS runs when the computer is switched on.
- It performs a Power On Self Test (POST) that checks that the hardware is functioning properly and the hardware devices are present.

5. **Ports and Interfaces:**
- Motherboard has a certain number of I/O sockets that are connected to the ports and interfaces found on the rear side of a computer. You can connect external devices to the ports and interfaces, which get connected to the computer's motherboard.

6. **Expansion Slots:**
- The expansion slots are located on the motherboard. The expansion cards are inserted in the expansion slots.
- These cards give the computer new features or increased performance. There are several types of slots as explained below:
  - **ISA (Industry Standard Architecture) Slot** is used to connect modem and input devices.
  - **PCI (Peripheral Component InterConnect) Slot** is used to connect audio, video and graphics. They are much faster than ISA cards.
  - **AGP (Accelerated Graphic Port) Slot** is a fast port for a graphics card.
  - **PC Card** is used in laptop computers. It includes Wi-Fi card, network card and external modem.

7. **CMOS Chip:**
- BIOS ROMs are accompanied by a smaller CMOS memory chip. When the computer is turned off, the power supply stops providing electricity to the motherboard.
- When the computer is turned on again, the system still displays the correct clock time. This is because the CMOS chip saves some system information, such as time, system date and essential system settings.

8. **Processor:**
- The processor or the CPU is the main component of the computer. The CPU acts like the brain of the computer. Select a processor based on factors like its speed, performance, reliability and motherboard support.
- A microprocessor is an Integrated Circuit (IC) chip containing the arithmetic, logic and control circuiting required to interpret and execute instructions of a program.
- Pentium Pro, Pentium 2 and Pentium 4 are some of the common examples of processors.

9. Ribbon Cables:

- Ribbon cables are flat, insulated and consist of several tiny wires moulded together that carry data to different components on the motherboard.

- There is a wire for each bit of the word or byte and additional wires to coordinate the activity of moving information. They also connect the floppy drives, disk drives and CD-ROM drives to the connectors in the motherboard.

- Now-a-days, Serial Advanced Technology Attachment (SATA) cables have replaced the ribbon cables to connect the drives to the motherboard.

10. Memory Chips:

- The RAM consists of chips on a small circuit board. Two types of memory chips— Single In-line Memory Module (SIMM) and Dual In-line Memory Module (DIMM) are used in desktop computers.

- The CPU can retrieve information from DIMM chip at 64 bits compared to 32 bits or 16 bits transfer with SIMM chips. DIMM chips are used in Pentium 4 onwards to increase the access speed.

7.4 | BIOS

- BIOS is an acronym for Basic Input/Output System.

- BIOS, also known as System BIOS, ROM BIOS or PC BIOS.

- BIOS consists of the basic input/output instructions and the information is stored in integrated chips as read only information.

- The instructions in BIOS are executed when the computer is powered ON. As stated earlier, computer requires an Operating System (OS) to do some basic tasks for its proper working.

- For a computer to run an operating system, a bootstrap program is required. This program is loaded from a known memory location and provides enough information to access the device in which the operating system is loaded.

- The fundamental purposes of the BIOS are to initialize and test the system hardware components, and to load a bootloader or an operating system from a mass memory device.

- BIOS software is stored on a ROM chip on the motherboard. It is specifically designed to work with each particular model of computer, interfacing with various devices that make up the complementary chipset of the system.

- BIOS chip is usually located near the memory socket in the motherboard. Certain BIOS chips are marked on their top surface. Two types of BIOS chips found in motherboards are shown in Fig. 7.6.

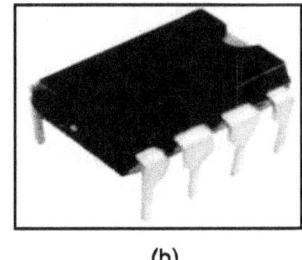

(a)   (b)

Fig. 7.6

Functions of a PC BIOS:

1. **POST:** Test the computer hardware and make sure no errors exist before loading the operating system.

2. **BIOS or CMOS Setup:** Configuration program that allows you to configure hardware settings including system settings such as computer passwords, time, and date.

3. **BIOS Drivers:** Low level drivers that give the computer basic operational control over your computer's hardware.

4. **Bootstrap Loader:** Locate the operating system. If a capable operating system is located, the BIOS will pass control to it.

7.5 NETWORK INTERFACE CARD (NIC)

- The Network Interface Card (NIC) is a hardware card that allows a PC to participate in passing and receiving data on a network.

- A NIC is also known as a Network Interface Controller, Local Area Network (LAN) Adapter, Ethernet Adapter or Network Adapter.

Characteristics of NICs:

1. The NIC constructs, transmits, receives, and processes data to and from a PC and the connected network.

2. Each NIC has a unique six-byte Media Access Control (MAC) address, which is typically permanently burned into the NIC when it is manufactured.

3. NICs manufactured by different vendors vary in speed, complexity, manageability, and cost.

4. Each device connected to a network must have a NIC installed.

5. The NIC requires drivers to operate on the network.

6. The NIC must be compatible with the network i.e., Ethernet-10baseT or token ring to operate properly.

- Fig. 7.7 shows typical NIC.

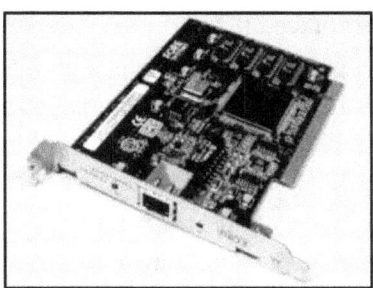

Fig. 7.7: NIC

- An Ethernet connection uses a standard interface known as a RJ45 connector. 'RJ' stands for 'Registered Jack.'

7.6 | GRAPHICS CARD

- A graphics card also called a video adapter, display card, video card, graphics board, display adapter, graphics adapter or frame buffer.
- A video card is an interface between the CPU and the monitor.
- It is an expansion card which generates a feed of output images to a display (such as a computer monitor).
- Frequently, these are advertised as discrete or dedicated graphics cards, emphasizing the distinction between these and integrated graphics.
- Fig. 7.8 shows internal computer video expansion card.

Fig. 7.8: Graphics Card

- In Fig. 7.8 the video card is inserted into the AGP expansion slot on the computer motherboard. Over the development of computers, there have been several types of expansion slots used for video cards.

- Today, the most common expansion slot for video cards is PCIe, which replaced AGP, which replaced PCI, which replaced ISA.

    1. **VGA** short for Video Graphics Array. VGA is a popular display standard developed by IBM and introduced in 1987. VGA provides 640 x 480 resolution color display screens with a refresh rate of 60Hz and 16 colors displayed at a time. If the resolution is lowered to 320 x 200, 256 colors are shown.

    2. **S-Video** short for Super Video and is a round connector interface and cable that transmits video luminance (Y) and chrominance (C) signals separately. When received by the TV or other display device this generates a better picture when compared to composite video. The picture shows an example of an S-Video connector on the back of a video card.

    3. **DVI** short for Digital Visual Interface. DVI is a video display interface. It was developed to be an industry standard for transmitting digital video content to display devices at resolutions as high as 2560 x 1600. Common devices that utilize the DVI connection are computer monitors and projectors.

    4. **AGP** short for Accelerated Graphics Port. AGP is an advanced port designed for Video cards and 3D accelerators. Designed by Intel and introduced in August of 1997, AGP introduces a dedicated point-to-point channel that allows the graphics controller direct access to the system memory.

    5. **PCI** short for Peripheral Component Interconnect. PCI was introduced by Intel in 1992. The PCI bus came in both 32-bit (133MBps) and 64-bit versions and was used to attach hardware to a computer. Although commonly used in computers from the late 1990s to the early 2000s, PCI has since been replaced with PCI Express.

    6. **ISA** short for Industry Standard Architecture. ISA was introduced by IBM and headed by Mark Dean. ISA was originally an 8-bit computer bus that was later expanded to a 16-bit bus in 1984.

PRACTICE QUESTIONS

    1. What is meant by computer hardware and software?
    2. What is port? Enlist its types.
    3. Write short note on a: PC Hardware.
    4. What is CPU? Explain its parts.
    5. Explain BIOS in detail.
    6. Describe graphics card in detail.
    7. What is NIC? Enlist its characteristics.
    8. Explain motherboard in detail.
    9. What are the functions of PC BIOS?

■■■

Troubleshooting and Preventing Problems

Contents ...

8.1 INTRODUCTION

- Troubleshooting is the process of determining the cause of a problem, and then resolving the problem.

- Basic computer troubleshooting techniques can help alleviate any frustration when facing a computer problem.

- Troubleshooting is the process of figuring out how to solve a computer problem.

- Below we describe some of the most commonly encountered technology issues:

  1. The printer is not working.

  2. A program is not responding.

  3. The keyboard is not working.

  4. New hardware or software is working incorrectly.

  5. The mouse is not working.

  6. The computer is slow.

  7. The browser's homepage suddenly changed.

- Troubleshooting is the process of identifying, planning and resolving a problem, error or fault within a software or computer system. It enables the repair and restoration of a computer or software when it becomes faulty, unresponsive or acts in an abnormal way.

- In computer there are following ways of troubleshooting:

1. Hardware Troubleshooting:

- Hardware troubleshooting is the process of reviewing, diagnosing and identifying operational or technical problems within a hardware device or equipment.

- It aims to resolve physical and/or logical problems and issues within a computing hardware.

- Hardware troubleshooting is done by hardware engineer or technical support technician.

- Hardware troubleshooting processes primarily aim to resolve computer hardware problems using a systematic approach.

2. Software Troubleshooting:

- Software troubleshooting is the process of scanning, identifying, diagnosing and resolving problems, errors and bugs in software.

- It is a systematic process that aims to filter out and resolve problems, and restore the software to normal operation. It is a subcategory of IT troubleshooting.

- Software troubleshooting is generally done to resolve technical or source-code-related problems in software. This can be both functional and non-functional in nature.

- Software troubleshooting can also be done when software needs to be configured correctly, such as resolving issues due to incorrect installation or restoring software after corruption or file deletion caused by a virus.

3. Network Troubleshooting:

- Network troubleshooting is the collective measures and processes used to identify, diagnose and resolve problems and issues within a computer network.

- It is a systematic process that aims to resolve problems and restore normal network operations within the network.

- Fig. 8.1 shows steps in troubleshooting.

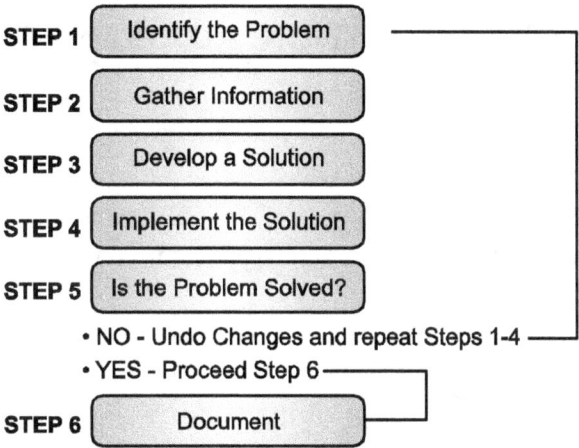

Fig. 8.1: Troubleshooting Steps

- Steps in Fig. 8.1 are explained below:

Step 1 : **Identify the Problem:** This step should provide a clear problem statement that defines the problem as a set of symptoms and associated causes. This is done by identifying the general symptoms and then determining the possible causes that could result in these symptoms. The outcome of this step should be a written set of ideas and possibilities.

Step 2 : **Gathering Information:** The information gathered here will be used to develop a solution to the problem. A technician will be able to make better decisions when the problem has been accurately described.

Step 3 : **Developing a Solution:** The technician will assess the gathered data and its definition. The technician will use experience, logic, reasoning, and common sense to develop a solution.

Step 4 : **Implementing the Solution:** This step involves the technician working on the computer. The technician attempts their solution through hands-on manipulation of the computer components, which might be hardware and software.

Step 5 : **Is the Problem Resolved?:** The technician is responsible for verifying that the system is operating correctly. If the system is operating properly, then the troubleshooting cycle ends successfully. If the system is not running correctly, the troubleshooting cycle will continue. If the technician needs more information, go back to identifying the problem (step one).

Step 6 : **Documenting the Solution:** It is important to always document all the changes that were introduced to the system as a result of solving one problem. This record can be the starting point for troubleshooting any future problems.

8.2 | LOGICAL FAULT ISOLATION: ADJUST METHOD

- Complex problems often yield to a structured analytic approach. The idea is to create a logical step-by-step procedure that will accurately identify the cause of a network problem, a process that is also repeatable.

- The idea is to isolate a problem using Logical Fault Isolation, and to find the correct solution the first time. In order to isolate a problem you should follow the following six basic steps known as ADJUST:

  1. **Assess** the level or concern and the priority the problem has. Not every problem is important, or requires an immediate solution.

  2. **Discover** all information related to the fault. This information is best gathered from a number of sources, such as user interviews, log analysis and other network activity information.

  3. **Justify** the cause of the fault and analyze the information found in discovery to suggest possible fault testing.

  4. **Unit** test to isolate the fault. The process should be test, evaluate and isolate.

  5. **Systematically** analyze the fault data. Perhaps your testing found the problem, then further work isn't required. However, many problems are complex and result from interactions of faults with other faults or complex systems. So in this step the idea is to review the fault data until you have isolated the problem.

  6. **Transcribe** the findings and document the process. It's a good idea to generate a record of the problem and its solution. You never know when it might crop up in the future.

8.3 | COMMON NETWORKING PROBLEMS

- A network is defined as a group more than two computer or device like printer that connect together for the purpose of sharing resources.

- Troubleshooting a network problem can take many forms. Before the network is even installed, decisions must be made about it that will affect the way it is troubleshot in the future.

- For example, Ethernet and token-ring networks use different data encoding schemes and connections, as well as different support software. Each has its own set of peculiar problems and solutions.

- Troubleshooting a network may take you down a hardware path (bad crimps on the cable connectors causing intermittent errors), a software path (the machine does not have its network addresses set up correctly), or both. There even may be nothing wrong with the network, addresses set up correctly or both.

- Today's network is more complex than ever before. The impact that the multitude of devices, applications, and locations have on network performance can be startling – increased congestion, slow application response time, loss of user productivity etc.

- Some most common problems in computer networking are given below:

  1. **Cable Problem:** Cables that connect different parts of a network can be cut or shorted. A short can happen when the wire conductor comes in contact with another conductive surface, changing the path of the signal. Cable testers can be used to test for many types of cable problems such as Cut cable, incorrect cable connections, Cable shorts, Interference level, Connector Problem.

  2. **Software Problem:** Network problems can often be traced to software configuration such as DNS configuration, WINS configuration, the registry etc.

  3. **Excessive Network Collisions:** These often lead to slow connectivity. The problem can occur as a result of bad network setup/plan, a user transferring a lot of information or jabbering network card.

  4. **Connectivity Problem:** A connectivity problem with one or more devices in a network can occur after a change is made in configuration or by a malfunction of a connectivity component, such as hub, a router or a switch.

  5. **Duplicate IP Addressing:** A common problem in many networking environments occurs when two machines try to use the same IP address. This can result in intermittent communications.

  6. **Entire Network Unreachable:** Networks rely on clearly defined, shared protocols. When, where, and how you say something makes all of the difference in whether you will be heard or ignored.

8.4 | TOOLS FOR GATHERING INFORMATION

- Many computer users do not know how to describe a problem beyond the statement "It's not doing what I want it to."

- Windows 7 is different from earlier versions of Windows, in that it has sophisticated methods to diagnose and repair as many problems as possible on its own. If it cannot diagnose or repair the problem, it can attempt to automatically connect to Microsoft and determine the best next course of action.

- The built-in diagnostic tools and repair wizards can work without the user having detailed and intimate knowledge of Windows 7. Windows XP and previous versions of Windows have limited methods for self-diagnosis and repair.

- The automated tools in Windows 7 may fix some problems, but even these tools have limits. In these cases the person repairing the computer must resort to traditional troubleshooting tools and techniques.

- The first step in efficient troubleshooting is collecting of details that describe the state of the computer and information that describes the problem.

- The best tools to start gathering information are Problem Steps Recorder, System Information, Computer Management, Action Center, Help and Support, and Microsoft Support Web site.

1. Problem Steps Recorder:

- Windows 7 OS includes Problem Steps Recorder to allows users to record the exact steps required to reproduce a problem.

- The recorded steps can then be forwarded to help desk staff for analysis. This tool can be used to accurately capture information about how a problem is caused when help desk staff are unavailable or when it is not possible. For help desk staff to remote control a computer.

- You can access Problem Steps Recorder by typing psr in the Start Menu search box.

2. System Information:

- This tool scans the current state of the computer and reports its findings in a searchable tree format.

- The System Information utility can export its findings to a text file or it can be saved to a System Information file.

- System Information files use the extension .NFO and store data in a compressed binary format.

- A System Information file can be e-mailed to another technician and reviewed by opening the file with the System Information utility. This is an efficient way to summarize the details of the current software and hardware running on the computer.

- The System Information utility can also report critical observations such as what programs are started automatically and what hardware conflicts are present.

3. Computer Management:

- The Computer Management utility is an MMC-based utility used to manage several key systems and operations for a computer.

- The Computer Management utility can also be used to connect to remote computers as long as the remote computer allows the communication through its Windows Firewall and recognizes that the user has administrative permission to interact with its systems the connection is allowed.

4. Action Center:
- The hub of Windows' troubleshooting tools can be found in the Action Center, which is accessible via the white flag icon in the Notification area of the taskbar.
- Clicking it may reveal that it's already aware of the problem plaguing you, allowing you to click the link and hopefully take steps to resolve it.

5. Help and Support:
- The Help and Support troubleshooting tool provides automatic resolutions for many troubleshooting issues. Click a button, and your problem is repaired. And for issues that cannot be resolved automatically, such as plugging your network cables into the correct ports, the Help and Support troubleshooting tool walks you through procedures to get your systems up and running quickly and easily.
- If the Help and Support troubleshooting tool cannot help you resolve your problem and your Internet connection is still active, you can contact a technical.
- The Help and Support troubleshooting tool can also help you improve your browser performance by enabling you to perform such tasks as automatically deleting temporary Internet files, empting the Recycle Bin, and disabling any proxy connections on your computer with a single click of the mouse.

6. Microsoft Support Web Site:
- It is a great source of information and is home of the Microsoft Knowledge Base (MS-KB) articles.

Additional Tools to Find out Information About Your Computer's Hardware:
- Knowing what hardware is present inside your computer by using just the tools present inside Windows might give you some idea, but it won't be terribly informative.

1. System Spec:
- System Spec displays a lot of the basic hardware information on its main window, and by clicking on the icons across the top, more in depth details are available for components such as CPU, memory, sound, USB etc.
- There are also a number of convenient menus with quick access to Control Panel functions and system tools such as System File Checker and Device Manager etc.

2. HWInfo:
- HWInfo is definitely one of our favorite free system and hardware information tools because there really is enough in it to suit everybody.
- There are in fact three different screens you can get your information from and you will be asked on startup; the Summary screen displays useful information about the core system components of processor, memory, graphics and motherboard. The Sensors window displays every temperature, voltage and frequency your system has available.

3. PC Wizard:

- PC Wizard is one of the most comprehensive free hardware information tools available.

- And in addition to the highly detailed and easy to understand information provided about hardware, it also scans several areas of your Windows system and can even pull things like your browser or instant messaging usernames and passwords.

4. System Information Viewer (SIV):

- SIV is a good tool to use. All the usual basic detail about CPU voltages and temps etc and memory clocks are in the main window, clicking the buttons across the bottom takes you to numbers loaded windows about almost everything you could wish to know about your hardware.

5. System Information for Windows (SIW):

- SIW is another comprehensive information tool and as well as displaying a good amount of hardware detail, there's an equally large amount of information about Windows or other software components, and also information about several parts of your network.

- Some useful tools are also present such as a broadband speed tester, a window password revealer, MAC address changer, a simple monitor tester and CPU, memory and network monitoring windows.

6. CPU-Z:

- CPU-Z has long been one of the techies favorite tools because it simply focuses on providing useful information relating to the four core component areas of your system i.e., processor, motherboard, memory and graphics.

- The supplied information is clear and concise and CPU-Z is a tool that's often recommended when overclocking because of the accuracy when reading the CPU or RAM frequencies.

8.5 | TROUBLESHOOTING PC HARDWARE

- Computer hardware is the physical part of a computer and it is frequently changed as compared to the software. Most computer hardware is inside the computer and cannot be seen by normal users.

- There are a large number of the computer hardware devices including Hard disk, CD-ROM, RAM, Motherboard, Monitor, Printer, Peripheral devices and other devices.

- One of the first steps in the troubleshooting is to sort out the hardware and software problems. You can use the event viewer utility in the Windows operating systems to identify the nature and cause of the hardware or software problem. Also you can identify the hardware problems by identifying the initial start up beeps.

- The beep pattern is telling you what part of the hardware is failing. Unfortunately there are different standards for the beep pattern and you will have to refer to your motherboard's user manual for the meaning of it.

Troubleshooting Motherboard:

- The motherboard is the computer, so the usual symptom of a failed motherboard is a completely dead system.

- Fans, drives, and other peripherals may spin up if the motherboard is dead, but more often nothing at all happens when you turn on the power. No beeps, no lights, no fans, nothing.

Troubleshooting Keyboard:

- Typical symptoms associated with keyboard failures include the following:

    1. No characters appear onscreen when entered from the keyboard.

    2. Some keys work, whereas others do not work.

    3. A keyboard error—keyboard test failure error appears.

    4. A interface error—keyboard test failure error appears.

    5. An error code of six short beeps is produced during bootup (BIOS dependent).

    6. The wrong characters are displayed.

- Clean your keyboard using dust cleaners. An unplugged keyboard, or one with a bad signal cable, also produces a keyboard error message during startup, so check cable connections.

Troubleshooting Mouse:

- There are many reasons why a computer mouse may not be functioning properly.

    1. **The mouse is not clean:** An optical-mechanical mouse (mouse with a ball) may not work well because the inside of the mouse is not clean.

    2. **Optical portion of mouse is blocked:** If you have an optical mouse (LED or laser) with erratic behavior, the optical eye is possibly blocked.

    3. **Bad surface:** Although most mice work on any surface, if you are having problems with the cursor, we suggest a different mouse pad or surface, such as a book or piece of paper.

    4. **Reconnect and try different port:** It is also possible that a loose connection or bad port can cause problems with the mouse. Make sure that it is not either of these problems by disconnecting the mouse from the current USB port and connecting to another USB port.

Troubleshooting Power Supply:

- The PC power supply is probably the most failure-prone item in a personal computer. It heats and cools each time it is used and receives the first in-rush of AC current when the PC is switched on.

- A typical failure of a PC power supply is often noticed as a burning smell just before the computer shuts down. Another problem could be the failure of the vital cooling fan, which allows components in the power supply to overheat.

- Following is a simple steps to help you zero in on common power supply–related problems:

  Step 1 : Check AC power input. Make sure the cord is firmly seated in the wall socket and in the power supply socket. Try a different cord.

  Step 2 : Check DC power connections. Make sure the motherboard and disk drive power connectors are firmly seated and making good contact. Check for loose screws.

  Step 3 : Check DC power output. Use a digital multimeter to check for proper voltages. If it's below spec, replace the power supply.

  Step 4 : Check installed peripherals. Remove all boards and drives and retest the system. If it works, add back in items one at a time until the system fails again. The last item added before the failure returns is likely defective.

Troubleshooting RAM (Memory):

- Computer memory problems are generally caused by defective memory chips, wrongly installed memory chips and wrong configuration of memory chips.

  1. **Computer fails to boot:** Many times your computer memory chips get loosened so you have to make sure that memory modules are completely installed. Also check your RAM chips when you have installed them for the first time.

  2. **Computer boots up with a blank screen:** You may have loose memory chips and you may be using some different type of memory which isn't compatible with your system. You need to check you VGA card as well if you see this type of problem.

  3. **Computer hangs and reboot:** This type of problem is generally caused by faulty RAM, faulty PSU or overheating. Reseat RAM and rotate RAM to different slots.

  4. **Three Short Beeps:** This certainly means some RAM issue like bad dim slots on the motherboard or faulty RAM chips. Try replacing them with new RAM.

Troubleshooting Hard Drive (HD):

- One of the most difficult areas to troubleshoot is the hard drive. Typical symptoms associated with hard disk drive failures include the following:
  1. The front panel indicator lights are visible, and the display is present on the monitor screen, but there is no disk drive action and no bootup.
  2. The computer boots up to a system disk in the A drive, but not to the hard drive, indicating that the system files on the Hard Disk Drive (HDD) are missing or have become corrupt.
  3. The computer does not boot up when turned on.
  4. A HDD controller failure message appears, indicating a failure to verify hard disk setup by system configuration file error.
  5. A no boot record found, a non-system disk or disk error, or an invalid system Disk message appears, indicating that the system boot files are not located in the root directory of the drive.
  6. An out of disk space message appears, indicating that the amount of space on the disk is insufficient to carry out the desired operation.
  7. A missing operating system or a hard drive boot failure message appears, indicating that the disk's MBR is missing or has become corrupt.
  8. A current drive no longer valid message appears, indicating that the HDD's CMOS configuration information is incorrect or has become corrupt.
- If you cannot access the hard disk drive, and its configuration settings are correct, you must troubleshoot the hardware components associated with the hard disk drive. These components include the drive, its signal cable and the Hard Disk Controller (HDC) on the system board.
- Check the HDD signal cable for proper connection at both ends. Exchange the signal cable for a known-good one. Check the Master/Slave jumper settings to ensure they are set correctly.

Troubleshooting Ports:

- Failures of the serial, parallel, and game ports tend to end with poor or no operation of the peripheral.
- Generally, there are only following four possible causes for a problem with a device connected to an I/O port:
  1. The port is defective.
  2. The software is not configured properly for the port (i.e., the resource allocation, speed, or protocol settings do not match).
  3. The connecting signal cable is bad.
  4. The attached device is not functional.

Troubleshooting Monitors:

1. **Monitor is blank after starting computer:**
   - Check to be sure that the monitor has power and that the light is on.
   - Check your cables connecting your monitor with your computer.
2. **The words on the monitor are too small and unreadable:**
   - You will need to change the monitor's screen resolution.
3. **The picture on the monitor is stretched, too bright/dark, or is not the way you like it:**
   - You will need to check the monitor settings. Look for a button on the bottom of the monitor which will open a menu to change monitor settings.
   - Find the default settings and return the monitor to default settings.
   - Use the vertical and horizontal settings to center the image and stretch to your liking.

Troubleshooting Printer:

1. **Cables not connected properly:** Your printer should have two cables connected to it i.e., the power cable and the data cable. Make sure the power and data cables (parallel cable or USB cable) are connected to both the printer and computer.
2. **Printer error (orange or blinking light):** After your printer has completed its initial startup, you should see a solid colored light. If the indicator is blinking or is orange, often this is an indication of a printer error, like a paper jam or an issue with the ink or toner cartridge. As there are not standards for all printers, if you see a blinking light, visit the manufacturer's site or review the printer manual for specific error details.
3. **No paper or paper jam:** Without paper, your printer will not be able to print. Make sure you have paper loaded into the printer paper cartridge or tray. Next, verify that no printer paper is jammed or partially fed into the printer.
4. **Inkjet printer ink related issues:** Often when you're encountering an ink related issue, your printer status indicator light (mentioned above) should be flashing. If this is not occurring, you may want to skip to the next section. However, if you've recently inserted a new ink cartridge, you may want to try the below suggestions.
5. **Printer self tests:** Most printers have a way of printing a test page. A printer test page allows you to determine if the printer is working. The printer self test is usually accomplished by holding down a series of keys. If you are not sure if your printer has this feature or how to perform it.
6. **Printer drivers:** If your printer does not have any flashing lights and is connected properly, it's possible you may be encountering a driver related issue. We suggest visiting our printer driver listing, which links to all major printer manufacturer driver pages, and download the latest drivers for your printer.

Troubleshooting CD-ROM and DVD Drives:

- A bad disc drive can cause an assortment of different issues on your computer. Below are just a few of the possible issues you may encounter.

  1. Error when reading CD or DVD.

  2. CDs or DVDs may not play audio or video properly.

  3. CD or DVD programs may not install or encounter errors after being installed.

  There are different ways to test your computer's disc drive and determine if it's bad or has flaws that are causing issues with your computer.

- Below is a listing of these recommendations:

(i) Software and Hardware solutions:

- CD and DVD disc drives can sometimes get dusty and dirty inside, causing problems with reading discs. You can use a CD/DVD Drive Cleaner kit to help clean the disc drive, which can be purchased at many office supply stores and electronics stores.

- Below is a listing of software programs available that are designed to test your computer's CD and DVD disc drives and discs.

  o **CDRoller:** Great program that is used to test and, if needed, recover data from CDs and DVDs.

  o **CDCheck:** Another great program used to help check CD drives (no DVD compatibility) and can also be used to help recover data from damaged discs.

(ii) Replace the Disc Drive:

- If the disc drive still appears to be bad after trying the above suggestions, we suggest replacing it.

Troubleshooting NIC:

- There are several common problems caused by the NIC driver failure which were worthy users' attention. Such as the low boot speed issue or the accidental destruction of the NIC driver. Some computer users complained about the low boot speed after installing the NIC driver in the system.

- First, they thought the NIC driver could be installed in an inappropriate way, so they reinstalled the driver for times but the problem still remained unsolved.

- Actually, the low boot speed problem was often caused by the connecting failure, as the NIC driver has to match with the transmission rate, otherwise, it would take time for the system to detect the network card. This deceleration problem was kind of normal, users could try to uninstall the NIC driver then reconfigure the NIC parameters.

- And the NIC driver damages might caused by a few reasons like power interruption, maloperation or antivirus detection. Once, the NIC driver was damaged in unexpected situations, the network card would be unable to work successfully and lose the connection because it has lost the needful supports from the driver software. For this case, the best solution for users to do is to reinstall the NIC driver manually.

PRACTICE QUESTIONS

1. What is meant by troubleshooting?
2. With the help of diagram describe steps in troubleshooting.
3. Write short note on: Common networking problems.
4. Enlist tools for gathering information about computer hardware.
5. Explain ADJUST method in detail.
6. List some common failures/problem in computer.
7. Write short note on: PC Hardware.

■■■